THE DAY
THE WORLD
SHUT DOWN

THE DAY THE WORLD SHUTDOWN

by Mike Hyatt and George Grant

WORD PUBLISHING

NASHVILLE

A Thomas Nelson Company

Word Publishing
Y2K: The Day the World Shut Down
Copyright © 1998 by Mike Hyatt and George Grant

All Scripture quotations are from the King James version of the Bible.

Library of Congress Cataloging-in-Publication Data

Hyatt, Michael S.
    Y2K : the day the world shut down / by Michael S. Hyatt and George E. Grant.
        p.   cm.
    ISBN 0-8499-1387-X
    I. Grant, George E., 1954–   . II. Title. III. Title: Year two thousand.
PS3558.Y345Y3   1998   98-31414
813′.54—dc21   CIP

ISBN 0-8499-1387-X

Printed in the United States of America
98 99 00 01 02 03 QBK 9 8 7 6 5 4 3 2 1

To our wives and children:
our hope and our future

Prelude

"But of that day and hour knoweth no man, no, not the angels of heaven, but my Father only." Matthew 24:36

DECEMBER 31, 999

The old church of St. Peter in Rome was thronged with the faithful. Originally erected by Constantine the Great some six and a half centuries previous, the vast decrepit basilica would not be revitalized by Michelangelo's artistry until some five centuries hence. Those who crowded into the transepts, around the apse, throughout the nave, and into the narthex that day would not have expected that the creaking timbers and worn stones around them would have any need to endure the long span of all those years. Weeping and wailing, they had gathered there to await the end of the world.

Just before midnight, a great liturgical procession began to slowly make its way along the shadowy aisles toward the iconostasis and the choir, altar, and focault beyond. The tormented cries of the people hung in the air, thick like incense. The great bells in the towers above the adjacent courtyard began to toll ominously. Every sight, sound, texture, and aroma bore the manifest taint of judgment. Grievous, they were observing a wake for the world.

The holy seers had all foretold this dreadful day—indeed, most had expected it for quite some time. Almost from the beginning of history men began to anticipate the end of history. Centuries prior, when Rome was sacked by the Vandals, the apocalypticists were certain that the end was nigh. Later, when successive waves of Persians and Moslems swept through Byzantium making the great Christian centers of Jerusalem, Alexandria, Damascus, and Antioch captive to fierce pagan warlords, they became convinced that the last days had finally come. It seemed that the *fin de siecle*—the end of each successive century—was nearly always marked by a new interest in the harbingers of doom. Up until now, the prophets had been inaccurate, erroneous, and premature, even in their most painstaking calculations.

But here at the end of the millennium, the signs were practically unmistakable. The beloved Pope Gregory, just before his untimely demise earlier that year, had assured good men and women of faith that the wars and rumors of wars, that the nations rising against nations and the kingdoms rising against kingdoms, the famines, the pestilences, and the earthquakes in divers places—all seen in abundance in recent days—were clear portents of the consummation of the ages. His successor in the office of the Holy See, with the concurrence of each of the venerable Patriarchs of the East, confirmed that time had run out for this, the terminal generation.

Some of those who were gathered at the Vatican that evening had rid themselves of all their earthly possessions as a final act of contrition. Some donated their lands, homes, money, foodstuffs, and household goods to the poor. Others simply left their fields, shops, and villages vacant. Still others gave themselves over to an "eat, drink, and be merry, for tomorrow we die" debauchery. In most cases, little or no preparation was made for the future—because of course, there was no future.

At long last, the hour arrived. A hush fell over the congregation as the bells slowly tolled the end of the year, the end of the century, the end of the millennium, the end of the world. And then . . . nothing happened. Nothing at all. The silence was deafening. Everyone looked around at one another in astonished relief. The terror was past.

And that was when the real trouble began. Preparing for the end, though perhaps dispiriting, is not nearly so difficult as preparing for what comes after the end.

One

*"He went out and dwelt in the land of Nod on the
east of Eden, and he builded a city." Genesis 4:16,17*

JANUARY 6, 2000

The air was pure, sharp, and cold, heavy laden with drama
and disquiet, as befitted Epiphany. A frosty mist hung along
the banks of the snaking river and a slip of it lingered in the
growing darkness of the little dell below. It was not yet quite
dusk, but the first stars had come into the sky, twinkling through
the snowy boughs and illuminating a narrow path toward the
crest of the hill.

Will Ajax looked out at the picture postcard panorama
before him. A little farmhouse was set snug into the hugging
hills. Surrounded by several carefully situated outbuildings,
barns, pens, and gardens, the homestead was crisscrossed by a
series of fences, walls, pathways, and hedgerows. A thin wisp of
wood smoke rose from the chimney. The aroma of fresh bread
wafted randomly upward. A kind of indescribable glow radiated

from the scene—with all the deep inglenooks of memory and of home.

The intoxicating spell was suddenly snapped by the harsh crackle of his radio headset. "The team is in position, Sir."

Ajax looked off to his left. Through the trees he could see eleven men arrayed along the crest of the hill. They wore winter woodland camouflage and were weighed down with a bevy of assault weapons, telecom appliances, magellan devices, and directional op-mechanisms. Their faces were obscured by night vision goggles. But their intentions were clear enough.

"Right. Recheck the perimeter. Containment is essential. We don't go until they're all in the house."

Ajax allowed himself a hint of a smile.

IT DIDN'T LOOK AT ALL the way he'd imagined the end of the world would look. If anything it looked more like its beginning.

Bob Priam was walking in the garden. A sharp moon, just visible over the tree-lined horizon, was fighting with the flying rags and tatters of a storm. He couldn't quite tell if it was coming or going—but he didn't really care one way or the other. He was lost in the magnificence of the moment.

A thin layer of soft snow and crystalline frost dusted the ground, clung to the prickly shrub stalks, weighed down the last remnants of the fall herbs, capped the long line of fence posts, hung off the low eaves of the barn, and flocked the stooping branches of the trees. Long rays of light from the farmhouse above the ridge diffused across the wan platinum landscape, sparkling and skittering to the edge of the woods. The lustrous spectacle before him combined with the sweet musky scent of sugar maple leaves carpeting the walkway and the lilting music of the rustling limbs in the woods to serve up a real feast for the senses.

He drew in a deep breath of the crisp evening air. A bracing winter wind whipped the top of the encircling hills, but only the slightest hint of a breeze reached him there. He felt safe, secure, and satisfied.

His house was in order. His preparations were complete. His barns were full. And the turn of events had vindicated him. Though he was not a prophet—nor was he the son of a prophet—at least this once, he had been right. And he savored that thought with glee.

He walked along the narrow, now-empty furrows of the vegetable beds to the iron gate leading to his favorite spot on the property: a carefully tended walled plot that just a few months ago had been bursting with color and fragrance. A slender brick-lined pathway wound through lush beds of forget-me-nots, polyanthus, and crown imperial fritillaries. What appeared to be haphazard clumps of lilac, viburnum, and philadelphus were linked integrally to one another by a wide wavy border planted with alchemilla, nepeta, and several other sturdy herbaceous plants that he had never quite been able to identify. There were the assorted remnants of blooming primroses, lilies, and Canterbury bells. There were also the frozen stalks of snapdragons, hardy geraniums, and lavender. Along one wall, in front of a magnificent wisteria, was a bed redolent with herbs—basil, thyme, oregano, rosemary, and cilantro. There was parsley among the hollyhocks, honeysuckle twisted round the roses, and the now-bare stems of tiger lilies peeking through the shrubby euphorbias. Even now, below the surface, lay garlic and shallots, along with rows of ornamental bulbs, waiting for the warmth of spring to rouse them. He pondered the world of unseen things—hidden in the secret places, under soil, or snow, or circumstance. The sense of both promise and portent was strong.

The garden was a hard-won vision of paradise planted in the midst of the hustle-bustle crises of life at the end of the millennium. Even now, dormant, muted, and glazed over by traces of wintry hoar, it was beautiful, luxuriant, fragrant, mysterious, and rich in surprises.

Its personal scale, its wide-ranging palette, and its orderly conception portrayed a distinctly practical vision of both the possibilities and the limitations of creation and were what had convinced him to buy the property in the first place. He was beginning to believe that gardening was a means of grace. There was just something about this garden that restored in him a sense of balance and serenity to a way of life harried by the tyranny of the urgent. He somehow saw in that little world how the holy might be derived from the wholly worldly.

"Dad?" A voice broke his concentration. "Hey, Dad? Are you out here?"

"Over here. Next to the gate in the wall," he answered.

It was Priam's daughter, Cassandra, silhouetted against the silvery hillside. "Dinner's ready. Mom asked me to come and get you. Whatcha doing?"

"OK, Cassie. I'm on my way. I just can't get over how much I love this place."

"Yeah, I know. It's really just too good to be true, isn't it?"

A sudden chill came over him and Priam shivered as he turned toward the house.

AJAX LOWERED HIS BINOCULARS as the two small figures below were caught in the light of the open doorway. His pulse was racing. He could taste the saccharined cusp of adrenaline at the back of his throat. It was now or never.

He looked over at the men fidgeting in their positions. One was rechecking his weapon for the umpteenth time. Another was repositioning his duffel carriers and tow straps. Yet another was toying with his goggles, trying to get a more comfortable fit across his brow. The rest were gazing down at the odd convergence of pristine beauty and desolate wonder that marked their target.

He took a deep breath and gave the signal to strike.

The men immediately scrambled to their feet and began to move across the frozen terrain down toward the house. Despite the weight of their gear, the steep embankment, and the necessity to maintain stealth, they kept themselves aligned in perfect formation all the way down to the house.

The moment felt like eternity, as moments of mere temporal consequence so often do—discerning the difference between what may be the beginning of the end and what may be the end of the beginning is almost always impossible.

Two

APRIL 13, 1998

Time. He just needed a little more time. Otherwise, he was sure to drown. His lungs were bursting. His heart was racing. His adrenaline was surging. Fear gripped every fiber of his being.

One last time Bob Priam squatted down as low as he could and then pushed off the spongy bottom with all the strength he could muster. The mud felt slimy and cold against his bare feet. Alas, he didn't go far—the water resisted his feeble launch. He felt a stab of panic as he wondered how in the world he would make it to the surface, so far above his head. He hesitated, suspended between the horror of a watery grave and the hope of warm sunshine and clean air, calculating the odds of making it.

He was fading fast. He could feel his very life ebbing away. Time. He just needed a little more time.

He tried to swim. Kicking feverishly upward, he stretched his arms toward the surface with all his might. Slowly, his aching body drifted toward the roiling waves above. But not fast enough. He could feel the pain deep inside his chest as his body drained the last of his oxygen reserve. He released some of the carbon dioxide to ease the pressure. But he knew he was running out of time. He kicked harder and engaged his arms, grabbing at the water above his head and then pulling it to his sides in large sweeping motions.

He could see only a few feet in front of his face. The water was murky and dark. But as he moved upward, the light slowly filled the cold liquid, robbing it of its life-choking power. By now, his lungs were empty. No oxygen. No carbon dioxide. Nothing. His head was throbbing. The panic, which had subsided when he put his body into motion, came back. He fought off an impulse to inhale. Then another and another.

He kept swimming—determined to live. He wasn't going to die. Not like this. Not so close to the surface. Not alone.

Just a little more time. That was all he needed.

After what seemed an eternity, his head burst through the surface of the water—and Priam woke up gasping aloud. Startled, his eyes opened wide. His heart was pounding. He was breathing quickly—and hard. He looked over at Abby, still fast asleep, peacefully oblivious to the ordeal he had just been through. He looked at the clock. Four twenty-five. In another five minutes, the alarm would go off and the day would officially begin. A day he had planned for for so long. And dreaded for just as long.

Time. He just needed a little more time.

IT HAD BEEN LATE LAST SUMMER when Priam first got concerned about the Y2K Millennium Bug problem. Initially, it didn't seem like that big of a deal. The embedded bug had lain dormant in the corporate computers for nearly a decade without a hint of any disruption. It could wait another month or two. But the more Priam learned about the problem, the more convinced he became that they were running out of time. And because he was the Chief Information Officer, it was *his* time they were squandering, making an already difficult job nearly impossible.

Priam had been at OfficeCentral for almost three years. With a B.A. in Humanities and an M.A. in Philosophy, he was hardly your typical CIO. While his peers at most of the other Fortune 1000 companies had earned their degrees in Computer Science or Math from all the right science and technical schools, he had gained his knowledge of computers by firsthand experience— hours of tinkering, hacking, and pouring over software manuals and programming books. For his colleagues, working on computers was a job. For Priam, it was an obsession that had filled nearly every moment of his discretionary time for years. Indeed, it had gradually crowded out every other pursuit, becoming a demanding and insatiable mistress.

He had discovered computers, innocently enough, while working on his masters' degree. He bought his first one as a replacement for his Selectric typewriter. He was confident a bona fide word processor would save him hundreds of hours in preparing his master's thesis. And he was right.

He found that he had a natural ability to recall scores of arcane software commands without having to go back to the manuals more than once. The computer had become a seamless extension of his brain. As his grandfather would have said, "he took to it like a duck to water."

Soon his toolbox grew to include a spreadsheet, a home accounting program, a database or two, and dozens of software utilities. He mastered them all and began to feel a growing frustration with off-the-shelf software. These point-and-click, plug-and-play, lowest-common-denominator packages never quite did things the way he would have liked. As a result, he became a beta-tester for several of his favorite programs. The newest versions promised to quench his thirst for more features and he radically reduced the time required to acquire them by signing on as a software guinea pig. This didn't involve any compensation, of course, but it did mean that he got the latest software developments earlier than the general public and had the opportunity to provide some input—albeit minor—to the developers.

But even this wasn't enough for Priam. The only way to get what he really wanted was to become a *programmer*. So, he did the logical thing: He signed up for a night class in Computer Programming 101 at the same university where he was working on his masters. But after a week, he dropped out. The class was too slow, and it bored him to tears. He didn't have time or patience to spend four years listening to teaching assistants with bad attitudes, thick accents, and inflated egos talk computer theory. Maybe *ordinary* students needed to walk this wearisome path, but not Bill Gates. Not Steve Jobs. And not Bob Priam. He needed "news he could use." He wanted to get to work implementing his design ideas and writing real software. He never stopped to ask why any of this was important. It just was.

He started with the simple stuff: macro processors that simply memorized commands like a tape recorder and then played them back when the user summoned them. This didn't add any new functionality to the software, but it did make it work faster and with greater elegance. Soon, however, he got bored with this, too. He pulled himself out of the shallow end of the pool, as it were, and headed for the diving board at the deep end.

He actually taught himself programming languages. He began with BASIC and then moved on to COBOL. He bought third-party manuals on programming, especially those that offered real-world solutions to the problems he was trying to address. He subscribed to several programming magazines and poured over each new issue like a cub reporter looking for a hot lead. He traded programming tips and sought out advice wherever he could get it. And little by little his knowledge grew. He quickly graduated from the simpler code languages, took on PASCAL, and then finally, the granddaddy of them all, C++. Within the space of two years, he could hold his own with any academically trained programmer in the country. In fact, a handful of professionals sought him out from time to time for solutions to their more difficult problems.

It was out of these informal discussions that he was offered his first computer job. Two months before he finished graduate school, a software consulting firm that specialized in sales automation offered him a position in Dallas as a Technical Support Engineer. Up until that moment, he had planned on getting his doctorate in literature and teaching at some prestigious, small college. He enjoyed the academic life, especially the give and take of heated debate and the refinement of ideas. Like an unfaithful husband caught up in the emotional muddle of a steamy affair, he had never considered leaving his first love and marrying his second. But then again, he had never had the opportunity. Now, the temptation was just too much.

Upon graduation, he took the job and quickly moved up through the ranks: Tech Support Engineer, Associate Programmer, Programmer, and Senior Programmer. Some four years into his career, Priam resigned to accept a position with a medium-sized manufacturing company in Omaha. He was in charge of managing their networked PCs. After a year, he caught the attention of the mainframe Project and Operations Manager and was moved into that department as a Systems Analyst/Programmer. He continued his climb to the summit: Senior Systems Analyst/Programmer, Project Lead, Manager, and finally Vice President of Information Systems Planning. He remained in that position for just under two years before he was hired by OfficeCentral in Nashville as Senior Vice President and Chief Information Officer.

It had taken him a mere fifteen years to climb the ladder and get to the top. Not bad for a guy who dropped out of the only computer course he ever took.

Part of what made him rise to the top so quickly was that he appeared to be more well-rounded than his geekish colleagues. His background in the arts and humanities had taught him to think laterally, which enabled him to grasp more quickly than his peers the problems they were trying to solve. He was articulate and could communicate compellingly in either written or oral form. And best of all, he could describe technical problems for the ordinary businessman without resorting to liberal doses of jargon.

From the very beginning of his career, he also *looked* like a senior executive. No worn-out Hush Puppies. No ill-fitting, short-sleeve, polyester-blend shirts. No dirty glasses, funny hats, or bad haircuts. And definitely no plastic pocket protectors. He was strictly button-down, Brooks Brothers—all the way. To the Board and the other executives, he possessed that texture of familiarity which made them comfortable in his presence. Admitting him into the inner sanctum of the Senior Executive Team was easy. He was already one of them.

WHEN PRIAM ARRIVED AT OfficeCentral's newly built facility that fine April morning, he slipped his security pass into the front door and immediately headed to his office. He glanced quickly at his watch. Five forty-five. Most of the offices were still dark, though he could smell the delightful aroma of freshly brewed coffee. Down the hall he saw Jill Homer, a sharply dressed, impeccably groomed marketing manager, filling her coffee cup. The pot was already half empty.

She glanced up and smiled. "Morning, Bob."

"You're here early, Jill. Did you ever go home?"

"Yeah. But just for a nap!"

Priam chuckled and gave her a knowing nod.

Jill continued. "Jerry's got me finishing up his report for the Executive Committee meeting."

"Oh great. How about telling him to cut back on the razzle-dazzle and give the rest of us a chance."

"I don't think you have to worry. I'm sure you can hold your own."

Priam smiled and seriously wondered if this time he would indeed be able to hold his own.

He finally got to his office on the second floor, flicked on the lights, and went back to the common area immediately outside to make his own pot of coffee. He would need it. *The first of many*, he thought. With this chore behind him, he returned to his office, opened his computer case, and removed his sleek, state-of-the-art laptop. One of the perks of being the CIO was that he always had the latest, greatest hardware and software. If someone else in the company needed a new computer, he always bought the newest generation, the latest iteration, the hottest technology on the market, and then handed down his. It was one of his unwritten policies, and it made everybody happy.

With a touch of the prompt pad, his thin magnesium slab instantly awoke from suspend mode and he was staring at the same document he had been working on just before he hit the rack the night before. He thought he was nearly done with it, but he wanted to carefully review it one more time before print-ing out the final draft. In truth, he read and reread it several more times over the course of the next two hours, making sure that everything was in order. It had to be perfect. The stakes for the company—and for his own future—were enormous.

WHEN PRIAM ENTERED THE Boardroom half the executives were already there. Most were standing around the vast mahogany conference table in groups of two or three making small talk. All had the obligatory cup of coffee and a few had already claimed a fresh bagel from one of the two oversized pastry platters at either end of the table. Priam poured himself a cup of coffee, adding sugar and creamer to change the elixir from black to beige. As he raised his head from the coffee caddy, Glenn Anchises greeted him with a warm smile and a firm handshake.

"How ya' doing, Bob?"

"Not bad. You?" Priam tried to calm the butterflies in his stomach and forced a half-smile.

"This is your big day, huh?" As Vice President of Operations, Anchises was Priam's biggest in-house customer. About 70 percent of the work the Information Technology staff did was for Operations. Over the past several years, he and Anchises interacted daily, sometimes several times a day. As a result, they had developed a close, working relationship. Even their wives enjoyed one another's company, so they often spent a weekend evening every couple of months or so to do some long-range planning and strategic analysis. In truth, they were about as close as a corporate friendship ever allowed.

Priam involuntarily let out a sigh. "Yep. It's show time."

"You're gonna do fine." Anchises gave him a "thumbs up."

Just as they finished their brief interchange, Frank Menelaus, OfficeCentral's President and Chief Executive Officer, entered the room. Without greeting anyone, he parked his files at his end of the conference table and bellowed, "Please find your seats, people, we have a lot to cover today and very little time to do it." He quickly sat down, put on his half-glasses, and glanced over the agenda as Nancy Briseis, his administrative assistant, distributed copies to the other executives.

Menelaus was small, thin, and hard as nails. He looked and acted a bit like Ross Perot only with a better haircut. He'd come to OfficeCentral from the Navy, after retiring at the age of forty-four. A graduate of Annapolis, he had risen through the ranks in the predictable order, becoming a Commander at the age of forty. But his wife had finally grown weary of his long excursions at sea and the frequent moves, insisting that he retire when he completed his twenty-year tenure and get a job in the private sector. She wanted to stay in one place, build a new home, and have a real, honest-to-goodness life. Being bored with the military himself, he agreed.

His first job at OfficeCentral was Vice President of Procurement. After a mere three years, during which he had managed to dramatically increase the company's gross margins and amaze his colleagues with his pluck, efficiency, and sheer energy, he was promoted to the position of Executive Vice President, overseeing every aspect of the company's business. This was an opportunity for him to grow intellectually and experientially as he learned every aspect of the company's business, except one—data processing.

Menelaus hated computers. He didn't use one and goaded any of the executives who did—publicly referring to laptops as "Game Boys." Deep down, he was probably afraid of them—though he would never admit as much. Having missed out on the personal computer revolution, he felt it was too late to get started. He didn't want to invest his now-precious time in what he was certain would be a long learning curve. The bottom line was that he was too embarrassed to ask anyone how to use one—and he tended to despise anything that he could not instantly master.

Interestingly, the big mainframe computers were another matter entirely. He didn't understand these any better, but then he wasn't expected to. This was the realm of techies, code junkies, wire wonks, and propeller heads—the professional geeks who spoke to one another in an algebraic syntax of jargon and pandect that no one else cared to understand. Menelaus, and the executives under his charge, were content to let the big machines crunch the numbers and provide them with the green-bar reports they used to manage the day-to-day operations of the business. So, even if he didn't understand these computers, he appreciated them. Without their assistance, OfficeCentral wouldn't be as profitable—or as competitive—as it was.

After four years as Executive Vice President, Menelaus's boss, the previous CEO, suddenly dropped dead of a heart attack at the ripe old age of fifty-two. The Board of Directors asked Menelaus to step in and assume command. He was the logical choice and a worthy candidate.

MENELAUS WASTED NO TIME in diving in. The first order of business, as it was every month, was a review of the previous month's financials. If the company had had a good month— meaning a *profitable* month—then the rest of the meeting would be pleasant, perhaps even stimulating. But if the previous month had not been profitable, then the meeting would be unpleasant—or worse, it would be more than a little brutal. It was a simple and predictable formula. The financials were always distributed a week in advance, so everyone came to the meeting knowing exactly what the tone of it would be. Fortunately for Priam, the previous month had been very profitable. He could only recall two occasions where the meeting had turned ugly in spite of a profitable previous month. He was praying this wouldn't be another one.

The review of the financials was quick and painless. A few problem areas were noted, but nothing serious. Menelaus then moved on to a look at the coming quarter. Each executive presented a brief report, outlining where they expected to be in terms of revenue and expenses three months hence. Most of the discussion centered around sales. Menelaus's philosophy was that there were no problems more revenue wouldn't fix.

After the numbers, Menelaus moved on to the other agenda items. Glenn Anchises, Priam's friend, was first. The Operations Division, for which Anchises was responsible, had been involved in a massive reengineering of OfficeCentral's warehouse and distribution system. This included automating virtually every aspect of the picking and packing process. The goal was to reduce the number of errors in fulfilling customer orders as well as the amount of time it took to get the order out the door. The project was proceeding right on schedule. There were no cost overruns and no surprises. Just the way Menelaus liked it.

Next, the Chief Marketing Officer presented a competitive analysis, comparing OfficeCentral with Office Depot and Staples, the company's two primary competitors. Jerry Virgil presented a true-to-form, razzle-dazzle presentation, complete with computerized slides and an attractive, bound presentation booklet. This also generated a good deal of discussion and some heated opinions.

When he was done, Menelaus said, "Good work, Jer," which was about as close as he got to handing anyone a bouquet. Priam was next.

"All righty, Bob. Look's like you're up. Try to speak in plain English, if you don't mind, so us poor simple folk can follow along."

Everyone chuckled at his mock-pained expression.

PRIAM HAD BEEN TRYING to get on the Executive Committee agenda for months. Menelaus had stonewalled him at every turn. Part of it was that Priam said he needed an hour, and Menelaus said they just didn't have that much time for one agenda item. Most of it was that Menelaus knew it was going to be an unpleasant subject—a subject beyond his own grasp—and so he just kept procrastinating, promising that they would get it on the agenda next month. Priam had not wanted to sound like an alarmist, so, for a few months, he let it slide. But he knew he was running out of time.

"Look, Frank, you gotta put the year 2000 problem on the agenda. I'm running out of time," Priam had insisted the previous month.

"What do you mean, *running out of time?*" Menelaus snapped.

"I mean we need to get working on this problem soon. If we don't, I can't be responsible for the consequences."

Menelaus glared at him for a moment. He wasn't sure if Priam's words were a threat or an ultimatum. Even though he knew he was out of excuses, he didn't like a subordinate backing him into a corner. But he didn't really have a choice. Sighing, he muttered, "Fine. You can have forty-five minutes at the next meeting." With that he dropped his head dismissively and went back to the memo he was reading when Priam had walked in, clearly signaling that the meeting was over.

As Priam left, he didn't know whether to laugh out loud or start crying. He had gotten what he wanted, but it felt like he'd just been handed a sentence.

PRIAM DIVIDED HIS REPORTS into two stacks, handing one stack to Glenn Anchises on his left and the other to Laura Jones, the CFO, on his right. "Please take a copy off the stack and then pass it around." Priam's palms were sweaty and his heart was racing. He forced himself to breathe deeply and relax.

"Most of you remember only too well the ill-fated Apollo 13 mission. Or maybe you saw the movie. When the NASA spacecraft departed the earth on April 11, 1970, everyone assumed it was just a routine space flight to the moon. American astronauts had successfully landed on the lunar surface twice, and by the time this third mission was launched, the public was bored with it. In fact, the mission was initially so routine that a television broadcast from the spacecraft scheduled for prime time viewing was cancelled because there wasn't sufficient interest.

"During the first two days of space flight, it was business as usual. Everything went according to plan. But as the three astronauts approached the moon, they heard an explosion. As it turned out, an oxygen tank blew up and took with it the Command Module's electricity and a few critical systems, including their ability to abort the mission and return to Earth.

"Immediately after the explosion, James Lovell, the ship's commander, informed Ground Control, '*Houston, we have a problem.*' For the next three days, the astronauts and their colleagues at NASA worked around the clock to cheat death and bring these guys safely back to earth. On April 17, after five frightening days in space, Apollo 13 successfully landed in the Pacific Ocean."

Priam paused, took a sip of coffee and continued. He hoped that his metaphor was hitting home—especially with the command-and-control Menelaus.

"In many ways, life at OfficeCentral has become routine, too. I know we have a lot of new initiatives and programs. We heard about a few of them today. But when we come to work each morning, we make a number of assumptions. We assume that people are going to continue showing up for work. We assume that our vendors are going to continue to deliver the products we resell to our customers. We assume the postal system will continue to deliver our shipments to those that ordered them. We assume that the office will be warm in the winter and cool in the summer. That the lights will come on and the water will flow from the taps. Most of all, we assume that the computers that run this stuff—all of it—are going to keep on running it."

Priam paused for effect, letting his words sink in. The mood of the meeting had begun to change. His colleagues were silent, leaning forward in their chairs. He had their full attention.

"People, we have a problem. A very big problem. Everything you and I have worked so hard to accomplish at OfficeCentral is threatened. What I'm talking about is the Year 2000 Computer Problem. Perhaps you've heard of it. Sometimes it is referred to as the Millennium Bug or simply Y2K for short.

"Y2K is a sort of digital time bomb. When the clock strikes midnight on January 1, 2000, computer systems all over the world will begin spewing out bad data or maybe even stop working altogether—unless they are fixed. The Millennium Bug infects almost every mainframe computer on earth, many micro-computers, and even embedded computer chips in various appliances, instruments, and other devices. And, from what we can tell so far, we've got one heck of a problem right here at OfficeCentral.

"By now you're probably wondering what this problem is. Let me give you a little history. Thirty years ago, at the beginning of the computer age, data storage was quite limited and very expensive. Those first computers used punch cards, and it took a handful of cards to store the amount of information we can store today in a space smaller than a speck of dust. Computer storage cost ten thousand times—that's 1 million percent—more than it does today. *Any* method that could save storage space was readily adopted. One method used was to shorten the year portion of dates. Instead of using four digits, they abbreviated them to two by deleting the century. For example, 1967 became 67; 1984 became 84. From the programmer's perspective, adding the 19 each time was a space-wasting redundancy.

"The problem is that dates are used in all kinds of business and even scientific calculations. When these programs were written, no one considered what would happen when you get to the year 1999. What happens when you add 99+1? Obviously, the answer is 100, but remember you only have two digits to work with. For most computers, 99+1=00. Because the computer assumes that the century is always 19, it will think the year is 1900."

Priam paused again and took another sip of coffee.

"This may not seem like such a big deal," Priam continued, "but, trust me, it's huge. Let me give you four real live examples of how the year 2000 will affect us if we don't fix our systems to deal with it:

"First, it starts with a 2. Some programs, especially some of our data validation routines, will only recognize years beginning with a 1. In other words, when users try to enter the year 2000, the computer will think it's a bad date and refuse to accept it. We've actually already encountered this problem in trying to enter inventory expiration dates. For the time being, we're simply entering 12/31/99.

"Second, it ends with zeros. Some random-number generators, which, for example, we use to create account numbers, use the computer's system date and divide by the last two numbers. These programs either lock up or crash when they try to divide by 00.

"Third, it starts on a Saturday. Many programs use a day-of-week function to perform certain tasks. These can be as simple as an automated backup procedure, which we use extensively, to automatically open the warehouse if it is Monday but lock it if it is Saturday or Sunday. The problem is that January 1, 1900, was a Monday; January 1, 2000, is a Saturday. If the computer thinks the year is 1900—as all noncompliant systems will—the warehouse doors will swing open on Saturday and lock shut on Thursday. This is a trivial example and one that we can work around, but there are other more serious problems, and we aren't even sure what they all are.

"Fourth, it is a leap year. Most people assume that every fourth year is a leap year. However, every fourth turn-of-the-century is a leap year, too. The year 1900 was *not* a leap year; the year 2000 is. Therefore, if the computer doesn't account for the fact that 2000 will, in fact, have a February 29, then all kinds of calculations will be off, including billing cycles. This will create an enormous problem for our accounting department." Priam glanced at Laura, whom he had already briefed on the problem. She nodded in agreement.

Burt Benson, the Marketing Manager, interjected, "So why can't you just reprogram the computers and be done with it?"

"Good question" Priam continued, "the problem is certainly simple enough. It's really not a technical problem at all. In fact, we know exactly how to fix it. The real challenge is securing and managing the resources. Time and money.

"For example, we have approximately 8 million lines of code to review and repair in our mainframe computer systems. It needs to be completely repaired by December 31, 1998, in order to allow a full year for testing. That gives us just over eight months. A good programmer can handle about 100,000 lines of code in that time. That means we are going to need an additional eighty full-time programmers, plus another fifteen or so system analysts and project supervisors. That's a total of ninety-five. At an average salary of $50,000 a year, that comes to nearly $5 million in additional salaries alone.

"That assumes that most of the code is fairly clean and well-documented, which it is not. Most of it is more than ten years old. Probably half of it is twenty years old. It was written before most of us were here. The guys that wrote the code never imagined that their programs would still be in use when the century rolled over. Obviously they were wrong. There are several systems we don't even have source code for, so we can't repair them—they will likely have to be replaced. As a result, I think we can probably only count on each programmer handling about 70,000 lines of code. And even that's a guess. If it's right, we will need even more programmers plus supervisors. That could push our salary costs into the $7 million range."

By this time Menelaus was clearly agitated. He couldn't believe what he was hearing. He started banging away on his calculator and jotting notes on the yellow legal pad in front of him. After a few moments, he interrupted Priam.

"For crying out loud, Bob, by the time you add benefits and basic operating overhead, you're probably talking about close to $8 million a year for just a few months of work."

"I know." Priam sighed. "And we really don't know how big the problem is. I need to hire an outside consulting firm to do an audit and assessment. Until that's done, everything is a guess."

"Why can't your people do that?"

"It's just too big a job. My people are working overtime as it is just to keep the systems we have running. Bringing the automated warehouse system online has got us stretched to the limit. For an assessment like we're considering, we need some outside specialists unencumbered with the ongoing day-to-day business operations."

"What will that cost?" Menelaus barked.

"I don't know yet. As soon as I have your approval, I'll start soliciting bids."

"Give me a ballpark," Menelaus pressed.

"At least a couple hundred thousand. Maybe a lot more."

"That much!? You gotta be kiddin' me. So, you're talkin' about a total project cost of close to $10 million."

"Yeah . . . but that doesn't include the final year of testing."

"And what's that gonna cost?" By now Menelaus's tone was almost mocking.

"I really don't have a clue, Frank. We've never had to deal with a project this massive. It's going to take some research before we can come up with a budget."

"If this project is so massive, why are you just now bringing it to my attention?" Menelaus demanded. He was now visibly flushed.

"Frank?! I've been trying to get this on the Executive Committee agenda for the last eight months."

"Well, you should have tried harder. I had no idea you were talking about something like . . . like this. Do you know what our entire bottom line was last year?"

Priam didn't respond. While he knew his divisional budget down to the last jot and tittle, he didn't have the corporate numbers on the tip of his tongue.

"Eighteen million, Bob. Do you know what the plan calls for this year? Almost twenty million. And it will probably top twenty-two million next year—if we don't royally screw up. And now you're asking me to spend almost half of that on some hare-brained computer project—one that you should have been taking care of all along? What happens if we don't fix this mess?"

"We'll be out of business."

"Out of business?" Menelaus stood up and began to pace around the room. "Come on. Couldn't we just revert to a manual system for a while?"

This time Laura Jones spoke up. "No way, Frank, we are pushing hundreds of thousands of transactions through our system daily. It would take a legion of bookkeepers to replace the computers. Bob's right. We either fix the problem or go out of business."

"Shoot. This is one awful mess," Menelaus said to no one in particular. "If we don't fix 'em, we're in the tank. If we do fix 'em, the company takes a major hit on the bottom line—and the stockholders revolt. I could lose my job!"

He glared at Priam. "Is that what you're after, Bob . . . my job?"

"No, Frank. I'm trying to solve a problem."

"O, yeah? Well, I don't think you're trying quite hard enough. You've really put me between a rock and a hard place."

"Look, I haven't put you anywhere. This is a problem we both inherited."

"Right. Try telling that to the stockholders." Frank returned to his chair, sat down, and cursed, shaking his head in utter frustration.

No one dared speak.

After a few moments, Menelaus looked up, scowling fiercely. He cleared his throat and fairly spat out his words. "If you think I'm going to take the fall for this high-tech boondoggle, Bob Priam, you're wrong. You should have been dealing with this problem years ago. You're a day late and a dollar short, bucko. I think it's about time I got myself a CIO who knows what he's doing."

His taut neck rippled with obvious rage.

"You're fired!"

And with that, Menelaus stood up and stormed out of the room scattering Priam's carefully prepared reports across the glossy tabletop.

Three

*"Give subtilty to the simple, to the young man
knowledge and discretion." Proverbs 1:4*

APRIL 13, 1998

N oah Kirk seemed to carefully cultivate his image as an
eccentric. In fact, he had practically turned oddity into an
art form. Apparently, the more out of fashion his clothes
were, the better he liked them—and though invariably neat and
clean, they were often deliberately, even wildly, mismatched. He
often wore cheap polyester bowling shirts and garish soccer
jerseys with classic English leather accessories and Scottish
waxed hunting jackets. He kept a pair of pince-nez spectacles on
a long ribbon and a pocket watch with a silver fob in his
omnipresent tweed waistcoat. His cargo khakis always bulged
with the gadgets, wires, cables, and electronic tools he was   forever toying with.

He was an excellent student, a computer wiz, a gifted
artist, and a self-taught musician. He carried himself with an

unpretentious air of self-confidence. And well he might. He was tall and strikingly handsome—with his muscular build, dark close-cropped hair, square jaw, icy gray eyes, and clear mocha complexion. Though he didn't seem to have many friends, he was anything but shy and retiring. He enjoyed class discussions, was invariably polite and kind, and had a riotous sense of humor. He was unabashedly outspoken and articulate. But, he was also very mysterious—a kind of loner.

He lived by himself in a small apartment just a block from school where he retreated almost immediately once his classes were over. No one ever really saw him after school or on weekends. As far as anyone could tell, he never dated, never hung out with classmates, and never attended school functions. The only extracurricular activities he went to at all were the regular meetings of the school's *Poetry Review*. And even those merely added to his mysterious air—after all, what interest could a strapping teenage guy like him possibly have in poetry?

No one seemed to know much about his background. Why, for instance, did he live alone? Where were his parents? How could he afford to attend a private school? How did he even find out about the Rivendell Academy? Rumors abounded—as they always do in small communities—but more often than not they were laughably wide of the mark.

Dr. Tristan Gylberd, the founder and professor of Humanities at the school, was probably the only person who really knew Noah's story. And he was characteristically mum about any and all details—he was after all, very nearly as eccentric as the young man he was apparently mentoring. On this particular day, the youngster had asked Gylberd to stop by the apartment after school to talk about a few things. It would be Noah's first visitor in nearly a year.

He was still scurrying around the three crowded rooms trying to tidy up when the doorbell rang.

"Hey, Doc. Come on in."

"Thanks. How're you doing?"

"Fine, thanks. Well, welcome to Command Central."

Gylberd looked around the apartment and recognized immediately that Command Central was an apt name for the place. The walls were covered, from floor to ceiling, with bookcases overflowing with books. From the looks of it, they were mostly used texts—not fine antiquarian editions, but good old reading copies of the classics, arcane histories, and obscure biographies. Gylberd's trained eye quickly scanned the collection—there were well-stocked sections devoted to theology, art, music, architecture, and *belles lettres*. He let out an appreciative whistle.

"Quite a library you've got here, Noah."

"Yeah, thanks. I haven't been able to do much with it for a while. But my Dad was a real discerning collector, so I've got lots of great titles and very little riffraff. It's a good start."

"I'll say."

But as remarkable as the small library was, it was actually not the most distinctive or dominating feature of the apartment. Everywhere Gylberd looked there were long folding tables stacked with complex electronic habiliments, digital machinery, and vintage computers. Wires, cables, and data lines splayed out across the floor and snaked up onto the tables. Processors of all shapes and sizes hummed with frenetic energy. Monitors blinked a kaleidoscope of colors onto the book-laden walls and lent an eerie glow to the entire place. It looked something like the willy-nilly trading floors of the Stock Exchange in New York or the Board of Trade in Chicago. The humming and whirring high-tech accouterments of data processing, number crunching, metaverse surfing, multitasking protocols, and telecommunications were strewn all throughout the apartment—literally everywhere.

Noah followed Gylberd's eye toward the banks of equipment.

"This is my own little collection."

"It appears to be more than just a little collection." Gylberd's voice revealed a healthy dose of amazement.

"Well, I've been at this for a good while—and I spend almost all my free time on it. Here, let me show you what I've got. There's some really cool stuff here."

He walked over to the first table. "I decided a long time ago that some of the earliest computer equipment—stuff that most people just get rid of once they've decided to upgrade to the latest and greatest improvements, advances, and releases—might be really helpful someday in some of my research and development work. This table is full of my antiques. Old computers that nobody wants anymore. You can't really buy software for any of them. There is little or no support. In fact, most of the companies that made these machines either don't even exist anymore or aren't manufacturing for this part of the computing market. But the equipment still works—and a lot of it is really interesting. Working with this stuff helps me think outside the box along primary programming lines rather than simply layering technology upon technology, application upon application."

On the table squatted the pioneer machines of an earlier computing era—all of them in perfect operating condition. Their bulky cases, ostentatious designs, and gawky features betrayed their vintage. Though nearly all of them were less than two decades old, they represented the extinct dinosaurs of the computing ecology.

"This is one of my favorites. It's a Kaypro. One of the very first attempts at a portable computer. It was really quite clever for the time. Great industrial design."

"I remember those," Gylberd exclaimed. "I almost bought one. They were a writer's dream back in the early eighties."

"Yeah. They were cheap, intuitive, reliable, and—for those days—relatively fast." Noah patted the boxy sheet metal case with the drop-down keyboard.

"What's this one?"

"Ah, that's another beauty. It's an Osborne. It was manufactured for only a few of years. It was also an early attempt at a portable. But this one was really designed for business applications. Check out the amber monitor and the sleek molded plastic shell. Most of these used the DOS operating system and proprietary software—not exactly user friendly, even for relatively simple operations like word processing and database management. That's why this one over here was so revolutionary."

"Oh my, you've got an original Mac."

"Yeah. It was such a great machine. And it really transformed the computing industry. More than any other innovation or development—except maybe the Internet—this little processor brought the power of computing to anyone and everyone. It was accessible, stylish, hip, versatile, and fun. I still love to use it."

Scattered atop the tables was a veritable museum of computing history. There were early versions of gaming systems like Atari, Nintendo, Commodore, Phalanx, and Amiga. There were long forgotten desktop machines like the Apple Lisa, the Next workstation, the NCR network server, and the Toshiba mediaplayer. There were experimental portables and laptops like the first Compaq dispenser-style portable, the early Apple flop-top portable, the initial Powerbooks and Thinkpads, and the revolutionary Omnibooks. There were rows of PDA machines including the earliest Newton, Sharp, Psion, Moblion, Palm Pilot, Omni Go, Mobile Pro, Phenom, and Velo palmtops. There were even a number of fairly recent iterations of the tiny new laptops—albeit with slower processing speeds or more limited memory than the current top-of-the-line models.

"How can you possibly afford this much equipment? Surely, you've got a fortune sitting here in this apartment," Gylberd worried.

"Well, actually, I didn't buy much of it at all. In fact, almost none of it."

"This stuff isn't . . . it isn't . . . stolen, is it?"

"Oh, no. No. You needn't worry about that, Doc. The fact is, virtually all of this equipment is—or at one time, was—absolutely worthless to the folks who owned it. Technology changes so fast that once these machines were outmoded by a couple of new generations of applications, memory chips, or operating systems, they were thrown out. Literally. This stuff is the flotsam and jetsam of progress."

"So where did you get it?"

"Out of the trash, mostly. Dumpsters."

"Garbage dumpsters?" Gylberd looked quizzically around the room at the jittering concourse of analytical appliances.

"When my Dad first started collecting books seriously, he told me that the key to finding a really great deal was simply in knowing where to look—and when. Well, the same is true about defunct or obsolete technology. And particularly, this kind of superannuated computer technology. You've got to know where to look—and when. And if you do, there is no telling what you'll find."

"So you're saying you've found all this equipment in the garbage."

"Yeah. It's amazing what people will throw away, isn't it?"

"You're serious?"

"Sure. Look, most of this stuff is worthless to business or operations managers. When an old unit is superceded by new technology, what are they supposed to do with it? Some companies donate their obsolescent equipment to schools, non-profit organizations, and churches for a tax write-off. Others try to find after-markets. But a lot of them just shove the old stuff into a utility closet. After a while, when they run out of storage space, someone will go on a tear, clean the whole place out, and into the dumpsters go the machines."

"But how do you know where and when that happens?"

"Well, partly it's trial and error. Partly it's experience. I've been dumpster-diving for a couple of years now. Every one of these tables I've reclaimed. All my computers, printers, external drives, modems—really, everything except my big server—came out of trash bins. Even most of my furniture—all except for my bed, of course. I usually go out to the big office developments late at night, after the cleaning crews have already come and gone. I can tell at a glance if a dumpster holds any treasures. I pull my pickup next to the bin and unload whatever looks interesting. After several stops, I'll come back here to the apartment and sort through what I've got. I'll throw out whatever I decide is unredeemable and keep the rest."

"And the stuff you find is generally in good condition?"

"Not always. But I may be able to cannibalize a couple of pieces of equipment in order to make up one complete restoration. Sometimes a machine will malfunction or break down and it is easier and more cost effective for the company to buy new gear rather than to fiddle with repairs—especially since the evolution of software and hardware moves along so quickly. Usually, with laptops, the first thing to break is the screen hinge. People drop them or they try to pick them up while they're open. With keyboards, storage media, and disk drives, it's usually something like spilled coffee or soft drinks. It's tedious, but repairing that stuff can be done without much of a problem. Then I just clean the unit up and add it to my collection. If a component is broken beyond repair, I take whatever else from the machine I can salvage—the screen, the processor, the motherboard, the case, whatever. Then if I find another one, I've got two sets of parts that I can pool together to make a single working model. This Apple II here was cobbled together using four different units. But look, it works great. And it's a wonderful little machine—the first really useful computer for educational purposes."

"Amazing."

"I know. It really is. America is a consumer society where everything has essentially become disposable. As a result, a whole dumpster-diving subculture has developed. Late at night in our urban centers an entire alternative world comes to life— a nocturnal world of thrashers, skaters, divers, and hackers. I first became aware of it lurking in online chat rooms. I decided to check it out—and I guess, one thing led to another."

Noah pulled up a chair—an ergonomic office model—and beckoned Gylberd to sit down. "Is there something I can get you to drink? I've got water, tea, and Dr. Pepper."

"Sure, a DP sounds great. Thanks."

He reached into a practically empty refrigerator and pulled out a couple of cans. "You'll have to excuse my informality," Noah said apologetically. "I don't really have a living room, or dining room, or even a bedroom—all this stuff pretty much takes up all my available space, and then some. Sorry."

"Not a problem. This is like a digital theme park. I love it."

"Yeah, well, it's serviceable. And it has given me the opportunity to learn an awful lot."

"I guess. So, tell me what it is you wanted to talk about. As wonderful as it is, I have a hunch you didn't ask me to come over here for an afternoon of show and tell."

"Well, it is related. I wanted to talk to you about your lecture this morning—or actually, I wanted to talk to you about some of the issues you raised in it."

"OK. Shoot. What issues exactly are you interested in?"

"The end of the world."

"Ah ha. Right. And this has something to do with my lecture this morning?"

"Well, you mentioned the Y2K problem—the Millennium Bug. How much exactly, do you know about it?"

"Umm. Gee, not a whole lot. Basically, what I mentioned in class today. It looks to be a pretty serious problem if businesses and governments fail to respond in a responsible manner. They could discover that their computers suddenly shut down—or give erroneous data. But, I don't really think we'll see that kind of a worst-case scenario, because most companies will realize the necessity of making their systems compliant, and they'll do whatever is necessary to beat the deadline."

"I don't think so."

"Really? You think that companies will just sit back and try to ignore this mess?"

"Yeah, I do. For the same reason that they throw out perfectly good equipment rather than take the time and the energy to fix it or upgrade it or whatever."

"You may have a point there. But, outdated equipment is one thing. Allowing entire infrastructure systems to expire is another matter altogether. The consequences of inaction, indecision, or inattention could be catastrophic. Surely business leaders recognize that fact."

"You know, Doc, I've been a Y2K skeptic for a long time. I've always had a very hard time believing that Civilization-As-We-Know-It was coming to an end simply because the date-sensitive codes in our computers are inappropriately abbreviated."

"You've been a skeptic for a long time? How long have you known about this? It's all pretty much new information to me."

"Well, I started reading bits and pieces about it a couple of years ago—but there have been articles, newsletters, and web sites devoted to it for a really long time. The thing is, I always figured that some cyber stud in Silicon Valley would come up with a silver bullet solution for all our looming technical glitches. I read the nay-saying newsletters, the doomsday Internet postings, and prophetic hand-wringing and just chalked it all up to all too predictable survivalist and *fin de siecle* hysteria."

"But not anymore?"

"Nope. Not anymore. There are less than 600 days remaining before the world's computer code must be made compliant—thus, able to read four digit dates (1998, 1999, 2000, 2001) instead of the current two digit standard (98, 99, 00, 01). It seems like this ought to be a simple upgrade process of search-and-replace. But it's not. It's a tedious process where codes literally have to be replaced one at a time. And there are billions of lines of code that must be replaced—at enormous costs that most assuredly will have negative effects on our economy."

"Yes, but that can be done."

"Well, yes. It's technically within the realm of conceivability. And that's the good news. But the bad news is that we probably don't have enough time left—even if we were willing to spend the money, hire the staff, and set the priorities necessary to accomplish the task. Most Fortune 500 companies simply won't be ready. And the government is woefully far behind—most agencies will not have mission-critical operations compliant until well into the first decade of the new millennium."

"That's not good. Not good at all—if you're right."

"I think I've done my homework on this one, Doc. I really wish I was wrong. Because, you're right, this situation is not good at all. The fact is, computers just can't think or reason, so if they get confused over whether the day is Saturday January 1, 2000, or Monday January 1, 1900, they simply shut down. Zap. Kaput. Nada. Zilch."

"So, Noah, what are you saying?"

"You said it yourself—in your lecture today. The problem we're facing as we enter the twenty-first century is only partly technological. To be sure, the thousands upon thousands of computers we have come to rely upon—for our electrical power grid, our telephone network, our fresh water supply, our hospital equipment, our planes, trains, and automobiles, our commercial system, our food distribution, our banking, our national defense, and a myriad of other daily necessities—are jeopardized by the domino effect of crashes, defaults, and failures due to confusing or conflicting commands. There are even embedded chips hidden in our cars, our household appliances, our medical equipment, and on and on and on. And no one even knows whether those chips are complaint. In fact, no one really knows where all those chips actually are. That is bad enough. What may be worse are the social ramifications of the Y2K debacle."

"OK, I see where you're headed."

"Doc, what would our communities be like if forced to go without power, phones, food, water, gas, or police protection for three days? What about three weeks? Or maybe, three months? Even a minor and short-lived disruption of basic services could have a catastrophic effect on our society."

"It would not be a pretty picture."

"Worse than that. January 1, 2000, may be the day the world shuts down. It could be the end."

"I don't know, Noah. That's pretty radical."

"I know. That's why I really wanted to talk this over with you. I've got lots of files on this. I even have a book or two over here somewhere. I've been hosting an online discussion forum so I've been able to tap into tons of links to related sites with oodles of information. This Zip disk is chock full of the best articles, charts, graphs, estimates, timelines, and raw data I've been able to accumulate over the past several months. And that's not all. There is a whole lot more where all this came from.

"So, what do you want me to do?"

"Read through it all. Or at least evaluate what I've pulled together. Then just tell me what you think. What I'm really hoping is that you'll see something that I haven't so far—that you'll tell me that this is all a bunch of harum-scarum nonsense. Maybe you'll even find a silver bullet solution out there somewhere."

"Well, thanks for the confidence, Noah, but I'm not so sure I'm the best person to ask for this sort of thing. I'm not exactly a technophile."

"Doc, I've heard you say that your aspiration is to be able to intelligently discuss any subject for at least five minutes. Well, here's your chance to add another subject to your already broad repertoire. Tell me that we're not looking over a gaping chasm into social oblivion. Tell me that I'm all wet about this thing. Tell me that I've got it all wrong. Find the good news in this bad news story."

"Noah, if I can, I will. But I'm afraid I'm in way over my head here."

"Well, if I'm right about this, I think we all are. And that's the problem."

Four

"All things work together for good." Romans 8:28

APRIL 13, 1998

P riam lived with his family in Brentwood, a historic town
turned upscale bedroom community about twenty miles
from his company's executive offices in downtown
Nashville. Typically, it took him thirty minutes to get home—
assuming he left from the office immediately following the peak
of rush-hour traffic. Tonight, however, he had left—or had been
forced to leave—early.

He hated traffic. He hated to wait. He avoided standing in
lines at the grocery store, the movie theater, or the mall. He
never checked luggage when he traveled. He simply didn't have
the patience. And he never drove in heavy traffic if he could help
it. But as he pulled out of the parking garage, he could already
see cars backed up for several blocks trying to get onto the freeway which looked to be stopped altogether. It seemed that he

was destined to spend almost an hour in rush-hour traffic, alone with his thoughts.

And there was little likelihood that they would be pleasant thoughts.

Quite simply, Priam was stunned. He wasn't really angry; rather, he was confused. He had never been fired from a job in his life. He had always tried to work hard, do his best, and maintain a good attitude. This formula had worked for his entire career.

Until now.

This can't be happening to me, he thought. *Why did I get the blame for a problem I didn't create? He can't do this to me. Surely he'll cool off and call me back when he can think of a face-saving way to do it. Maybe Jill or Glenn will talk some sense into him. They understood the problem.* Alas, the realities of office politics made him uneasy over this last point. No, Menelaus meant what he said. And he was going to stick to it, come hell or high water.

Priam played back the meeting in his mind again and again, trying to make sense out of it. But it just didn't add up. He tried to think how he might have presented this information in a less threatening manner. But he realized there wasn't anything he could have done to change the magnitude of the problem. Someone's head had to roll. Everyone else in the meeting was probably relieved that the problem was finally identified—but that they had not been chosen as the sacrificial lamb. The thought stung. He knew it wasn't personal, though. Just business as usual.

His first inclination was to blame the entire mess on Menelaus. After all, he'd done his homework and followed every appropriate procedure. The facts spoke for themselves. Ignoring them wouldn't help anyone or anything. Menelaus seemed to be operating from a fatally flawed proposition that might very well sink the company: *if you don't like the message, shoot the messenger.*

But as much as he wanted to shift the responsibility to Menelaus, he simply could not escape a plaguing sense of self-doubt. *You've just always got to rush in where even angels fear to tread, don't you? You're impetuous. You're pompous. You always think that you can pull the fat out of the fire by your own self-reliance, pluck, or ingenuity. What gall! Well, it finally caught up with you, didn't it, Bobbie-boy? You're just reaping what you've sown—or haven't sown! Be sure, your sins will find you out. And this is just the beginning!*

"Stop it! Just stop it!" Priam cried out in protest.

As soon as the words left his lips, he felt like a fool. "Oh great, now I'm talking to myself," he muttered. "This is unbelievable. I can't believe I'm actually torturing myself like this—all for doing my job well."

But he somehow knew that his self-examination, however tortuous, had uncovered an uncomfortable truth: he was a prideful, domineering, and self-absorbed man. His life had become terribly unbalanced.

Priam's meteoric career advancement had given him an excuse to put everything else on the back burner. Family, friends, and faith were all relegated to the background of this everyday life, to the precincts of the catch as catch can. He wasn't involved in his community. He didn't know his neighbors. He wasn't particularly regular in his church attendance. His relationship with his children, though tender, was hurried and harried. And though he really wanted to, he didn't even spend much time alone with his wife.

It wasn't that his work demanded so much of him. He was simply obsessive. He had high expectations for himself. So, he spent every spare minute thinking about his job. He would often make promises to himself, to his wife, to his children—and sometimes to God—that he would recover a bit of balance as soon as things slowed down. But, of course, they never did. The days turned into weeks, the weeks turned into months, and the months turned into years.

Why does it always seem to take a crisis to make me reexamine my priorities? Why is balance always such an all-or-nothing struggle? He hit the steering wheel with his fist and looked for an open space to advance in the snail's pace traffic.

PRIAM HAD ALWAYS BEEN fascinated by high wire acts. He could still recall with vivid clarity the very first time he craned his neck up toward the pinnacle of the Big Top to witness the astonishing spectacle of a beautiful woman prancing across the wide span of the tent with nothing beneath her but a thin cable. He was transfixed by the ultimate risk of everything.

He was probably about five years old when his father— finally giving in to his relentless begging—had taken him to the circus to see the lions and tigers and bears. The pungent closeness of the sawdust-covered arena floor, the wafting aromas of popcorn and cotton candy, the dazzling sights of clowns on motorcycles, acrobats on horseback, and daredevils in cages with roaring beasts captivated his imagination to be sure. He was wide-eyed with wonder. But the moment the high wire act began, nothing else seemed to matter. Though there were three rings of furious and fabulous activity spread out before him, he only had eyes for the daring woman balanced a hundred feet above.

He was hooked.

For the next several years he learned everything he could about high wire acts. He followed the amazing careers of the

Flying Wallendas—a single family that somehow produced three generations of the greatest performers the circus world has ever known. He collected their stats, figures, and memorabilia as relentlessly as any baseball fan.

As he looked back on it now, he was not entirely sure what it was that so gripped his imagination. He'd always been just a tad afraid of heights—so it wasn't as if he ever wanted to actually do what the Wallendas did. Certainly he did not relish the thought of living the life of a circus performer—even as a youngster he was a committed homebody. Perhaps it was simply a recognition of the phenomenal sense of balance the acts demanded—the ability to avoid the extremes of either left or right, of forward or backward. It seemed as if he was always striving for balance—whether he was learning to ride his bike, or climbing into the highest branches of a tree in his backyard, or seesawing with his friends on the school playground. A sense of balance lends grace and agility to almost any activity—and he'd always desired that. Maybe that is why the Wallendas and their high wire kith and kin were always so attractive to him. Maybe that is why they made such an indelible impression on him— risking everything while remaining in perfect balance.

Now as an adult, he had often considered how much like a high wire act his daily life tended to be. Again and again he found himself dangerously shuffling a hundred urgent tasks, precariously perched high above his circumstances, hanging by what seemed to be just a thread—and all without a net. It made single-level situations excruciatingly boring to him—like most social occasions, or even his wife's nightly recital of the day's activities.

Sitting on the freeway on this particular day, he felt as if he really ought to have the balance of a Flying Wallenda. And that was no mean feat—especially since this was no circus act. What he needed to balance was his life—and that at a time when everything seemed to be going wrong.

Of course, everyone struggles with the competing concerns of life, he thought. So, how do people successfully juggle their obligations at work with their responsibilities at home? How do they give proportionate weight to the things that they know they need to do and the things that they just want to do? How do they keep their priorities at the forefront of their daily agenda even in the face of the tyranny of the urgent? How do they maintain a clearheaded perspective in this fast-paced, willy-nilly, fly-by-the-seat-of-our-pants world?

Everyone he loved benefited from his success, although they might complain about some of its consequences. He knew they didn't want an ambitionless, passive husband and father to replace him. Like a high wire act, he yearned for—he needed—balance.

But he wanted something more than a compromised life, a surly détente of pragmatic resignation. He wanted something more than a conservative suppression of wilder urges, a kind of taming of residual barbarian impulses. He wanted something more than a happy medium between virtue and vice. Instead, the kind of balance he was after was a well-rounded, whole-hearted, fully-integrated life. It was an animated life-style of symmetry and stability, of equilibrium and equanimity, of imperturbability and unflappability. It was a happy melding of devotion and action, being and doing, patience and passion. It was a careful integration of the inner life and the outer life—manifesting word and deed, faith and works, forgiveness and discipline. It was more practical than pragmatism, more thoughtful than rationalism, more experienced than existentialism, and more romantic than sentimentalism. It was more stable than conservatism and more progressive than liberalism.

He knew the key was probably spiritual, but that thought made him more than a little uneasy. He just wanted it all. *If wanting it all was balance, then so be it. But did such a balance exist? Could it? Or were such longings little more than Flying Wallenda fantasies?*

FOR ABBY, PRIAM'S WIFE of nineteen years, it was a fairly typical day. After an hour of nonstop rushing around, she finally got the children out the door to catch the carpool to school. After a quick kiss, an "I love you" for each, and a cheerful wave, she shut the front door, and breathed a sigh of relief. Less than an hour later the school office had called. Hector, their twelve-year old, had a sore throat and was running a fever. Abby uttered another sigh and headed out the door. So much for her plans to have lunch with her mom and spend the afternoon running errands.

The Priams were upstanding members of a local evangelical church, St. Andrew's. However, Abby and the children were the only regular attendees in the family. Priam usually made it to the Sunday worship service only once or twice a month. He always had some seemingly reasonable excuse—a big presentation he had to prepare for, an unexpected emergency at the office, or he was just too tired from the demands of the previous week. Abby wished her husband placed a higher value on spiritual things, but she had grown weary of pressing the issue—and wary of the price she paid when she did. Whenever she brought it up, it only seemed to push him further away. After all, he was a wonderful husband and good provider. If he wasn't spiritually motivated at this time in his life, well, that was between him and God. She wasn't about to be a nag like her mother—her dad's resultant stony silence had drummed that determination into her long ago.

Abby was more than just a frequent church attendee. She was actively involved in a variety of spiritual pursuits. She was vice president of the women's fellowship at church, led a small group Bible study in her home once a week, and taught the sixth grade Sunday school class. Though not a perfect Christian by any means, she was serious and substantive when it came to matters of faith.

Abby had learned to see everything that came to her throughout the day—whether good or bad—as having been sent by the Lord. As her grandfather used to say, "The devil may sometimes bring it, but the Lord always sends it."

The call from the school was no different. "Thank you, Lord, for Hector's sickness," she prayed on the fly. "Restore him quickly. And give me the grace to deal with it as more than just an interruption to our schedule." Abby then jumped into the family's new minivan and headed for the school.

Although Hector was definitely too sick to stay in school, he was not too sick to command his Mom's attention for most of the day. Except for an hour-and-a-half nap after lunch, the two spent the day playing cards, watching the *Hoosiers* video (for the upteenth time), and putting together a puzzle. He took full advantage of the unshared attention.

ABBY WAS JUST STARTING to prepare dinner when she heard the automatic garage door opener kick in and the unmistakable sound of her husband's Jeep Cherokee a few moments later. *I wonder why he's home so early*, Abby thought. She wiped her hands on her apron and opened the door into the garage.

"Hi, Sweetie. You're home early."

Priam was just making his way up the steps to the kitchen. "Yeah. It's been quite a day," he said with a sigh.

"Sounds like it. I, uh, prayed for you this morning," she replied, trying to sound cheerful.

"Thanks," he said without any emotion. As he entered the kitchen, he set his briefcase down, and then offered Abby a faint smile and an obligatory kiss. As he hugged her, he sighed again.

"Good grief. What's wrong, Bob? You look like you've got the world on your shoulders."

He took off his coat and opened the closet door to hang it up. "Not the whole world. Just ours."

"Tell me about the meeting. I've been dying to hear how the presentation went." Actually, from his demeanor, Abby was not at all certain she wanted to hear about it. She began chopping vegetables for the salad, trying to appear at ease.

"You're not gonna believe it, Abby." He shook his head.

"What happened?" She wiped her hands and sat down at the kitchen table. Priam fell into the chair across the table from her. She forced herself to meet his eyes.

"Well, I thought everything was going to be fine. We had a great month last month and Frank seemed to be in a really good mood. I'd already briefed the other guys individually, so I knew they weren't gonna give me any static. I started with the *Apollo 13* analogy, hoping it would get everyone's attention, especially Frank's. Everything seemed to be going just great until I started talking about what it was going to cost to fix the problem."

As he was talking, he got up, walked across the room, opened the refrigerator, and helped himself to a Coke. He paused, popped the top, took a deep swallow, and then continued.

Abby bit her tongue to keep from asking him to get to the point. *What had happened?*

"When I started giving him the numbers, his face started to get red. Everything seemed to shift into slow motion. I felt like

51

I was watching a really bad B-movie. He asked me why I didn't bring this whole thing to his attention sooner. Can you believe it?"

"You're kidding?" Abby said in disbelief.

"No! Then he started lecturing *me* on how the Y2K repairs were going to adversely affect the bottom line, the value of the company's stock, the shareholders' equity, yada-yada-yada. Then he actually asked me what would happen if we *didn't* fix the computers—as if we could just brush the whole thing under the rug and be done with it. I was amazed. I told him we'd be out of business. Even Laura backed me on that one. You know what he asked me then?"

"What?"

"He asked me if I was trying to get him fired!"

Abby frowned and shook her head, empathizing with his predicament. Frank Menelaus had a difficult ego to deal with. She thought again of his wife with compassion.

"He then blamed the whole thing on me. He said I should have been working on this problem years ago. I mean, he went on a tirade, Abby. He said he thought it was about time he got a CIO that knew what he was doing. He actually started swearing at me . . . in front of everyone! I've never been so humiliated."

"So what happened then?" Abby demanded.

"Well, he . . . he fired me." Priam could hardly get the words out of his mouth. They hung thick and pregnant in the air. The full force of the emotion hit him again like a kick in the stomach. He sat down under the weight of it, and his eyes filled with tears.

ALTHOUGH ABBY TRIED to comfort and reassure him, what Priam needed most was some time alone to think through his options. So, after he'd settled down a bit, he changed into his running gear and headed out the front door. When he was feeling under stress, there was nothing he liked better than a good, long, hard workout.

Priam was a regular jogger—typically running three or four miles a day, focusing more on time than distance. Thirty minutes was generally all the time he could afford, but that seemed more than adequate for keeping his body—and especially his cardiovascular system—in shape. However, the primary reason Priam ran was for his mind. He found this was just about the only time he could really get away and think. He often solved some of his most perplexing problems and came up with his most creative solutions when he was alone on the road. It was usually a time when his mind cleared and everything came into sharp focus. This was something he needed now more than ever.

In stark contrast to his emotions, the pavement felt solid under his feet. In a way, it was reassuring and familiar. As his feet fell into their accustomed rhythm, his inner turmoil began to adjust itself to the shape of the road—a few gentle ups and downs but mostly flat and even. Priam was pushing himself harder than usual. After about ten minutes, it was as though his head popped out of the clouds, like an airliner finding the sunshine above the thunderheads. He felt a gentle peace envelop his whole being. Somehow, at that moment, he intuitively knew everything was going to be all right.

Maybe the Lord is trying to get my attention, he thought. *The truth is, it could be a lot worse!* He then thought of Ed Wright, one of his business associates, who had dropped dead of a heart attack at forty-six. He remembered how that had been such a "wake-up call" when it had happened, reminding him of his own mortality. Unfortunately, it was a lesson he quickly forgot. He thought of the couple—long-time friends—he and Abby knew that were in the midst of a messy divorce. He also thought of several of the other guys at work whose kids were on drugs or in some other kind of trouble.

I have a lot to be thankful for, he acknowledged. *I'm in reasonably good health. My wife loves me, even though, I'm afraid, I haven't been much of a husband in the last few years. My kids are doing well in school and seem to be relatively normal. None of us have been sick or in a serious car accident. I guess if you are going to experience some adversity, then work is the best place to have it.* For the first time in a very long time—longer than he cared to contemplate—Bob felt gratitude. *What a strange emotion to be feeling after losing my job,* he thought.

By now, a full twenty minutes into his run, Priam suspected that losing his job might be, in actuality, a divine gift—a life preserver in a storm of inverted priorities and misplaced affections. Perhaps this was the only way he could—or would—be ready, willing, and able to find the balance in his life that he so desperately needed.

His work had become an idol. And now, the idol had been knocked from its pedestal and smashed.

As the realization dawned on him, his eyes began to fill once again with tears. *How could I have been so stupid? How could I have drifted so far from the things that matter most? I know better than this!* He actually began to pray—again, for the first time in a very long time.

As he returned to his house, the sun had already begun to set. He stepped through the front door into the light and warmth within. He could smell the pleasing aroma of dinner wafting in from the kitchen. He felt as if he was coming home from afar, at long last.

ONE OF THE THINGS Abby had brought into the family when she and Priam were newly married was the tradition of "best things." Each night, as the family sat down together for dinner, each person around the table would share with the family the best thing that had happened to them that day. No one was allowed to complain, and everyone was forced to think of something positive, even if it had been a really bad day. Even when she was too tired, one of the children would speak up and insist that they do "best things." Tonight was no different.

After the prayer, Hector, without wasting a moment, said, "Dad, don't forget best things."

Although Priam was feeling better about his day, he was ready to forget the whole thing and try to deal with the fallout tomorrow. But he knew it was futile; the kids would never let him get away with it. So, after taking a deep breath and letting out an equally long sigh, he began, as the food was being passed around the table. "Okay, Hector, why don't you begin. What was the best thing that happened to you today?"

"Well," he began with a smile on his face, "I came home sick from school today. But Mom and I spent a lot of time together. We played cards, watched a video, and put together a puzzle. It was just the two of us. I guess that was my best thing."

This was the first that he had heard about Hector's sickness, so he asked, "How are you feeling now?"

Hector shrugged his shoulders and said, "Purdy good, I guess."

Priam glanced at Abby, and she rolled her eyes. Both of them had the same thought: *it's amazing how fast kids rebound from an illness—especially once school is out.*

"Good," he acknowledged. "Troy, what about you?"

Troy was their fifteen-year-old son. His life revolved around pick-up basketball, noisome music, and computer games—and he tended to be melancholy by nature.

"I don't have a best thing. The whole day sucked."

"We don't say the word *sucked* in this family, young man!" Abby snapped.

"Well, it did!" Troy insisted.

"That's not the point," Priam jumped in. "Your Mother and I don't want you using that kind of language in this house, and I don't want to hear it again. Is that understood, young man?"

"Yeah," Troy almost whispered.

"Yes, what?" Abby asked.

"Yes, sir," Troy conceded.

"That's better," Abby affirmed. "Now what was your best thing? You know the rules. Even if you had a really bad day, you have to think of something positive." Of course, everyone knew the rules. They had been drilled into them night after night. This was simply how the kids—and sometimes even Priam— offered their protest.

"Well, I didn't get run over by the bus," Troy offered with a wry grin.

His mother only scowled and gave him one of those you're-about-to-get-yourself-grounded-but-good looks.

"Okay, I got an A-minus on my Humanities test."

"Great." Abby said, a little surprised. Hector broke out clapping and everyone else joined in, too.

"No big deal," Troy muttered, somewhat embarrassed.

"Okay, what about you, Cassie . . . what was your best thing?"

Cassandra was the family's perky first-born. At seventeen, she already had the world by the tail. She rarely had a bad day, even after her monthly visit to the orthodontist to get her braces tightened. Gregarious and affable, she seemed to be everyone's best friend.

"Well, I really have two, Mom. Can I share 'em both?"

Generally, Abby tried to hold it to one item per person;

otherwise, the exercise became too tedious and everyone got restless. But tonight Abby knew that they were going to come up short on the best things scoreboard, especially once her husband shared the news about his job. "Sure. Why not?" she responded.

"Thanks, Mom. I'm *sooo* excited. I got an A on my Humanities paper and . . ."

Once again everyone broke out in applause before she could finish. Hector even whistled. After ten seconds she continued. "And I was chosen as the editor for the *Poetry Review*!" Cassie beamed. Hector high-fived her and the others followed suit. Except for Troy.

"Yeah, big deal," he grumbled under his breath. The truth was that Troy was very proud of his sister but it wouldn't be cool to admit it. Fortunately, no one else heard him. Or, if they did, they ignored it.

"Congratulations, Cassie," Priam said, trying to muster up all the excitement he could. "You'll be the best." He leaned over and gave her a peck on the cheek. "How about you, Abby, what was your best thing?"

Abby had been so concerned about what Priam was going to say when it was his turn that she had forgotten to think of something for herself. "Well, I guess spending time with Hector was my best thing, too." She flashed a smile at Hector, who looked like someone had just given him a medal. He was beaming.

"Ooooh, that's so sweet," Cassie cooed.

Now it was the moment of truth. "What about you, Bob, what was your best thing?" Abby honestly didn't know how in the world he was going to come up with anything positive about today. Frankly, it wouldn't have surprised her if, like Troy, he had said the whole day *sucked*. If there was ever an appropriate time to use *that* word, this was it.

Priam put his fork down and said something even more shocking. "This was probably one of the best days I've had in a *very* long time."

The peace in his countenance seemed to confirm it. Abby couldn't believe her ears. He went on to recount how he had lost his job and how the situation had caused him to reevaluate his priorities. Then, to Abby's utter amazement, he confessed how, over the years, he had let his priorities get all jumbled up and how he had slowly crowded faith and family out of his life. Life had become a high wire act, but he'd lost his balance. The kids were completely silent. Abby felt the tears welling up in her eyes. She knew she was witnessing firsthand the answer to a prayer she had uttered daily for more years than she could count.

"The truth is, I have been a lousy example and not much of a father, I'm afraid." Priam had to stop. The emotion was welling up inside his chest, and he knew he would be in tears if he continued. After a few moments, he regained his composure and continued. "I want to ask you all—especially you, Abby—to forgive me. I've been wrong and, starting today, I want to change." Another moment or two passed. "Will you forgive me?" As he looked up at Abby a teardrop spilled onto his right cheek and he let it fall to the table without wiping it away. Abby was sobbing quietly. She pulled a napkin to her nose and futilely tried to stop the torrent of tears streaming down her face. Despite the emotion, she felt like laughing out loud with joy.

"Oh, Bob . . ." was all she could get out.

Five

"He delivered them into the hands of spoilers
who spoiled them." Judges 2:14

APRIL 13, 1998

That night, Noah went out scavenging—taking his regular route. He went to several office buildings, industrial parks, and commercial developments. Each had yielded lucrative treasures in the past. But not tonight. After almost four hours of fruitless searching, he was about to call it an evening when he remembered seeing in the local paper that a large hospital management company was completely remodeling its executive offices. Often, such renovations would produce a rich haul of discarded equipment.

As he drove into the parking lot of the sleek low rise complex, he saw that he had been beaten to the punch. A couple of other dumpster-divers were already milling around the disposal site out behind the maintenance facilities. Noah recognized them right away. He had seen them often. They worked as a team and were very efficient. They were rarely interested in the same kinds of things he was though—generally they were after consumer items like radios, TV sets, and video players as well as office supplies, furniture, and tools.

Divers usually guarded their turf with a fierce jealousy. But these two immediately called him over. They apparently recognized him too. One of the men was tall and thin, about thirty years old, and extremely haggard. The other was short and stocky, a little younger perhaps, and a good deal less unkempt. It looked as if they hadn't recovered anything yet from the large bin behind them.

"It's locked," the tall one offered.

"Must be some good stuff for them to go to all this trouble," said the other. "Locked it up, tight as a drum."

As he walked toward the men, Noah reached into one of the pockets of his cargo khakis. "So, let's unlock it," he replied. He produced a tumbler pick set and held it up to the light. "Not a problem if you've got the tools for it."

"Good deal," said the tall one.

Both crowded in close to watch as Noah slid a wire pick into the padlock on the front of the dumpster. "Did you check the big construction bins on the other side of the parking lot?" he asked them over his shoulder.

"Yeah. Nothing but Sheetrock scrap and some rubbish."

He thought he had it for a moment but the wire slipped free and the tumblers held. The lock scraped his knuckles. "Arrrh. I hate it when that happens." He was about to select another wire when a flash of light swept across the dumpster.

"Where did that come from?"

"I'm not sure." The two men began to back away toward the shadows beside the maintenance building. The tall one seemed especially skittish.

"Security guards?"

"Yeah. Maybe." Noah went back to work on the lock, apparently unconcerned.

"Look, there it is. Over there. It's in the building. Someone's in the building. Man, we better get outta here. Come on, let's go. Look, there it is again."

"Yeah, I see it. That doesn't look like security guards though. Why would security guards be walking around inside the building with flashlights?"

"I have no idea. And I don't much care to find out, quite frankly. Hey, the dumpster's locked. Let's just get outta here. This kinda stuff spooks me."

The two men started walking quickly toward their truck. "You comin' man?"

"Naw. I'm gonna stick around. Check it out. Ya'll go on ahead. Take it easy."

"Right. See ya." The men hopped in their pickup and sped off into the night.

Noah continued to work on the lock while keeping an eye out for the lights in the building. At last the tumblers released. He slid the long rusted panel open and scanned the interior of the bin. Immediately, he knew he'd hit the jackpot. Right on top were three old ink jet printers and a tangle of serial cables. He could see several external Zip drives. And peeking out from under several garbage bags filled with office trash was the corner of a massive graphics monitor.

He went to work immediately. He ran over to his pickup, started it up, and pulled it inches away from the hulking container. He climbed into the dumpster—his Mini Maglite scanning the prize before him. In less than ten minutes, he recovered more than a dozen fine, serviceable pieces of equipment. There were no desktop processors and only one laptop—and it looked to be in pretty bad shape, with a shattered LCD screen and a cracked case. But all in all, it was a worthy haul.

He had all but forgotten about the lights in the building when he heard voices coming from that direction. And once again, a beam of light swept across the front of the dumpster.

Time to go, he thought to himself.

Crawling out of the dumpster, he walked around the front of the truck. Just then he noticed a rear emergency door in the nearest building was propped open. There was a large cargo van parked just adjacent to it. And the beams of light he'd seen earlier seemed to have converged there. Now, he was getting curious.

Throwing all caution to the wind, Noah walked through the parking lot, over a low retainer wall, across the landscaped median, and into the open space between the maintenance facility and the office building. It was a nondescript edifice. A smoky gray curtain of glass and steel sheathed the entire structure in the kind of anonymity only modern architecture can achieve. It was featureless and efficient, like a factory, like a machine, like a computer—like a dumpster. Corporate planners prefer such a masque for being less serious, less heroic, and less evocative than that to which architecture has always aspired before. Such a building might disguise anything—anything at all, from business to pleasure, pragmatism to pretentiousness, or want to excess. And tonight apparently it did.

Noah knelt in the cool, damp grass beside a small clump of ornamental bushes. The men were hurrying out of the building and making their way toward the van. They were dressed entirely in black, from top to bottom, head to toe, and hand to foot. The dim reflecting lights from the parking lot seemed to be swallowed up in their ominous silhouettes. Oddly, they didn't appear to be carrying anything. *Definitely not security guards*, Noah thought. *But who then? If they are thieves, you would have thought that they would be carrying their stolen goods out to the van. They all appear to be empty-handed. So, what are they up to?*

Then one of the men turned to scan the area and Noah saw that at least he was carrying something. Something rather unexpected. *Uh oh. A gun. What am I doing here? That guy's got a gun. It's some kind of an automatic. An Uzi or something. Yikes, this is some pretty serious hooey here.*

The man with the gun began giving orders to the others. Noah couldn't quite make out what it was he was saying, but it was obvious that he was trying to get them to hurry up. They appeared to be rigging something—maybe, resetting the alarm system.

"Move it, move it, move it," he thought he heard someone say.

"Look, Ajax. I'm going as fast as I can."

"We're behind schedule."

"Hey, with this kind of a system, you just can't skip steps. Relax. Patience will insure that the operation goes without a hitch. Get too antsy, and mistakes will happen. Just loosen up. We've got this under control." He said something else, but the words drifted away in the cool evening breeze.

The man with the gun was still clearly nervous. He was pacing. Whatever it was that the other men were doing at the doorway was taking far more time than he was comfortable with—regardless of the other man's explanations and assurances.

Noah could really identify. The whole scene before him was more than he was comfortable with. He decided he'd better beat a hasty retreat. He wasn't sure what it was that he had seen. But whatever it was, he'd seen enough of it. Crouching low and moving gingerly over the lawn, he retraced his steps. He slipped over the median and headed toward the lot where his truck was parked.

But he forgot about the retainer wall. It was veiled in the patchy shadows, and in his haste he stumbled over it and plunged headlong into the waxleaf hedge below. *Uh oh. I've done it now.*

"Hey, who's there?" The voice of the man with the gun pierced the evening quiet.

Noah held his breath. His adrenaline was surging. His heart was racing. And his head and shoulder were aching where he'd crashed to the ground.

He heard footsteps pounding toward him. *Oh, man. Am I ever in trouble now. Do I hide? Do I try to sneak past these guys? Do I . . . No, forget it, I gotta get outta here.*

He tried to spring to his feet, but his shirt was caught in the hedge. He heard shouts from the building. And the footsteps were getting closer. They were less than a hundred yards away. He tore free and lunged into the parking lot. Scrambling to his feet he started running.

"Stop right there."

Noah ran harder and faster. He was panic stricken. He looked behind him. The man with the gun was less than fifty yards away—and several of the other men were close behind.

"I'm warning you. Stop."

Noah ran with all his might. He rounded the corner of the maintenance building. His truck was there, door still ajar. *Thank goodness.* He jumped into the cab and slammed the door just as the men came into sight again.

The keys. Where are the keys? Oh, here. OK. OK. You got it. You're all right.

The man with the gun opened fire just as the key turned in the ignition. The first rounds went wide. Noah pumped the gas and the engine sprang to life. *Almost home. Just drive. Drive.* A shot grazed the top of the cab and clanged into the side of the dumpster.

Screeching away from the curb, he steered away from the men and toward the street. By the time he reached the corner he was doing forty-five. He burst out of the parking lot, through a stop sign, and onto the two-lane blacktop.

Man, that was as close as I ever want to get, he thought.

And then he saw the van in his rear view mirror. Careening out of the parking lot and onto the street, the men were in hot pursuit. *Great. Just great. Here they come. They're chasing me.*

It would not be hard to follow him—even though he had a good head start—because the roads were virtually empty this time of night. They could see for a mile. He could run, but he could not hide. *Lord, help me. What have I gotten myself into here?*

His best hope was to make it to the freeway. Whatever it was the men were doing in the building, it was not likely that they wanted to draw too much attention to themselves. So Noah thought that if he could just get into a well-trafficked area, they might decide to break off the chase.

The roads that wind through the rolling hills of middle Tennessee are a delight to drive—unless you're in a hurry. Noah squealed around blind curves, over the crests of dangerous ridges, and down through narrow hollers with utter abandon. And though he was able to maintain the distance between himself and his adversaries, he couldn't lose them.

As he bore down on the entrance to the freeway, he had the sense to lead them away from his neighborhood. Instead of aiming back toward Brentwood, he headed north toward downtown Nashville. He slammed the little truck into overdrive as he pulled onto the frontage road. It lurched forward. Before long, he was speeding along, faster than he had ever driven. But his heart was racing faster still.

After a few moments, he glanced back. No sign of them. The van was nowhere to be found. Apparently, the men had never gotten on the freeway. Still, Noah drove on, unrelenting, towards the burgeoning skyline ahead.

NASHVILLE WAS A BOOMTOWN. Its forward-thinking leadership was attempting to shed the city's image as little more than the capital of country music and home of the Grand Ole Opry. The once decaying downtown was bustling with renewal efforts. A new outdoor stadium, a vast new art museum, a new downtown library, a sprawling new public park, and a new indoor arena were all either under negotiation or already under construction. A vibrant restaurant and shopping district had revitalized the riverfront—once a tawdry example of urban blight. And high-tech businesses with flashy corporate headquarters were moving in at a record pace, attracted by intentionally structured tax-incentives.

The music and media industries were investing huge sums in the city's infrastructure—as more and more companies decided to leave Los Angeles for more hospitable cultures and climes. Several fine universities and colleges, a massive medical research and training complex, an easily accessed world-class airport, and stunning natural beauty all made Nashville an attractive site for relocation. It had become a hub for a myriad of graphic design, printing, publishing, video production, digital information systems, and telecommunications businesses. As a result, the small-town hospitality of the old South was married to the hip progressivism of the corporate, academic, artistic, and entertainment worlds—an invigorating and inviting combination.

In addition, all those things meant that you could always find a good cup of coffee in town—no matter what time it might happen to be. Noah needed a cup of strong java to settle his nerves. So he headed toward one of his favorite places, a little coffee shop appropriately named HavaJava.

As he pulled into the lot, he noticed several of the late-night regulars relaxing around the small, round oak tables, listening to alternative music, and reading subversive poetry. His favorite waitress was working that shift.

In the prosaic blue-collar neighborhood where Clara Rachman grew up, resentment was as common as hedgerows. She was a part of that spoiled post-war generation that was rudely awakened to the fact that they might never be able to attain the prosperity of their parents—at least not without paying the grueling price their parents had.

Their tightly packed row houses and tiny hip-pocket gardens became emblematic for them of a society where no one is ever alone but is always lonely nonetheless. As prosperity passed them by, they gradually came to believe that their own chance at affluence—indeed, that the very vehicle of their civilization—was merely the luxurious giant whim of powerful malefactors, that the narrow suburban streets they had played on as children were paved with the gold of avarice, and the traffic there was fitfully directed by robber barons.

By the time she had won a full academic scholarship to Vanderbilt University, Clara was already well-versed in the rhetoric of rancor and envy—she had become a thoroughly modern and liberated woman. She wore all of the right clothes, the uniform of her rebellion—dark and dismal. She listened to all of the right music, the standard of her defiance—angry and discordant. She went to all of the right meetings, the hallmark of her insubordination—strident and bombastic. And she believed all of the right things, the conformity of her mutiny—nihilistic and angst-ridden.

She was the picture of pampered insolence.

She committed much of her free time perusing out-of-date issues of *Feng Shui* that she kept stacked by her futon in the little loft apartment she shared with a college friend. She regularly worked herself into a piqued frenzy over such things as chlorofluorocarbons, plastic milk cartons, and styrofoam McDonalds packages. She waxed eloquent about apartheid in South Africa, deforestation in Brazil, whale harvesting in Japan, acid rain in Canada, and the international conspiracy of the Elders of Zion. She was heartbroken over what she was sure was the fraudulent electoral rejection of Daniel Ortega in Nicaragua. She was dumbfounded by the collapse of the workers' paradise in Eastern Europe brought about by the desovietization of Gorbachev's *perestroika*. And she was flabbergasted by the popularity of the likes of Rush Limbaugh, G. Gordon Liddy, Randall Terry, Ollie North, and the rest of the resurgent conservative movement across America.

Early on, Clara had become lemminglike in her hipper-than-thou, perennially indignant, and compulsively correct political associations. She joined Greenpeace, of course. And Amnesty International. But she also became a member of the Committee in Solidarity with the People of El Salvador, Housing Now, People for the Ethical Treatment of Animals, the African National Congress, Sierra Club, and the New Internationalist Women's Cooperative. She even bathed with Body Shop soaps, ate Ben and Jerry's ice cream, and wore Birkenstock knockoffs and a cheap dangling nose ring.

Like any good Materialistic Atheist, she knew what she knew. But like any good New Age Agnostic, she did not know what she did not know.

Noah loved engaging her in conversation—just to see if he could get a rise out of her. The fact was, he thought she was beautiful when she got angry—her gray eyes flashed, her short auburn hair fluttered, and her creamy smooth complexion flushed. He even thought that their conversations had struck a nerve with her from time to time—she actually seemed to enjoy their little squabbles. And tonight, he could use a bit of a friendly diversion.

"Hey, Clara. How's my favorite feminazi?"

She looked up over the counter and smiled broadly. "Great. How's my favorite fascist?"

Boy, it sure feels good to be someplace normal, safe, and sane, he thought. He pulled up a stool and ordered a triple cappuccino. He looked up at the clock. It was just a few seconds before midnight—and he watched as the day ebbed away with a sweep of the second hand.

Six

APRIL 14, 1998

P riam awoke promptly at 5:30 A.M., just before his alarm
clock was set to go off. Although he had no place to go,
he had failed to inform his body.

He turned the alarm off, and, for half a second, began men-
tally preparing to get ready and head to the office as usual.
Then, like being rudely awakened from a nap by a bucket of ice
water in the face, it dawned on him: *I don't have a job!* Priam felt
a flash of panic and then a cloud of melancholy descended upon
him. It wasn't exactly depression—he had worked through the
whole matter yesterday during his run. At least intellectually. He
was simply feeling the inevitable emotional response that accom-
panies any significant loss. So much of his self-esteem was
wrapped up in what he did. Now that that was gone, he felt
confused.

What am I supposed to do now? he wondered.

Priam folded his hands behind his head and remained in bed, staring at the ceiling. He let out a long, deep sigh and looked over at Abby, who was still sleeping. Again, he felt the gratitude he had experienced last night when he was running. *Thank the Lord, I don't have to go through this alone.*

After the kids had gone to bed, Priam and Abby had talked through their options. They had stayed up until almost midnight. They hadn't talked that much to each other in years. Priam became painfully aware of how much he had missed by not sharing with Abby his deepest fears and dreams. The truth was that no one loved him more than she did. She also possessed great intuition and keen spiritual insight. She was a great help in sorting out the options and keeping things in perspective. Frankly, he needed her objectivity and optimism. He wondered why in the world he had failed to avail himself of her counsel until now.

In the rush and embarrassment of leaving the office, Priam had forgotten to ask about severance pay. Based on similar situations in the past, he was fairly certain they would give him at least three months pay and benefits and possibly as much as six. He wouldn't know for sure until he called the Human Resources Department. Regardless, whether it was three or six, it wasn't a lot of breathing room. He and Abby had almost no savings, so when the severance ran out, they would be in real trouble. Abby was certain that he would find a job before that happened, but, secretly, Priam wasn't so sure. The experience of being fired had already dealt a serious blow to his self-esteem.

As Priam thought about trying to find a job, he felt a wave of dread wash over him. He had not been in this position since his first job out of college. Every job he'd had since then had found him. Now the shoe was on the other foot, so to speak. He let out yet another deep sigh and closed his eyes.

At that moment he felt Abby's hand slide over his chest and her warm body draw close to his. He opened his eyes and glanced at her. She offered a reassuring smile, as if she knew exactly what he was thinking—and needed. She gave him a hug and whispered, "Good morning." Priam didn't say anything but returned her hug. A shiver ran down his spine.

They lay together on the bed, enjoying one another's silent company. Neither of them wanted to break the spell. Priam wished the moment could last forever. He desperately wanted to avoid confronting the challenge that lay before him. Finally though, he realized it was futile. Facing the day was inevitable. After a few moments, he spoke.

"Are you worried?" he asked. Priam wasn't quite sure he was willing to admit that he was, in fact, the one who was worried. Without quite consciously thinking about it, he thought it might be easier to share his fears if she acknowledged hers first.

She raised her head slightly from his chest and looked deeply into his eyes. She had the look of total confidence and trust. "Not one bit," she answered deliberately. She brushed his hair off his forehead and propped herself up on one elbow. She smiled and then said, "Honey, you'll have so many options . . . your biggest problem will be deciding which one to take!"

Priam wasn't sure Abby was right, but her confidence was contagious and he could feel his spirits lifting. His sense of dread began to melt.

"Well, then . . . I guess I'd better get busy." He kissed her on the cheek and headed for the bathroom to shave.

UNLIKE EVERY OTHER MORNING for as long as Priam could remember, he wasn't in a hurry. He ate breakfast with the kids and even helped them get ready for school. In doing so, he felt a new sense of appreciation for what Abby went through every day. Getting three kids fed, clothed, and out the door was no small task. By 8:05, he and Abby were alone in the house.

"You go through that every morning?" Priam asked.

"Yep. But it's down hill from there," she chuckled.

"So what do you do next?" Priam asked.

"Next comes my favorite part of the day," she said with a twinkle in her eye. "First, we get a fresh cup of coffee." They walked into the kitchen and filled their cups. "Now, we get to go sit out on the porch, watch the birds, enjoy the flowers, pray, think, dream, read, and drink in the quiet."

Abby had created a sanctuary all across the front of the house. Within a rustic picket fence a variegated palate of colors and textures mimicked the very best of the old English cottage gardens. Already, the first of the spring flowers and bulbs lined the long walk, surrounded the shade trees, and enfolded the house. Huge herb beds bestowed a complex bouquet of scents, fragrances, and aromas over the entire yard. Several birdhouses and feeders marked the perimeter of this demi-paradise and a large stone birdbath sat in its center like a brazen oasis of refreshment and delight.

They sat together for a long time in silence imbibing the rich libations of beauty and rest that enveloped them. Chickadees and goldfinches fluttered around them. A pair of bees buzzed from flower to flower. The gentle music of leaves rustling rose and fell in an even, certain, and rhythmical cadence.

Priam wondered at all that he had missed by never savoring moments like this before.

HIS STRATEGY FOR GETTING A JOB was simple. Priam planned to call some of his contacts at other companies and begin getting the word out. He then wanted to follow-up with a résumé. The only problem was that he had never prepared one. He hadn't needed to. He had reviewed scores of résumés as a manager, but he had never paid much attention to what they should include or the format that was used. So, after his brief morning sojourn on the porch with Abby, he packed up his laptop computer and headed for the neighborhood library. He had spent most of the morning researching the subject and had succeeded in duplicating the best of the information he had found. He finished reading his résumé through for the second time, put his laptop into suspend mode, and drove home.

It was a beautiful spring day in middle Tennessee. The trees were budding—the pears were a luminescent white, the redbuds were a rich scarlet, and the sugar maples were a golden yellow. The cicadas were humming, the goldfinches were chirping, and the daffodils were blooming. *It won't be long until the lawn has to be mowed for the first time this season,* Priam noted. *I guess I'll cancel the service and do it myself, at least for now.*

When Priam got home, he found a note from Abby.

"Bob—I've gone to the hospital to visit Jill. There's some turkey in the fridge if you want to make a sandwich for lunch. See ya about 2. Love, Abby." He silently thanked her for not hovering, an impulse he knew she had resisted.

Before making lunch, Priam walked out to the mailbox and got the mail. There were the usual bills and reams of junk mail, but there was also the new issue of *Business Week*. The cover story was about the Millennium Bug and was entitled, "Zap! How the Year 2000 Bug Will Hurt the Economy: It's Worse Than You Think."

Up to this point, most of his focus on the problem had been on the corporate consequences of not getting the bug fixed. Priam had not spent a lot of time thinking about the global impact or what effect it might have on the economy—or on him and his family.

"Hmmm," he said out loud. "This sounds interesting."

Priam made lunch, sat down at the kitchen table, and began reading. Several statements struck him as extremely significant:

- Up to now, skeptics have been able to pooh-pooh Year 2000 as a relatively easy-to-fix bug, an example of over-heated hype by consultants looking for a quick buck. But there's growing alarm in Washington and elsewhere. . . .

- Indeed, the Y2K bug is shaping up to have a profoundly negative impact on the U.S. economy—starting almost immediately. . . .

- It's not only the growth rate that will be affected. Starting in 1999, inflation will be higher than it otherwise would have been and productivity growth will be lower. . . .

- And the amount of skilled labor needed is enormous. Finding, fixing, and testing all Y2K-affected software would require over 700,000 person-years, calculates Capers Jones, head of Software Productivity Research, a firm that tracks programmer productivity. . . .

- A December, 1997, survey by Howard Rubin, a computer science professor at Hunter College in New York, indicated that two out of three large companies did not yet have detailed plans in place to address Year 2000. Small companies and government agencies are even further behind. . .

- Some analysts worry that Y2K could send the economy into a recession. Edward E. Yardeni, chief economist at investment bank Deutsche Morgan Grenfell Inc., sees a 40% chance of a sharp downturn. One way that could happen is if there's a major failure in the government's computer systems. Each week, the federal government sends out $32 billion in Social Security and payroll checks and payments for such mundane items as rent. Even a short delay could be a major shock to the economy. . . .

- Electric utilities are only now becoming aware that programmable controllers—which have replaced mechanical relays in virtually all electricity-generating plants and control rooms—may behave badly or even freeze up when 2000 arrives. . . .

- Closer to home, state and local governments are lagging even further behind the federal government. . . . Only about one-third of states are in decent shape. . . .

- "If you are not well on your way to fixing the Year 2000 problem, you just don't have time to do everything." . . .

- Most managers, though, are going to have to start thinking about contingency plans and workarounds. "There's no question that things will fail," says Judith List, who runs the Year 2000 effort for Bellcore. . . .

For the first time, Priam began to think about the personal consequences of the Year 2000 problem. *What happens if they don't get it fixed in time? What happens if the government can't send out Social Security checks . . . or welfare checks? How long will the recipients be patient? What happens if there is a serious downturn in the economy? What happens if the electrical grid goes down? How will we heat our home? How will we survive? Is all this hype just doomsday paranoia or is this for real?*

After thinking about it for a few moments, Priam made a mental note to get on the Internet and do some more research.

But right now he had more immediate concerns—like finding a job. The end of the world would have to wait. He had to concern himself with the end of the month.

As much as he dreaded making the calls, he decided there was no use procrastinating. He might as well get started. The sooner he had something nailed down, the sooner he could relax. He made a fresh pot of coffee and headed upstairs to his office.

As Priam sat down at his desk, it suddenly dawned on him that he had still forgotten to check on the status of his severance pay. "Good grief. What have I been thinking about?" he said out loud. He immediately dialed Harv McConnell, Vice President of Human Resources. Unfortunately, he got Harv's voice mail.

"Harv, this is Bob Priam. I'm sure by now you've heard about my little run-in with Frank yesterday . . . actually, it was more like a train wreck. Anyway, in the confusion I forgot to ask about severance pay. I'm assuming that because I was terminated without cause I will get the maximum amount possible. Could you call me back to confirm this? I also need to know what happens to my health insurance and retirement fund. I'd be grateful for any help you could give me, ol' buddy."

Harv was a friend, so Priam knew he would do what he could for him. However, he also knew that Menelaus had a mean streak in him and might order the minimum out of spite. If so, Harv wouldn't have a choice. Priam offered a silent prayer and hung up the phone.

"Well, I might as well wait to worry," Priam sighed, trying to set his mind at ease.

Priam made a "hit list" of priority contacts in his day planner. These were people he had met through the years at various industry functions. Most of them were either Chief Executive Officers or Chief Information Officers at other companies. These would be the people who had the power to authorize hiring him if they chose to do so. If possible, Priam wanted to avoid the delay of having to get a position approved by the corporate bureaucracy and all that entailed. From his own experience, he knew this could take forever.

Fortunately, Priam already had all the addresses and phone numbers he would need—right in his contact management software. This would make the initial calls and subsequent follow-up a breeze. All he needed was someone on the other end of the phone with an urgent need to hire an Information Technology professional with his qualifications. He thought about Abby's encouraging words earlier that day and picked up the phone to make the first call.

By the end of the afternoon he had made thirty-five phone calls. He took a moment to tally the results. He had left twenty-three voice mail messages, spoken with eight administrative assistants, and actually had conversations with four decision-makers. The hardest part of the conversations was explaining why he had been fired. Frankly, he was embarrassed. On the one hand, he wanted to be professional and not whine— he knew that would not prove attractive to a prospective employer. But on the other hand, he felt a need to explain what had happened. The bottom line was that he had become a scapegoat for a CEO who had refused to heed his innumerable pleadings to make Y2K repairs a priority.

All four of the CIOs he had spoken with—three men and one woman—were understanding. A couple of them were facing similar scenarios in their own companies. The last man he spoke with actually got angry and suggested Priam should go over Menelaus's head and appeal directly to OfficeCentral's Board of Directors. For about thirty minutes, Priam seriously entertained the idea. Surely the Board would be reasonable. They would understand the significance of the problem. He could even document for them how he had repeatedly brought the Millennium Bug to Menelaus's attention and that he had refused to deal with it. He knew he could make a compelling case. He imagined himself ousting Menelaus and saving the company. Heck, if he played his cards right, the Board might even make him the new CEO.

But then reality let the air out of Priam's fantasy. He realized that the Board would know even less about the real situation than Menelaus. In the final analysis, they would side with him, and Priam would be left out in the cold. He would have expended a tremendous amount of energy and time with nothing to show for it. These were two scarce resources that he could not afford to waste on a war he was all but certain to lose.

Although all four of the people he spoke with were sympathetic, none of them had anything concrete to offer. Of course, they all insisted that Priam send them a copy of his résumé, but he knew that this was simply a way of politely ending the conversation. He had done it to others hundreds of times himself. Nevertheless, he dutifully faxed a cover letter with a copy of his résumé to each person he spoke with. Because he could fax directly out of his computer, he made sure each recipient received the correspondence within minutes of their conversation. He hoped this quick response would make for a positive impression.

He felt discouraged but he still had ten names on his list. As he was debating whether or not to call them now or wait until tomorrow morning the phone rang. It was Harv McConnell.

"Hey, Bob. This is Harv. I just heard the news this morning. I can't believe it! What happened in there yesterday?"

Of course, he knew that Harv had probably heard the

whole story—at least Menelaus's version of it. But Priam felt compelled to tell his side of it, just to set the record straight. For the next ten minutes, he gave Harv a blow-by-blow account.

When he finished, Harv extended his condolences. "Buddy, I am so sorry. It sure doesn't seem fair, does it? I don't know what to say. What are you going to do?"

"Well, I'm not sure. I've spent the day polishing up my résumé and putting out some feelers. So far, I haven't had any bites."

"Well, I sure wouldn't get discouraged yet. You've only been unemployed for one day! With your brains and experience, I have no doubt you'll end up with multiple offers."

"You really think so?" Priam asked, remembering how Abby had offered him similar encouragement.

"You bet! You won't last a month on the open market. Good CIOs are in short supply these days, especially with the Y2K problem scarfing 'em up." As a Human Resources professional, Harv was well aware of the labor shortage that had been created in recent months as corporations scrambled to staff Y2K projects. "My guess is that you'll end up making significantly more money." Priam certainly liked the sound of that.

"That brings me to the $64,000 question, Harv. . . . How much severance has Menelaus authorized?"

"Well, I wish I had better news. He's going strictly by the book: two weeks of severance pay for each year of service."

"Six weeks? That's it! Are you kiddin' me, Harv?" Priam was incredulous. He knew what the Corporate Policy was, but he had never seen it applied to senior executives. He knew that Menelaus had the authority to extend it for a variety of "extenuating circumstances" and almost always did.

"I wish I were. I got a memo from Frank this morning outlining the details. I'm really sorry."

Suddenly Priam knew why Harv had been so upbeat with him, insisting that he would have a new job within a month. He felt sick to his stomach.

"I can't believe it," Priam mumbled. He sighed deeply, told Harv goodbye, and hung up.

He put his face in his hands and felt a fresh wave of discouragement cascade through his body. *What am I going to do if I don't get a job in the next six weeks?* he wondered. *Maybe we can borrow some money from Abby's parents.* The idea made him even more nauseated. He visualized himself flipping hamburgers at McDonalds or bussing tables at a greasy spoon café as he had done when he was in high school. It wasn't a particularly comforting thought. In fact, a shudder of panic ran up and down his spine.

What if we end up on welfare? How will I face Abby? How will I face the kids? What in the world am I going to do?

Seven

APRIL 14, 1998

D r. Gylberd spent a sleepless night pouring over the material Noah had given him, perusing online resources, following links, and verifying data. He spent three hours reading
through one web site alone. The amount of material available
was staggering.

It seemed that the more he knew about the coming Y2K
computer crisis, the more concerned he became. And what
concerned him most was that there appeared to be very few
moderate opinions on the subject. Y2K seemed to be one of
those subjects that either caused people to resort to an alarmist
extremism or defer to a detached denial—and there was little or
nothing in between. Most of the experts—those who seemed to
have a fairly educated grasp of the technical issues involved—
seemed to believe that the Millennium Bug would bring about

the ultimate collapse of civilization, or something terrifyingly close to that. Those who downplayed the whole thing as little more than a tempest in a teapot seemed to be appallingly uninformed. It was a choice between shrill or shill.

Gylberd's strong intuition told him that the truth lay somewhere between the two extremes. But he also recognized the fact that you can't fight something with nothing. And those few voices that might well take a moderate position on the subject were essentially being shouted down by the catastrophists on the one hand or the dismissivists on the other.

That was nothing new. Sundry millenarian apocalypticists had been predicting the end of the world almost since the beginning of the world—and they were invariably loud, obnoxious, and weighted down with tomes of evidence. Gylberd was not at all surprised that the year 2000 would attract the attentions of conspiracy theorists, prophetic doomsayers, eschatological seers, eternal pessimists, and various other worry-warts. The Y2K computer crisis had obviously become the latest Armageddon option: a convenient catastrophe for those who had alternately looked to killer bees, Beast-coded Social Security checks, hitch-hiking angels, conflict in the Middle East, secret federal cover-ups, biological warfare, Area 51 alien invasions, botched genetic engineering, and black helicopter deployments to usher in the last days of this, the terminal generation.

As a result, most observers tended to ignore the whole affair as little more than another Oliver Stone obsession or a Chris Carter plot idea. Gylberd was beginning to believe that perhaps the radical and conspiratorial tone of the Y2K rhetoric was precisely what kept sane and sensible people from giving it the credence it was due. It seemed evident to him that Y2K really did present formidable challenges. But the very people with the most helpful information about the challenges and how to face them were so rabid and fanatical that their frantic protestations went unheeded by cooler heads.

He didn't want to fall into that trap. But neither did he want to be gullible.

The more things change, the more they stay the same.

In the end, despite the reams of evidence he'd accumulated, he was forced to log off, suspend his inquiry, and begin his workday with far more uneasy questions than certain answers.

INTERESTINGLY, GYLBERD HAD first been introduced to Noah over the Internet. A couple of years earlier he had created a web site for the fledgling private school he had founded. Rivendell Academy pioneered a distinctive model of education that adopted the traditional elements of classical academics and applied them to the modern challenges of leadership training—identifying, raising up, encouraging, mentoring, and equipping the next generation of leaders was his passion. Almost by accident he found himself on the cutting edge of a remarkable new grassroots movement.

It quickly became apparent to him that this movement was hungry for a recovery and a rediscovery of the legacy of truth that had given rise to the remarkable flowering of beauty, progress, and freedom in Western civilization. Curriculums would be needed. New co-ops would have to be established. Networks of communication and support would need to be put into place. Training would have to be provided. Resources would need to be developed and made available.

The now-carelessly discarded traditional medieval *Trivium*—emphasizing the basic classical scholastic categories of grammar, logic, and rhetoric—had equipped earlier generations of students with the tools for a lifetime of learning: a working knowledge of the timetables of history, a background

understanding of the great literary classics, a structural competency in Greek- and Latin-based grammars, a familiarity with the
sweep of art, music, and ideas, a grasp of research and writing
skills, a worldview comprehension for math and science basics, a
prin-ciple approach to current events, and an emphasis on a
Christian life paradigm.

Gylberd was convinced that a return to that kind of rigorous
training would better prepare young men and women for the
challenges of the twenty-first century than any of the other
razzle-dazzle approaches to educational reform then in vogue.
At the same time, he was adamant that it was not a system of
education for intellectuals only. Rather, he argued, classical education was a simple affirmation that all of us need to be ground-
ed in the good things, the beautiful things, the true things. With
the utter failure of most modern educational methodologies
finally evident to all but the most hardened bureaucrat, he saw
the opportunity to really make a difference.

The thing was, he wasn't even an educator. Instead, he was
a musician. For years, he and his wife, Lois, had been mainstays
of the folk music circuit in Texas. At one time or another, they
had played every nightclub, beer hall, street fair, barbecue joint,
dinner theater, coffee house, honky tonk, showcase venue, cock-
tail lounge, chili festival, rodeo, and fund-raiser in the state—
and Texas is a big state. They were never able to have children,
so the road became a way of life to them. Though they kept a
small garage apartment in the Montrose arts district of
Houston, they were rarely ever there.

Even so, Lois had a knack for making him feel at home
wherever they were. Their rumbling little camper was always
adorned with wildflowers—bluebonnets and Indian paintbrush-
es in the spring, black-eyed Susans and Queen Anne's lace in the
summer, chrysanthemums and marigolds in the fall, and pots of
African violets and orchids in the winter. Their little foldout

table was always elegantly draped with a fresh lace tablecloth and romantically lit by candles. And their constant companionship was suffused with an indescribable tenderness and joy.

After a rich decade of marriage, Lois was struck down by a virulent strain of liver cancer. One week after they had played at the big Texas Renaissance Festival in October—they had always fancied themselves as jongleurs and troubadours so they relished the opportunity to play there—she began complaining of constant fatigue and an ache in her abdomen. The doctors initiated immediate treatments—but as is so often the case, the malignancy proved to be inoperable. And there was little that they could do to stop the rapid growth of the feral cells. By Christmas she was gone.

Gylberd was utterly lost without her.

At first, he just holed up in the little apartment. For weeks he did little more than subsist—wracked by grief, wearied by loneliness, and worn by restlessness. He couldn't sleep. And he couldn't stand to be awake. He despaired of ever returning to even a modicum of normalcy.

But then, just before Easter, he began to read—searchingly and substantively. For several months he resolved to read through all the classics of what traditional educators have called the Western Canon. He read and read and read. He read widely. He read seriously. He found that the books afforded not only solace for the heartache of his unimaginable loss but vision for his unfathomable future.

He quickly discovered, though, that the problem with serious reading is part and parcel with virtually all the other problems of modernity—serious reading is often laborious work requiring unflinching discipline, and if there is anything that most moderns have an aversion to, it is disciplined work. In this odd to-whom-it-may-concern, instant-everything day of microwaveable meals, prefab buildings, drive-through windows, no-wait credit approvals, and predigested formula-entertainment, his very nature tended to want to reduce everything to the level of the least common denominator and the fastest turnaround—which seems to be getting lower and lower and faster and faster with every passing day.

Whenever he had read before—which was admittedly, a rarity—he had really preferred literary junk food. The vapid factoids of *USA Today* were much easier to swallow than Cotton Mather's *Magnalia Christi Americana*. For him, John Grisham, Dean Koontz, Stephen King, and Tom Clancy were easier to digest than William Shakespeare, John Milton, and G.K. Chesterton. Reading is a discipline—and all discipline is difficult. But of course, he realized, that is the way it is with anything worthwhile, really. The best things in life invariably cost us something. We must sacrifice to attain them, to achieve them, to keep them, even to enjoy them. It slowly began to dawn on him that a flippant, shallow, and imprecise approach to anything—be it sports or academics or the trades or business or marriage—is ultimately self-defeating. It is not likely to satisfy any appetite—at least, not for long.

And so he began to fill his loneliness with new friends—Chaucer, Mandeville, Coleridge, Luther, Cervantes, Knox, Melville, Hawthorne, Longfellow, Wordsworth, Dickens, Trollope, and Austen. He determined to dispense with all the nifty gadgets, gimmicks, and bright ideas of modern pop-psychology that had brought him such little comfort and turned instead to Augustine, Dante, Buchan, Plutarch, Belloc, Chalmers, and Vasari. Self-taught, he became conversant in the ideas of Seneca, Ptolemy, Virgil, Kuyper, Noyes, Bunyan, and Mallory. The notions of Athanasius, Chrysostom, Anselm, Bonaventure, Aquinas, Machiavelli, Calvin, Abelard, and Wyclif began to inform his thinking and shape his worldview. And of course, undergirding all of these other books was *the book*, the

Bible. He read as if with new eyes and began to make logical connections between specializations. He thus began to recover a heritage of real substance. And a vision for the rest of his life. He became passionate about the art, music, and ideas that had provoked the great flowering of culture throughout Christendom.

In the process, his faith was restored, his hope was revitalized, and his love was rejuvenated.

He enrolled in a graduate program at the University of Houston—and though he found most of the classwork rather pedestrian, he loved the academic environment. He picked up a dual doctorate in literature and philosophy in record time.

He had come to Nashville shortly afterward as a studio player, orchestrator, sideman, and song writer in the burgeoning contemporary Christian music industry. He had always been fascinated with traditional Celtic and Gaelic folk music—and his versatility on tin whistles, uilleann pipes, Irish harp, recorders, and bagpipes enabled him to make a very respectable living on Music Row.

His job was music. But it was now clear to him that his calling was education. He wanted to somehow help others to see what he had begun to see, to share what he had begun to recover of the great legacy of truth.

At first, he just taught a few classes on History and Literature to some homeschooling familes he had met. Then gradually, the idea for the Rivendell school began to emerge. Renting space in a small local church, the little academy quickly outstripped the capacity of both the building and the infrastructure. He began to publish a newsletter. He was invited to speak at conferences. He even created a site on the world wide web arguing for his classical ideas and illustrating the successes of Rivendell—and there were indeed, great successes. Enrollment grew quickly and dramatically—as did enthusiasm in the community for the work. Families reveled in the great adventure of substantive intellectual discipleship.

Noah Kirk had somehow stumbled across the home page and began a lively correspondence with Gylberd. And that was the beginning of a remarkable relationship of contrasts and comparisons.

AT THE TIME, NOAH was living in Southern California with his parents. He was a precocious teen with a voracious appetite for music, movies, programming, and politics. His father worked for the federal Immigration and Naturalization Service, but his real passions were antiquarian books and surfing. With his vintage 1978 Yater Spoon 9' 6" longboard, he was a "local"—and a very respected one—at Rincon, California's premier winter break. His mother was gaining renown as a fine regional sculptor—but it was gardening that was her real delight. Their home was a stimulating smorgasbord of art, music, and ideas.

In those halcyon days, Noah realized later, he was happy beyond anyone's wildest expectations.

But then, tragedy struck with the same stunning intensity that it had in Gylberd's life. At the beginning of his senior year in high school, Noah's parents were both killed in a catastrophic automobile accident. Actually, investigators harbored suspicions that it may not have been an accident at all. They thought that it might somehow be connected to a drug-related deportation case his father had been working on for some time—but in the end they were unable to prove the link between the two. The crash remained an unsolved, unprosecuted mystery.

Alas, there was no mystery to Noah's sudden change of fortunes. Because he was the sole heir, and no longer a minor according to California law, Noah inherited the entire estate of his parents and was the beneficiary of a large insurance settlement. But that was little comfort.

He had no other family members. At least, there were none that he knew of—the family had splintered and disintegrated a generation earlier when his father was scandalously born out of wedlock, the unwanted child of a biracial teenage affair. The stigma remained with him the rest of his life. Years later, when he was dating Noah's mother, her family disinherited her—prejudice runs deep, even in the enlightened West.

So, he was alone.

Like Gylberd, for several months Noah did very little of anything. He oversaw the liquidation of his family's assets. He moved into a small apartment adjacent to Balboa Park near downtown San Diego. And he plunged into his solitary lifestyle of Internet surfing, dumpster-diving, and skate thrashing. Mechanical, emotionless things were the only relief from grieving that he had found.

His one continuing link with normalcy in the outside world was his e-mail correspondence with Gylberd at the Rivendell site. He was both impressed and stirred by the taped lectures Dr. Gylberd sent him from the school—they were historically informed, artistically astute, and immediately relevant. They were also fervent. And that was what Noah liked best—even when he was dead wrong, at least Gylberd was ardently, enthusiastically, and passionately dead wrong.

Eventually, he determined to pick up and move to Tennessee. He decided that he would complete—or rather, repeat—his senior year there. He loaded up a large U-Haul with his books and his growing collection of computer hardware, and drove himself across the country. He rented an apartment. He bought a new pickup. He launched his Internet forum. And he waited for summer to end.

Then, on the first day of school, he simply showed up, entirely unannounced—not exactly the sort of situation secretaries or headmasters in small private schools are used to handling on the first day of a new school year. Initially there was a flurry of confusion. Though he was no less taken aback, Dr. Gylberd smoothed over the necessary details, and Noah was officially enrolled.

It proved to be a good year for him. Though he had not actually come out of his shell, he had grown and matured. And he had begun to cherish dreams of some kind of a happy life again.

"So, WHAT DO YOU think, Doc?"

Noah had caught up with Gylberd in the hall on the way to the first class of the morning.

"I think I need a cup of coffee."

"I drank enough last night for you and me both. So, what do you think? About Y2K? Did you dig through all the stuff I gave you last night?"

"I did indeed. Thanks a lot for a sleepless night."

"Yeah, well, if it's any solace, I didn't get any sleep either."

"Working on your paper?"

"Uh, oops. No. Just a little high-speed chase down the freeway."

"Uh, yeah. Right. Very funny."

"Well, you know, I've got to while away the hours somehow or another. So now. Tell me. After reading through all the research, what do you think?"

"I think you've got a one-track mind. That's what I think. But, I also think that the Y2K crisis warrants serious consideration. The problem is for real and it is not going away. In fact, the longer we dilly-dally around, the worse it is going to get."

"I knew it. I knew it. We're really looking at a technological disaster, aren't we."

"Actually, Noah, I'm not so sure about that. No one really knows what Y2K may bring. Our future will be determined by people not machines. I think you hit on the truth when we first discussed this last night. It isn't some arcane technological problem that threatens to shut the world down. Instead, it is a social problem. If history is any indication, that is what we really need to be concerned about."

"What do you mean?"

"It's just what you indicated last night. Technological problems are eminently fixable. They always have been. They always will be. But social problems are a different matter altogether. Machines can be reconfigured, refurbished, or replaced. Just take a look at your museum of discarded hardware. But people are not nearly so malleable. Systems are adjustable. Cultures are implacable."

"So, what's the bottom line, Doc?"

"Well, the best estimates are that the Y2K computer crisis will affect only a small proportion of the world's total computer technology—less than 30 percent of all mainframe operations, less than 20 percent of all proprietary software packages, less than 10 percent of all desktop processors, and less than 5 percent of all embedded chip applications. But, it might very well wreak havoc in the most delicate, sensitive, and vital of the world's systems of all: society. It really all depends upon how people react to the disruptions—or even just the threat of disruptions—that Y2K might bring."

By now, several other students had gathered around to listen to the conversation.

"If that's the case," Cassie Priam chimed in, "then widespread panic could actually begin to set in months in advance of the calendar change."

"That's a possibility," Gylberd agreed.

"On the other hand, it may be that nothing will happen at all," Noah added.

"You're right. That too is also a very distinct possibility."

"So, what do we know for certain?"

"Not an awful lot. And therein lies the real risk."

Realizing that this rabbit trail—as interesting as it may have been—carried with it another risk, the loss of a productive class, he quickly shooed the students into their seats and began his scheduled lecture.

Not coincidentally, his lecture explored the hubris of early twentieth-century science. It was an examination of the most basic assumptions of many pioneers of modernist thinking. The students did not miss the connection.

"A utopian vision of the future was spawned early in the century by a peculiar and innovative worldview," Gylberd began. "It was a system of thought rooted in the superiority—even the supremacy—of science over every other discipline or concern. A fantastic world could be expected in the days just ahead because the sovereign prerogative of science would, no doubt, make short work of curing every cultural ill, correcting every irrational thought, and subverting every cantankerous disturbance. There was no obstacle too great, no objection too considerable, and no resistance too substantial to restrain the onward and upward march of the scientific evolution of human society."

Of course, the future that the prophets, pundits, and futurists of modernity predicted never actually happened. Reality took an altogether different path, he asserted. "Even though that future never happened the way they said that it would, we are quite familiar with what it might have looked like if their vision really had been realized. From old science fiction reruns, tattered comic book collections, juvenile penny-dreadfuls, and yellowed pulp magazines, we are actually able to recognize the profile of their future—a future that never was."

With that, he began to describe that imagined future. "A distant gleaming skyline soars up from the fruited plains through plump cumulus clouds to sleek zeppelin docks and mad neon spires. Roads of crystal unfold between the towers like an origami trick. They are crossed and recrossed by thousands of satiny silver vehicles like choreographed beads of running mercury. The air above the city crackles with remote radio-laser signals. It is simultaneously thick with ships: giant delta-wing liners, dragonfly-like gyro-copters, electro-magneto aerial cars, and vast hovering helium blimps. Searchlights sweep surreally across the horizon illuminating streamlined buildings ringed with bright radiator flanges."

The students began to smile as Gylberd's vivid picture began to take shape in their minds. "Thronging the broad plazas of pristine marble below are the happy citizens of this jaunty utopia. Orderly and alert, their bright eyes shine with enthusiasm for their floodlit avenues, their shark-fin robots, their carefree conveniences, and their elysian prosperity. They all look wise and strong, striking a uniform pose of youthful health, energy, and cooperation. It is a heroic world of fluted aluminum, slipstream chrome, lustrous lucite, burnished bronze, and the unfettered dreams of progress. Every scene, every nook and cranny, every high-flung portal of this great technological trophy seems to generate eager bursts of raw industrial achievement. It is a marvelous world, fit for Flash Gordon, Tom Swift, Buck Rogers, and Dave Dashaway—humming with a kind of totalitarian optimism. It is a triumph of science like a triumph of will—imagined by Horatio Alger and H.G. Wells or, perhaps, Albert Speer and Herman Goering. Its brave new world has been deliberately engineered to be very nearly perfect—or something frighteningly close to that."

He then paused for effect. "But of course, it never happened. Thankfully, that imagined future collapsed under the weight of its own fantastical illusions—and its coercive predilections. It is only remembered nostalgically as a kind of architecture of broken dreams. Today, its vast vision of a compulsory utopia is widely recognized as little more than an immaculate deception. Aside from late night cable TV reruns, its relics survive only on the most disreputable fringes of our culture. We might find hints of it in a few depressing strips of the urban landscape beneath the crumbling layers of neglect and the dust of decrepitude. It might be seen along highways pockmarked with rocket-ship motif transient motels, Alcoa-sheathed mattress wholesalers, and fifth-run drive-in movie theaters bedecked with gaudy geometric marquees. From the mad scientist deco-style of the thirties to the stripped down ultra-pragmatism of the fifties, the future that never quite happened was born of a pretentious spirit of modernism that is laughably passé today. Were it not so relentlessly tacky, perhaps it could even be considered quaint."

He drove home his point. "The same defunct science fiction ideology that conjured up handy ray guns, personal jet shoes, and atomic food pills also manufactured millennial dreams of a technologically edenic, worry-free society. That kind of unswerving confidence in the good providence of industry and technology gave its adherents a conceited algebraic certainty about their forecasts and predictions."

According to Gylberd, for all those who shared this Flash Gordon worldview, science was a kind of new secular predestination. "It not only affirmed what could be, it confirmed what would be. And more, it discerned what should be. Scientific experts were thus not only the caretakers of the future, they were the guardians of Truth. They were a kind of superhuman elite—not at all unlike Plato's philosopher-kings—who ruled the hoi polloi with a firm but beneficent hand in order to realize the high ideals of progress."

Of course, that meant that science had to necessarily be intermingled with ideology, he argued. "It had to become an instrument of social transformation. It had to be harnessed with the idealism of the farsighted elite. It had to be wielded by the *cognoscenti* as a tool for the preordained task of human and cultural engineering. It had to be politicized. Thus, in the early days of the twentieth century, science and millenarian politics were woven together into a crazy quilt of idealism, fanaticism, and ambition. It enabled a few powerful men and movements to believe the unbelievable, conceive the inconceivable, and imagine the unimaginable. This potent admixture of unquestionable science and coercive politics became the ideological craze of a new orthodoxy and the starry-eyed bludgeon of a new plutocracy. Thus was produced a new vocabulary of modern mumbo-jumbo. It was all hardheaded, scientific, and relentless."

This peculiarity of modernist thought was the fruit of a strange innovation in the affairs of men, he said. "With the decline of clerical power in the nineteenth century, a new kind of mentor emerged to fill the vacuum and capture the ear of society. The secular intellectual might be deist, skeptic, or atheist. But he was just as ready as any pontiff or presbyter to tell mankind how to conduct its affairs. This new breed of prophet, priest, and king brought a tragic compulsion to his task of remaking the world in which he lived. He proclaimed from the start a special devotion to the interests of humanity and an evangelical duty to advance them by his teaching. He brought to this self-appointed task a far more radical approach than his clerical predecessors. He felt himself bound by no corpus of revealed religion. The collective wisdom of the past, the legacy of tradition, the prescriptive codes of ancestral experience existed to be selectively followed or wholly rejected entirely as his own good sense might decide. For the first time in human history, and with growing confidence and audacity, men arose to assert that they could diagnose the ills of society and cure them with their own unaided intellects: more, that they could devise formulae whereby not merely the structure of society but the fundamental habits of human beings could be transformed for the better. Unlike their sacerdotal predecessors, they were not servants and interpreters of the gods but substitutes. Their hero was Prometheus, who stole celestial fire and brought it to earth.

"As a result," he asserted, "this motley band of social engineers marshaled little more than their wits in their attempts at reinventing humankind—a task no less arduous and no less ludicrous than reinventing the wheel. The result was predictably deleterious."

Of course, something rather unexpected happened along the way to this predetermined, preprogrammed, and presumptive utopia. "Ultimately the new world order of these Flash Gordon futurists was dashed against the hard reality of history. The sad experience of the twentieth century—two devastating world wars, unnumbered holocausts and genocides, the fierce tyrannies of communism's evil empire, and the embarrassing foibles of liberalism's welfare state—ultimately exposed its high flying ideals as the noisome eccentricities that they are. Nevertheless, despite history's stern rebuke, the foundations of this ever-hopeful worldview still undergird our society."

Thus, he concluded. "Science is not infallible. Society is not perfectible. Utopia is not attainable. All the money, all the educational programs, all the technological breakthroughs, and all the compulsion our philosopher-kings can muster cannot make it so. There is one fact that contravenes their fondest hopes and most fantastic dreams. It is the one fact that the Flash Gordon futurists never reckoned with. It is the one fact that insured that their messianic vision of the future never happened."

Again, he paused. "It is the fact of the Fall."

He then discussed the harbingers of the failure of scientism to achieve its lofty dreams—from the sinking of the *Titanic* and the incineration of the *Hindenberg* to the horrors of *Auschwitz* and the brutality of the *Gulag*. The applications were all too obvious. And thus, the end of the lecture found the students all abuzz as they considered the implications of the twentieth century's cautionary tale for the twenty-first.

AFTER CLASS, GYLBERD walked across the room to Noah who was gathering up his notebook and several paperback texts into his backpack. "You were kidding about the high-speed chase down the freeway last night, weren't you?"

"Great lecture, Doc."

"You didn't answer my question, Noah."

"Uh, no. I didn't."

"So, you were kidding, right?"

"Well, not really."

"Not really? What do you mean, not really?"

"You still need that coffee? I know a great place. You're done with your classes for a couple of hours, aren't you? I think we've got lots to talk over."

"Why do I get the feeling that I'm just about to entangle myself in some kind of a horrendous mess?"

Cassie Priam walking past quipped, "Beware of this guy, Doc. He looks like trouble."

Noah smiled. But Gylberd threw up his hands in mock exasperation. "I'm never really sure when anyone is kidding around here anymore."

Eight

"Lean not unto thine own understanding."
Proverbs 3:5

APRIL 26, 1998

P riam felt like he was a character in the movie *Ground Hog Day*. It seemed that he was destined to relive his first day of unemployment over and over again for the next two weeks. Each day he made his calls and each day he ended up with the same results—nothing.

He had retained an executive search committee. His contact management system was a treasure trove of old business acquaintances, friends, clients, and customers, but it had not yielded a single promising lead. Not one. He went by a local mega-bookstore and picked up several career strategy books. He tried every suggestion, every tactic, and every ploy. And still, nothing.

Sure, there were plenty of programmer jobs available, even some senior analyst positions, but he had not come across anyone who was looking for a Chief Information Officer. Although he was discouraged, he was not quite ready to take a step back in his career. For one thing, he didn't know how he could support his family on less than he had been making at OfficeCentral. Like most Americans, he was spending everything he made—and then some.

For most of his adult life, his work had defined his sense of identity. It established his standards of worth, purpose, and value. Now that he had no work—or at least, now that he had no job—he was struggling in the throes of a full-fledged crisis.

Who was he really? What was he supposed to do with his life?

Though he was resolved to reorient his priorities and regain a balanced perspective of faith, family, and work, he found it pretty tough sledding—with every passing day, he became more and more depressed. He had become so used to the protective environs of success that he had practically forgotten how to deal with adversity.

On the flip side, he was now working out of the house. And that gave him continual access to Abby. She was there to encourage him when he got discouraged and celebrate with him when he had had something positive happen—which was all too rare. Sometimes, just by having someone to bounce ideas off of, it helped him regain his perspective and focus. Where he had compartmentalized his life before, the dividing lines were fading and Abby was becoming his partner in every area of his life. He was more than chagrined at the years he had ignored the value of this kind of partnership, and he was determined to somehow correct the imbalance once he was reemployed. He was only too well aware that the tyranny of the urgent would more than likely attempt to segment their lives again. If they weren't careful, Abby would take over home and family, he would take over the role of provider, and they would meet at the end of the day exhausted—two good people with not a lot in common. That's the way it was with virtually every successful, prosperous, and ambitious man he knew. In the end, wives were little more than members of their support teams. How would he be able to guard against that trap? He wasn't certain, but he knew he had to try.

On Friday evening, after a particularly discouraging day—and week—he decided to reevaluate his strategy with Abby and solicit her input. Whatever it was that he was doing wasn't working, and he was running out of time. His severance pay would last only another month. Although he was trying to trust the Lord with the results and exercise his faith, he was also beginning to feel a low level of panic set in. He was having difficulty sleeping. He didn't think he could endure another day of the same old routine. He needed hope.

"Abby, I need your input. What I'm doing isn't working, and we only have two more paychecks before the severance pay runs out. To be honest, I'm beginning to feel a little desperate."

It was awfully hard for Priam to admit this. He had always tried to appear strong for the sake of his family. But the results of the previous two weeks had stripped that pretense away. All he wanted now was to provide for them. And if he had to eat a little crow and solicit Abby's help, he was willing to do so. He needed direction, and he was willing to take it from anyone who could offer it.

"That's perfectly understandable. After all, you don't have a lot of experience being unemployed." Abby smiled, trying in her usual way to turn a negative into a positive.

"Yeah, Thank God. And, frankly, I don't want any more experience. There's gotta be something I can do to speed up the process. I mean look at the facts, Abby. There are probably scores of companies out there that could use someone with my qualifications; I just can't seem to find them!"

"I'm sure you're right."

"So what can I do differently? I feel like I've hit the wall."

"I guess it's time to break down the wall."

"Yeah well, that's easier said than done."

"Most things are."

"So, how do I go about actually doing it then? Pray tell."

"Well, actually I have an idea." Again, Abby smiled. This time her expression indicated that she was hiding a secret, like a surprise gift behind her back.

"Really? So, spill the beans."

"This may seem really radical, but I've been thinking about it an awful lot for the last three days. I wasn't sure I should say anything, so I prayed that maybe *you* would open the door. Are you ready?"

"Of course, I'm ready. Can't you tell? I'd ask for Mitten's advice if I thought I could understand cat-talk."

Abby chuckled. Though it was clear that Priam wasn't kidding. She reached over and patted him on the hand affectionately.

"Okay, how about becoming a Year 2000 computer consultant?"

Priam sat expressionless.

"You've said this Y2K thing is getting a lot of attention and that companies can't fix the problem using their existing personnel, right?"

"Right."

"You've also said how much you've enjoyed working out of the house, seeing the kids when they leave for school in the morning and greeting them when they come home in the afternoon, right?"

"Right."

"I think you may even enjoy being around me . . . right?" Abby's eyes twinkled.

"I'm not sure I would go *that* far." Priam winked back and grinned.

"Well, it seems if you were a consultant, you could do a lot of the work right here at home. I think it would be great for our family life. You could transform this very difficult situation into an incredible opportunity. You could be your own boss. Set your own hours. Do work that you really believe in—and enjoy. Turn this lemon into lemonade. You might even be able to make *more* money than you were making. I don't really see much of a downside."

Secretly, Abby dreaded the thought of him going back into the corporate world. She had had her husband back for only a couple of weeks and she wasn't quite willing to send him off into battle again—not if they had another viable option.

"Well, it's not a bad idea. I've actually daydreamed about it a bit myself. But I've always assumed that it's just a dream—and a pipe dream at that. See, the problem is that I would still have to find the work. Consultants need clients. It seems like we're back to square one."

"Well, maybe. But maybe not. It seems like hiring someone for a *specific* project is an easier decision than hiring a new employee. There's a lot less risk and a lot less overhead. Right?"

"Yeah, that's true. Virtually all corporate information technology departments have a budget for consultants. I would just have to prove I'm the right guy for the job."

"Exactly. And you've said yourself that most of this Y2K stuff is now being done by outside consultants."

"Yep. And they're paid pretty well from what I've read."

"There you go."

"The thing is, I've never really gotten excited about going into business for myself because I didn't want to leave the security of a corporate job. Obviously that doesn't matter now. Still, I don't even have a clue as to where to start."

"Coming up with a game plan has never been a problem for you, Bob Priam. If you set your mind to it, I know you can do this—and be successful at it. Very successful."

"I just don't want to jump from the frying pan into the fire."

"Well, you've got to jump somewhere—otherwise we're cooked. Look before you leap, and I'm sure we'll be fine."

THEY TALKED THROUGH the implications of the decision over the weekend. Priam found that he could think about little else. Every time he turned around, he found himself imagining what it would be like to hang out the shingle and own his own business. No boss. No stupid, demoralizing corporate policies. No meaningless corporate procedures. No fixed schedule. He could come and go as he pleased. He could keep everything he made, less Uncle Sam's cut. And most important, he could be there for his family, participating in their joys and sorrows directly rather than simply hearing about them after the fact.

These thoughts checked his panic, and he began to feel a new sense of excitement building. Frankly, he hadn't felt this positive about anything in years.

On Sunday morning, as they were getting ready for church, Priam said to Abby, "Honey, you know, I am really excited about this whole idea of going into business for myself. I can hardly think of anything else."

Abby was busy curling her hair. Priam had everything on but his coat and tie. The kids were hunting for their shoes and Bibles.

"Me, too. I think it could be a great move. I just know you could pull it off."

"What I really need though is some kind of confirmation that this is the right direction for us to go. We can't afford to go down any blind alleys. We just don't have enough time to backtrack. If I could just get a good lead, a couple of references, a foot in the door, I'd feel a lot better about this. I need a jump-start to get me going."

"You mean money? Venture capital?"

"No, not that."

"You don't think it would take a lot of money to start a business?"

"Well, it would for some businesses. If we were to start a retail business, for example, we would have to buy inventory, lease space, and hire a staff—all of which can cost a *lot* of money. If we were to start a manufacturing business, we would have to buy supplies and equipment. But for a consulting business, all we need is a phone, a fax, and a computer—and we've already got all that. As you've already pointed out, I can work out of the house, so I don't even need to lease office space. There's really not much overhead. The only thing I really need to invest in is some letterhead, so I can look like we have a real business."

"Well, there's one other thing you'll probably want to get besides some new letterhead."

"What's that?"

"A client."

"Uh, yeah. That's what I meant about the jump-start—the foot in the door. It should be easier for the CIO to make a decision about bringing in an outside consultant than hiring a new employee. At least that's the theory."

"OK. So, what we need is that breakthrough first client."

"Yeah, and right now that is the one thing that I don't have the foggiest idea of how to find."

THE DRIVE TO CHURCH was peaceful. When Priam went to church, he was usually preoccupied with something else—a problem at work, a golf swing he was trying to perfect, or the news on the radio. The kids, needing some attention from dad, would often resort to teasing one another or fighting to get it. He had little tolerance for this kind of thing and would usually overreact. As a result, the family would often arrive at church with some in tears and others nursing hurt feelings. Priam always felt guilty, knowing that he was responsible, but he was too proud to admit it and too selfish to change.

But today was different. He was completely present, interacting with Abby and the kids. Everyone was in a jovial mood. They joked with one another and—at Hector's request—even sang a couple of old hymns together. He peered into the rearview mirror. He had expected to see Troy rolling his eyes, but he was actually quietly singing along. Priam's eyes grew moist. Though he had had a difficult week, he felt an enormous sense of gratitude for all that the Lord had given him. He may not have a job, but he had a wonderful, loving wife, three affectionate children, and his health. He also had a renewed sense of purpose and calling. For that, he was especially grateful.

The church service was uneventful but satisfying. The pastor, Tom Cullen, was a "meat and potatoes" kind of guy. Nothing fancy, but he served up a healthy portion of spiritual food week after week. Tall and lanky, he preached without notes and paced around the front of the church as he spoke. His wire rim glasses made him look erudite, although he spoke plainly and without pretense. He had been with the church for eleven years and nearly everyone loved him.

In the south, it seemed that every church, regardless of its denominational distinctives, had a "coffee hour" following the service. It was one of the things nearly all Christians could agree on. St. Andrew's was no different. Usually Priam hated going. He thought it was a waste of time and only delayed his favorite part of the week—the Sunday afternoon nap. But today he felt energized and was actually looking forward to the fellowship.

As he helped himself to a cup of coffee, Burt Virgil, a CIO with Tennessee Electric Corporation (TEC) greeted him.

"Good morning, Bob. How are you doing?"

Priam turned around and shook Virgil's hand. He was in his mid-fifties, slightly overweight, and looking disheveled, as usual. Although the electric utility where he worked was publicly held, for all practical purposes it was run like a lumbering government agency. And Virgil looked like a bumbling government bureaucrat.

"Not bad. You?"

"Better than I deserve . . . What's the latest with your job situation? I heard you've left OfficeCentral."

"Yep. It's a long story. You want the short version?"

"Sure. I heard you left over a Y2K disagreement," Virgil offered.

"Well . . . yeah. Actually, I got fired. I tried for months to get the CEO to take the problem seriously. By the time I finally got him to listen, he panicked. The magnitude of the problem—in both dollars and man hours—threatened his sense of security. It was pretty much a case of shoot the messenger rather than deal with the real issue."

Priam shook his head in disbelief. Even though he had had a few weeks to cool off, he still couldn't believe what had happened to him. Like picking at the scab of a nearly healed wound, retelling the story brought the pain to the surface of his consciousness.

"Unbelievable," Virgil acknowledged, also shaking his head. "It's probably no consolation, but a buddy of mine in Philly just went through the same thing."

"Really?" Priam exclaimed.

"Yeah, same situation as you. And I've heard through the grapevine that you two aren't the only ones—you're members of a rapidly growing club."

"I'm sure you're right. The sad thing is that firing a good CIO only makes matters worse."

"Exactly. Well, I guess there's no rule saying the boss has to be rational . . . So what are you going to do?"

"Well, believe it or not, I'm planning on going into business as a Y2K consultant. I want to help companies assess their problem and develop a plan for dealing with it." Priam liked the sound of what he was saying. There was something about saying it out loud that gave life to his plans.

"Are you going to do the actual repair work, too?" Virgil asked.

"Nope. I may be involved in overseeing it—depending on what the client wants—but I don't want to be involved in hiring and managing staff. I want to keep it clean and simple."

"That's probably a good idea. How soon are you wanting to get started?"

"Right away. Frankly, OfficeCentral didn't provide much of a severance package, and I need to start generating income ASAP."

"Well, I might be able to help you. The truth is, my CEO has been stalling on the issue, too. He just gave me approval last week to hire an outside firm to do the assessment and develop a plan for managing the repairs."

Virgil grinned, realizing that his encounter with Priam might well be more than just a coincidence.

"You're kidding?" Priam could hardly believe what he was hearing.

"Nope, and I'm ready to move on it right away. I'm already behind the eightball."

"Great! What do we need to do to make this happen." Priam hoped his excitement didn't make him look too eager.

"Why don't you come by the office to see me tomorrow. Say, about ten o'clock." He pulled out his electronic palm planner to make sure there would be no scheduling conflicts. "You'll need to bring a capabilities letter or brochure with you, along with a résumé. Not so much for me—I know how qualified you are—but for our management team. A utility company like TEC is a lot like a government bureaucracy—you have to have your paperwork in order before you can do anything. We also need to talk about fees and a timetable."

"I'll be there!"

Priam shook Virgil's hand and walked away with a spring in his step.

SUNDAY EVENING FOUND Priam sitting in front of the TV with his laptop. He wanted to write the capabilities brochure Virgil had requested. He also wanted to watch *60 Minutes.* The kids were at youth group and Abby was at the kitchen table, surrounded by seed and plant catalogs, so he had the den to himself.

Writing the capabilities letter was fairly easy. He simply included a list of what his new firm—he thought he'd call it Apollo Information Systems—was capable of doing. He then outlined a synopsis of his résumé. He couldn't actually include a bid, of course; he didn't know how extensive TEC's computer systems were. He would have to do some preliminary analysis before he could offer anything concrete. That would have to wait until tomorrow.

Just as he was finishing up, Ed Bradley's familiar face popped onto the screen for the two-minute overview of stories that would be included in this edition of *60 Minutes.* There were new allegations about the President's sex life, of course. This had been going on for weeks—or months or years. Hardly newsworthy. But there was also going to be a special report on the federal government's progress in dealing with the Y2K computer problem. Ed promised "startling new revelations that may threaten our way of life." *Now that's news.*

Priam could care less about the latest scandal surrounding the President. The only thing that disappointed him more than the President's most recent escapades was the American public's response to it—or lack of response. No one seemed to care as long as the economy was healthy—though this time the allegations were so serious, he just didn't see how the spin doctors could continue to portray the President in a positive light. Regardless, Priam muted the TV and proofread his letter one more time. He then set his computer down and went to the kitchen to grab a Coke and make himself a sandwich. When he returned to the den, the Y2K segment was just starting.

For nearly fifteen minutes—a very long time in the world of television—Leslie Stahl, the segment's reporter, examined several aspects of the federal government's progress in dealing with the Year 2000 Problem.

She began by profiling the Social Security Administration. This agency had, initially, become the federal government's "poster child" for Y2K progress. The SSA had started early and worked hard. They first learned they had a significant problem in 1989. By 1991 they had finished their assessment of the problem, believing they had 30 million lines of computer code to review and repair. For the next several years, four hundred full-time programmers worked hard with the goal of completing the project by December 31, 1998. This would allow one full year for testing before the century rolled over.

Before long, however, the SSA reported that it had completed the renovation on only 6 million lines of code—20 percent of the total. Their progress accelerated over the next year. But then, in November 1997, the SSA made two startling admissions: rather than having 30 million lines of code to review and repair in its main systems, it actually had 34 million. And, worse, there were an additional 33 million lines of code in its state offices that it had completely overlooked. The frightening thing about this is that many of the most important federal government agencies have far bigger Y2K problems and yet got started far later than the Social Security Administration.

For example, the Internal Revenue Service has more than 100 million lines of code to review and repair in its systems. The Department of Defense has some one billion lines of code! Stahl wondered aloud, "How in the world will these critical government agencies finish in time?" According to the House Subcommittee on Government Management, Information and Technology, they won't. Based on current rates of progress, fourteen of twenty-four key federal agencies will not be successful in repairing their mission-critical applications prior to January 1, 2000. These agencies will not complete their year 2000 projects until:

Early 2000:	National Aeronautics and Space Adminstration
Mid-2000:	Department of Education
Mid-2000:	Agency for International Development
Mid-2000:	Federal Emergency Management Agency
2001:	Department of Health and Human Services
2001:	Department of Justice
2002:	General Services Administration
2004:	Department of Treasury
2005:	Department of Agriculture
2010:	Department of Transportation
2010:	Office of Personnel Management
2012:	Department of Defense

2019:   Department of Energy
2019:   Department of Labor

The segment ended with this sobering fact: the federal government sends out 80 million checks a month in benefits and payments. What happens if they are unable to do this accurately—or at all—because of a computer glitch?

Priam turned off the TV and sat bewildered. Once again he was confronted with the fact that the Year 2000 Problem was not merely a professional concern—it was intensely personal. What the *Sixty Minutes* segment had intimated but not said was that there was the potential for a significant disruption in the American life—and in particular, its economic life.

Priam quickly connected the dots and realized that there might actually be the potential for a complete meltdown of society. If the Y2K problem was not repaired in time, life in the twenty-first century could be radically different than it was now. The computers would think it was the year 1900, and for all practical purposes it would be.

The average Joe was completely unaware of how much computers had to do with everyday life in the modern world—and this ignorance would ultimately prove to be the most dangerous aspect of the Y2K bug. It would lull people, businesses, and even governments into complacency until it was too late.

FROM THE MOMENT THEIR meeting started, it was apparent to Priam that Virgil had already decided to hire him. It was only a matter of negotiating a fee and schedule.

The truth was that Priam solved a very important dilemma for TEC. The only firms that Virgil could locate who were doing credible Y2K work were large companies like IBM and EDS. Because there was so much demand for their services, they were unwilling to do just an assessment. They wanted to do it all—assessment, repairs, and testing—or nothing. The problem was that Virgil couldn't get his CEO to approve the whole project. He wanted to see the assessment first and then make the decision. Because of Priam's extensive experience, he was the perfect candidate. Virgil knew he could pay Priam well and still save a small fortune compared to what the big guys would charge.

After walking Priam through the plant, Virgil brought him back to his office in the basement.

"So we basically have three large systems," Virgil summarized, "the business system that handles our accounting, the production system that handles power generation, and the embedded chip systems that are scattered throughout the production system, including the substations."

"And each of these large systems is made up of a number of separate, smaller systems, right?" Priam asked.

"Exactly. Some are one-of-a-kind proprietary systems, some are legacy systems with layer upon layer of add-on applications, and some are highly sophisticated, modern, upgradable systems. It's a real hodgepodge."

"Yeah. It's a mess. But it's a fixable mess. Time is our real enemy, not technology here."

"Right, so how quickly can we begin the assessment?"

"As soon as I get your approval to start, we put together an initial budget, sign a contract, and get rolling."

"Well, let's do it. Time's a wasting."

And just like that, Priam was in business.

Nine

"For I perceive that thou art in the gall of bitterness,
and in the bond of iniquity." Acts 8:23

NOVEMBER 23, 1998

For several years now, he had watched as one after another of his friends, peers, colleagues, and fellow workers had become millionaires. In Silicon Valley, success stories seemed to be a dime a dozen. Everywhere he looked, he saw some high-tech start-up raking in the boodle following a successful software launch or initial public offering.

Will Ajax was a competent programmer and an even better manager. In fact, he was far more talented than half the people who were now sitting pretty in the lap of luxury. He knew that—and so did most of them. And yet he was still struggling—at least in relative terms. He was hardly poor. Good programmers and administrators could actually make near six figures if they made the most of their opportunities—nothing to sneeze at. But he was hardly rich either. And that really stuck in his craw.

At one time or another in his career, he was the manager responsible for several killer apps that helped to revolutionize the computer industry. When he was living on the West Coast—first just outside San Francisco and later near Seattle—he was a part of the launch team for several small entrepreneurial efforts. But they never seemed to make it big until after he had already moved on. He had been on development teams at both Apple in Cupertino and Microsoft in Redmond. But his positions always seemed to fall victim to the latest corporate downsizing efforts—so he never was able to stay long enough for his putative genius to be adequately recognized.

So, for the last decade he had moved from job to job, project to project, and company to company. He was perpetually in search of the Next-New-Thing. And he had a real knack for somehow always just missing it. As a result, he was bitter. He simply had never gotten his due. He felt he had been cheated out of what was his by all rights.

By all counts, he had everything necessary for success—he was at the very least procedurally proficient. But he was also a natural leader and team builder. He was charismatic and likable. As a result he always seemed to pull together a group of followers—the geeky codeheads and okatu who actually did the technical work. He worked long and hard at nurturing those loyal relationships—and so he was able to earn both the respect and the trust of the coworkers who might be able to make him look good to his superiors.

In addition, he struck an imposing figure—his passion for weight training had made him a remarkable physical specimen. His biceps strained at the sleeves of his crisply starched oxford dress shirts. His washboard abs and trim waist were evident even beneath his tailored Armani suits. He was ripped from top to

bottom, head to toe. All that combined with impeccable groom-
ing, understated accessorizing, stylish hair, and rugged good
looks made him appear more like a fashion model than a computer programmer. He was, as the public relations executive at
one of the companies he had worked for said, "the complete
package."

Even so, his suave exterior was little compensation for his
modest successes. And he seemed to have a penchant for
impatience, a fiery quick temper, a surprising lack of tact and
propriety, and perhaps worst of all, a brazen outspokenness that
combined with all of his other deficiencies to create a pattern of
corporate self-destructiveness. Ajax found it impossible to display patience when so much high-tech decision-making was left
up to suits who couldn't even install their own spreadsheet or
contact management programs.

For a time he worked in New York—having given up on the
traditional West Coast computer industry—in a last-ditch effort
to attain fame and fortune as a freelance software developer and
programming consultant. He sublet a small brownstone walk-up
on the lower east side of Manhattan and began to gather
together a network of similarly disaffected souls.

And that is how, where, and why the Chernobyl team came
together.

JUST BEYOND THE FAMED Cooper Union, between Astor
Place and Tompkins Square, is an odd little neighborhood affectionately dubbed the East Village by its residents. Like so much
of the rest of New York, it is a community of violent contrasts:
historic Stuyvesant Street is lined with stately landmark homes
while shabby boutiques, disreputable tenements, and shooting
galleries dominate the surrounding blocks; homeless men and
women sleep in the doorways of chic art galleries and along the

sidewalk in front of fashionable lofts and condominiums; impeccably tailored Wall Street moguls and would-be moguls hurry to work amidst peddlers hawking their dilapidated wares; petition gatherers for every imaginable cause desperately distribute their leaflets to world-weary commuters and gawk-eyed tourists; fly-by-night hucksters vie for sales outside vintage establishments like the Strand, the Yiddish Theater, and Pageant Book and Print.

It was once a comfortable literary neighborhood where James Fenimore Cooper, W.H. Auden, Allen Ginsberg, and Jacob Adler lived and worked. In the sixties it became a haven for the hippie drug culture. Rock-and-roll came alive at the Electric Circus on St. Mark's Place and at Fillmore East on Second Avenue. When Greenwich Village rents began to soar in the seventies, gentrification began in earnest and the substantial Jewish, Polish, and Ukrainian populations were gradually displaced by uptown yuppies.

The St. Mark's Church-in-the-Bowery on Tenth Street was built in 1660 as a Dutch Reformed chapel on Governor Peter Stuyvesant's farm—"bowery" or "bouerie" literally means "farm." Late in the seventeenth century it became an Episcopal parish church for the emerging community of small freeholders and yeomen and has been in continuous use ever since. In the late seventies the church helped to launch the famed Poetry Project and by the early eighties it had become the neighborhood's center of avant garde radicalism, activism, and dissent. But the continuing evolution of the East Village has made even its most adventurous forays into the uncharted realms of multicultural political-correctness seem terribly tame in comparison.

By the early nineties the neighborhood had become the fulcrum of New York's hacker and net community. Just around the corner from the old church on St. Mark's Place—near the site of Cooper's last knickerbocker home—there were several Internet cafés, coffee bars, and bistros. Rehabbed and gentrified by the easily procurred venture capital that overvalued high-tech brokerage houses poured into such enterprises, the small neighborhood quickly came to symbolically dominate the social, cultural, and political life of the community.

That is where Ajax first met Mike Locrian.

They were both standing in line outside the popular CyberJoint, anxious to get in. It was a dismal gray New York afternoon. A wintry witchery hung in the air. The shivering file was as quiet, as servile, and as sullen as a welfare queue. It was a paradox as strange as almost any Ajax had ever witnessed. A straggle of men and women on the precipice of their intended visionary gaiety looked for all the world like lambs being led to the slaughter.

Locrian appeared to be about twenty-five or so. His haircut was close-cropped around the sides but with a tumble of coiffed dark curls on top. Dressed in the outre hip-hop fashion of the day—loose slacker jeans, layered shirts, a bulky stadium jacket, and expensive Nikes—the hesitation in his voice belied the cocky pose he struck.

The line didn't seem to be moving, so Ajax struck up a conversation. The two men immediately hit it off. They were both frustrated by the way their ambitions had been quashed by the powers-that-be. They had similar interests and ideas. They had similar passions and loathings.

Ajax could tell that his new friend was technically adept, creative, and hungry—the very attributes he was looking for in his new team members. A persuasive recruiter, Ajax convinced Locrian to join him in a new venture certain to make them both rich beyond their wildest dreams.

A COUPLE OF DOORS DOWN from the CyberJoint was the St. Mark's Bookshop. It was a thriving store that specialized in small-press books, philosophy, poetry, and women's studies. It was just about all that remains of a hypnotically fascinating row of secondhand and antiquarian bookstores that once made the East Village a bargain hunter's paradise.

It was there that Ajax met Athena Scully.

She was a strikingly beautiful woman who seemed to have gone to extraordinary lengths to hide that fact from the world. She wore baggy parachute pants, an oversized lumberjack flannel shirt, and hiking boots. Her hair was bobbed short and she wore no makeup or jewelry. She was, however, adorned with a bevy of buttons bearing the slogans of various hard-core conservative political groups: "Refuse and Resist," "Hack Us Back to Medievalism," "Save-the-Starving-Third-World-Lesbian-CoDependent-Whales," "I'm Just to the Right of Atilla," "Vote for Nixon: He's Tanned, Rested, and Ready," "AU H$_2$O," "Jesse Helms Is Too Liberal," "Braveheart for Sheriff," and "Impeach Clinton, Impale Gore." They were pinned willy-nilly all over her khaki photojournalist's vest.

She was browsing among the sundry literary offerings in the Self-Help section—which somehow did not seem to fit her profile, but then, not much else in the East Village was particularly consistent either. It struck Ajax as more than a little strange that virtually all of the titles that were not brazenly sophomoric seemed to focus on some kind of eastern mystical or spiritual quest: *A Zen Soul-Guide to the Zeitgeist, Buddhist Love Lessons, Psychic Cross-Dependency, The Sensual Satisfaction of the Soul-Spirit, Beautiful Bodhisattvah,* and *Shamanistic Existentialism.*

Athena seemed to be merely scanning the shelves. So, Ajax thought he might try his luck at a bit of conversation—she was clearly a fascinating character, and fascinating characters were his forte.

"Are you interested in spiritual things?" he asked her.

She turned and smiled cordially but her eyes betrayed an unmistakable look—that canny, shrewd, disabused, *"tres gauche* coast" look—conveying an experienced suspicion of any and all comers. She chuckled. "What are you? Some kind of shrink or salesman or pickup artist or something?"

"Yeah. Something."

She chuckled again. "Well, I have to tell you, I don't believe in any of this stuff. In fact, I actually despise all these odd psychoanalyzing cults." She pointed toward the shelf of books. "And this co-dependency business with all its New Age corollaries *really* leaves me cold. Pop psychology is so banal."

Her friendly manner and her easy articulateness seemed to contrast oddly with where she was and what she was doing. She continued with a wry winsomeness. "You name it, Muktananda, Sri Rajneesh, Divine Light Mission, Branch Davidian, EST, Transcendental Meditation, Dianetics, Synanon, Eckankar, B'hai, Rhema Faith, Baba Ram Dass—they're all hoaxes. Their promises are like pie crust—made to be broken. You know what I mean?"

"Well, uh . . ."

"Just nonsense. Junk. Fads. All of them are essentially the same. I come here to see what it is that folks are clogging up their lives and debilitating their wills with. It's even more informative of the crisis of American culture than daytime TV."

Then, she leaned toward him and showed him a thick tome with a colorful embossed cover. "Check this one out. It's my favorite. It's a best-selling transcript of a Prosperity Visualization Seminar. It's like a combination of all of the worst aspects of Arica, Zen, Jung, Freud, Rand, and—get this—even Christianity."

"Oh." At first, he couldn't tell if she was kidding.

She wasn't.

She looked back toward the shelf and began gesturing enthusiastically. "It is supposedly for people who have a big problem with affluence, you know, really visualizing it. As a result they are stuck at a kind of preternatural bourgeois level. So, according to this author, they just can't get a handle on who they are supposed to be. Or even *what* they are supposed to be. They simply can't appreciate themselves. They can't find a way to affirm their longings or passions. But now, thanks to Prosperity Visualization therapy, they can get in touch with their feelings. And they can actually *own* them—for perhaps the first time."

"So, this procedure somehow helps people get rich? Or does it just help those who are already rich?"

"Both. Definitely both, according to the back cover copy. See, with this one paperback book people can overcome all their problems and hurdle over all their obstacles to wealth. They can be rid of their anima. All their bad karma can vanish in an instant."

"Sounds a little weird to me."

"Just a little? Come on." She tossed the book aside. "This is nut-case stuff. The problem is that people believe it. They are suckers for this kind of nonsense. It's horrifying. They should know better. But the one thing Americans seem to have no shortage of these days is gullibility. It's like spamming the soul."

Fascinated, Ajax invited her out for a cup of coffee. They wound up spending several hours together talking about her wildly varied passions—everything from spiritual counterfeits to seventeenth century brocade, from kick boxing to chivalric poetry, from software daeliaforcation to Robin Hood ethics, from libertarian politics to free market economics, and from net freeloading to shareware virus hunting.

The one concern that Ajax had about her was her inflated view of justice and her exaggerated moral conscience. But he saw an almost indispensable technical promise in her, nevertheless. He decided she was worth the gamble. And so, before the night was over, Athena had been recruited into his programming partnership—or the computer cabal Chernobyl, as Ajax now liked to call it.

AJAX'S PLAN FOR THE GROUP was simply to make money. As much as they could. As fast as they could. Any way that they could. He was not very particular—he had few moral compunctions. His only concern was how to rake in the filthy lucre. That meant that he had to be very careful about what he did and did not tell Athena and Locrian—he knew that some projects might be appropriate for one but not the other and vice versa. But the bottom line for him was the bottom line. And he felt certain that a sure cure for any pangs of conscience either of them might have could be assuaged by the money they stood to make on each successive deal.

At first, the only jobs they could get were fairly typical hacker gigs—gathering addresses from the online service chatrooms for advertisers and pollsters, spamming e-mail accounts and corporate sites, doing web searches for private investigators and financial institutions, and prospecting competitor's hits for protocol monitors and net developers. They also did a little html coding and page designs for pay sites on the web—for a percentage of the action. Though actually relatively profitable, working on those projects proved to be a bit tricky for Ajax—he knew that Athena would refuse to work on code for pornographers, and they were the biggest, most munificent, and best-paying customers for that kind of work. But Athena was the best designer and the most savvy programmer he had. So he just did a some fancy footwork—he had her work on those projects piecemeal, never seeing the final product.

By the end of the first year, they had cobbled together a little more than a half a million dollar a year consultancy business from these varied enterprises—with a modicum of additional income from property royalties and contract margins. Long-term prosperity seemed certain—though it came at great cost in both time and energy.

Still, Ajax was not satisfied. He didn't want hardscrabble prosperity. He wanted the big bucks. He was after the easy money. And he realized that he would have to make some strategic changes in his enterprise if he was ever to get there.

When he began to notice in the trade journals that the entertainment industry was beginning to shift much of its locus from the East and West Coasts to Nashville, he decided that he needed to move Chernobyl's base of operations there as well. His assumption was that media types always tend to have more money than sense—a perfect prescription for his pilfering transactions. And, he believed, ignorant Southerners would be easy to impress with computer jargon baby talk.

Leaving New York was quite a stretch for both Athena and Locrian, but Ajax convinced them that they were all on the verge of making it big. Chernobyl was due for a breakthrough and Nashville was hot—where the action was. Reluctantly, they left their East Village digs behind and made the move.

They set up shop in a decrepit warehouse along the Cumberland River right downtown—an area that had already undergone an expensive and expansive renewal program. Ajax designed the space himself. He transformed the old metal building into a stunning high-tech paradise. Architecture like all art forms—though often neglected or taken for granted—is a vital aspect of our productive environment. Ajax wanted the architecture to be an integrative ecology, uniting form and function, medium and message, ethos and aesthetics.

Thus, he had to make sure that a kind of planned pandemonium would sideswipe the members of his team the moment they stepped inside. He wanted it to pulsate like the Times Square subway station at rush hour. His plan was to have a whole host of technicians swarm through the rambunctious technology-crammed space, their faces perpetually rapt with the pressure of projects, agendas, and deadlines. He wanted it to seem like a carefully plotted explosion, a premeditated meltdown, a planned Chernobyl.

It was to be his answer to the laid-back virtual office environment—he wanted none of the sleek, silent future where employees need only walk a few steps to their fully operational home offices, blissfully telecommute, and take meetings in deep cyberspace. Instead of streamlined silence, he believed in the productive qualities of noise and cataclysm. His theory was simple: shove lots of talented rebels and upstarts together into a small raucous space for long hours, give them the best equipment possible, and he would get magic. He wanted a jangling rock-and-roll environment fit for creative anarchy and productive chaos. He wanted to build a team, a community, a cabal of interactive and technological fusion. He would have young, Southern, New York-sophisticate-wannabes in his pocket the second the good old boys entered the room.

Running up the spine of the soaring, spare space, connecting three levels of lofts with the main floor, was a wide spiral staircase. But what looked like a staircase was actually a vertical meeting room. And then there was the food court. Set off by perpetually blinking monitors, the minimall along the side of the building offered everything from sodas to fresh fruit, cereal to candy bars. His idea was to create a frenetic, self-contained information milieu that his team would come alive in—and then never really want to leave.

The up front investment was heady—it took nearly everything that they had made in New York. The equipment alone cost them nearly a hundred grand. Remodeling, furnishing, and stocking the space took double that. But Ajax believed it was worth it.

AGAIN, FOR THE FIRST FEW months, Ajax was able to drum up only fairly pedestrian sorts of jobs for the team—web site design for various media and entertainment companies, online shopping links, and focused-search marketing campaigns. But then along came Y2K.

Ajax met Bob Priam at an information technology expo. Priam's consulting business had just been established and was already doing respectable business. But because he only did compliancy analysis, he was looking for programming teams who could actually repair the faulty or antiquated code. Priam didn't want to do the work himself. He didn't even want to subcontract it out. He just wanted to offer his clients a few good referrals.

But the repair work was just the sort of thing that Ajax was most interested in. It would give him the opportunity to survey the information systems and data banks of all sorts of enterprises while their security firewalls were down. In other words, he could lurk in the sensitive files of companies, extract whatever information he thought might be of value later, and never be detected—and he would be able to escape all suspicion. He might even be able to program in backdoor access to sensitive financial accounts enabling him to make withdrawals and transfers without ever being detected. He would come in like a savior and waltz out like a bandit—and the client would never know the difference.

It was a hacker's dream come true.

He could play the coveted roles of Robin Hood, Guy Fawkes, William Wallace, and John Barleycorn simultaneously. He could at last be the gallant Highwayman he had always dreamed of being.

He could be rich.

Ten

"Because thou sayest, 'I am rich, and increased with-goods and have need of nothing.'" Revelation 3:17

NOVEMBER 26, 1998

It was Thanksgiving day and the Priam family had much to be thankful for. It had been a very prosperous year. In fact, it had been prosperous beyond their wildest dreams. And it appeared that the best was yet to come. The sky was the limit.

Just a few months earlier—by about the middle of the summer—the media had begun to report on the Y2K crisis with increasing regularity, intensity, and alarm. Every major newspaper, magazine, and journal carried stories—sometimes even series of stories—on the potential that the computer glitch had for serious social, political, and economic disruption. Politicians began speaking out. Financial institutions, private sector organizations, and publicly traded companies began to disclose the magnitude of their compliancy efforts—and the cost to the bottom line.

Most Americans began to realize that it was either a problem that would cause planes to fall from the skies, water reservoirs to poison cities, and stock markets around the globe to crash, or else it was the biggest case of hype since Comet Kohoutek. They were told that it might affect just about every technological device in existence and cause them to shut down or go haywire on or before January 1, 2000, throwing the world into chaos. Or else we all would muddle through just fine. Experts were split about 70-30 in favor of disaster.

For an increasingly wary populace, it was beginning to look as if Y2K could turn into an unwanted crash course on the sundry subtleties of Murphy's Law—and that on a global scale.

In a widely publicized speech, Andy Grove warned congress that the federal government faced an ugly situation if it did not step up efforts to correct the programming error in its agencies' computers. And he asserted that businesses faced catastrophic losses if they did not do the same. The chief executive of chip maker Intel—and widely considered the most powerful man in the computer industry besides Microsoft's Bill Gates—was sounding the alarms, he said, in an effort to avert a global disaster of monumental proportions.

Then the President and the Vice President addressed the nation on the subject in a unique joint appearance. Having been accused by Republicans of ignoring a problem that was occurring on their watch, they announced that the Millennium Bug had become the biggest problem they had faced in their six years in office—or at least, the biggest one that did not involve an independent counsel. Indeed, they asserted that solving the crisis had necessarily become the nation's number one priority— more important than health care reform, tax cuts, bureaucratic downsizing, rapprochement with old foreign enemies, reinventing government, revitalizing industry, or saving the whales. Addressing the National Academy of Sciences, they warned of gaping holes in efforts by both government and private industry to prepare their computer systems for the end of the millennium. Bringing the nation's computer-run technological systems—both great and small—into compliance would be one of the greatest technological challenges in history, they said. And failure to deal with it might very well result in a series of shutdowns, inaccurate data, and faulty calculations that could affect the whole fabric of society.

While it appeared that American government agencies and private companies were very much behind the eightball on compliancy issues, the rest of the world was lagging even further behind.

- A June survey of 378 German companies by Frankfurt-based KHK software consortium found that 57 percent had done nothing to address the Y2K problem; only 3 percent had budgeted for it.

- About 70 percent of France's roughly one million small businesses had likewise taken no steps toward complaince according to the information department of the national Chamber of Commerce and Industry.

- Of the 50 largest financial institutions in Russia, only a third were even aware of the Millennium Bug, according to the systems analysis of Coopers and Lybrand.

- Britain's government had committed to spend about $5 billion on the problem, according to the Action 2000 accountancy group—but it was still expected to be able to fix only the most urgent mission-critical operations.

- Zhang Qi, the information ministry official responsible for China's Y2K efforts, testified before the International Monetary Fund review board that the government had not yet begun to seriously consider the problem.

- Likewise, Ravindra Gupta, the top spokesman for India's federal electronics department, said that the government was only beginning to examine the problem.

The impact of possible power, service, and social disruptions worldwide seemed to bode ill for the global economic future. This was at a time when the Asian currency crisis was already creating a negative ripple effect throughout markets everywhere.

And with every dire warning, every indication of impending disaster, and every harbinger of doom, Bob Priam cheered. For him, all bad news was good news. The fact was, he couldn't have bought better advertising for his fledgling consulting business. Suddenly, with Y2K in the headlines and at the top of the national agenda, demand for his services outstripped his most optimistic expectations. He had more clients than he knew what to do with. Since August he had adjusted his fee structure three times, added two full-time staff analysts, hammered out a licensing agreement with a diagnostic software firm, and retained exclusive referral relationships with several programming teams who could do the actual repair work at selected sites—and still he had clients waiting in line for his services.

In the seven months since he had lost his job at OfficeCentral, he had already made more than triple his former salary. What had been a very comfortable life before had become very nearly luxuriant in recent months. Priam felt like a mogul. Both *Success* magazine and *Working At Home* wanted to do feature stories on him. He was quickly becoming a high-tech celebrity—one of the talking heads networks regularly turned to when Y2K stories made the evening news.

With every passing day, more and more companies were coming to the realization that their computer compliance issues were far more complex and far reaching than their in-house information and technology staffs could handle. They were calling Priam in droves. And since he was one of the only games in town, he had a virtual corner on the market for Y2K systems analysis. He had clients all over the Southeast and Midwest. As the gravity of the situation began to break down the stern resistance of the corporate boardrooms, opportunities for his little company abounded. Just the previous month, he had even gotten a desperate call from his successor at OfficeCentral, begging for help and offering a premium consulting contract in an effort to save the company from disaster.

Frank Menelaus had given the go-ahead to hire him—just before the gruff CEO had been given the sack during a brawling and bloodthirsty stockholder meeting. *My how fortunes change,* he thought with no little irony at the time.

Although they splurged a bit of their new-found prosperity, Priam made certain that he put his family's house in financial order as well. He paid off their cars and their home. He did away with all of his credit card debt and started an aggressive savings and investment program. They had never been so far ahead, so secure, or so confident about their future together.

Indeed, the Priam family had much to be thankful for on this Thanksgiving day. And so they gathered around their table to express their deep and abiding gratitude—just as so many before them had.

THE VERY FIRST WINTER on American shores was incredibly treacherous for the colonists of New England. In the

Plymouth Colony, for instance, the settlers died in droves from both sickness and starvation. Though they were blessed with abundant moral reserves, they had little of anything else. At one point they were forced to ration their meager food stores—a mere five kernels of corn per person per day. Nevertheless, a small remnant survived—and eventually thrived in their new homeland. Early on those courageous settlers expressed their thanksgiving for the evidence of God's good providence in their lives. Despite all the hardships they faced, they recognized the peculiar opportunity they had been afforded. Thus, they outwardly affirmed their fealty to God and His ways.

In the years that followed, the valor, longsuffering, faithfulness, and gratitude of those stalwart Pilgrims have often been memorialized during Thanksgiving prayers, celebrations, toasts, services, and meals. In New England, for instance, it has long been a part of the traditional New England holiday tradition to serve each member of the family a mere five kernels of corn. Then, before the turkey is carved, before the table is laden high with delicacies, and before grace is said over the cornucopia of their abundance, they recite together a remarkable traditional verse. Thus, for many, this remembrance of the pioneers of Plymouth has become a symbol of the incredible blessing of American liberty.

Abby Priam loved traditions like that. She had always tried everything she could to build lasting and meaningful legacies of faith, hope, and love for her family. In fact, she often encouraged her brood with the words, "Come on, let's make a memory." Admittedly, the kids had to be cajoled into participating in more than a few of her grand schemes, but in the end they always appreciated her special attention to details, her knack for making even ordinary times extraordinary, and her penchant to add meaning to every family gathering.

On this day, though, there were no reluctant participants. The succulent aroma of turkey roasting in the broiler, the sweet fragrance of pies cooling on the racks, and the rich yeasty bouquet of fluffy rolls browning in the oven had lured the whole family around the long dining table. Even Troy was in a cheerful, anticipatory mood.

"All right everybody, let's pass out the corn," Abby directed them.

"I love this part," Hector enthused.

Against the oyster white porcelain china, the tiny kernels afforded them a stark reminder of just how much they had to be grateful for. Once they were served their symbolic rations, Abby passed around rolled parchment sheets inscribed with the verse. She had spent hours preparing the beautiful calligraphy—and it showed.

"Wow. These are awesome Mom," Cassie said.

"I think you've really outdone yourself this year," Troy agreed.

Abby just smiled.

Looking over his happy family, Bob Priam could only stand in utter amazement. How quickly his fortunes had changed. "Well, let's recite together then."

And so they did. Together their voices were lifted up in a kind of hymn of thanks. Originally penned by the American folk poet, Hezekiah Butterworth, the words rang out with renewed vim, vigor, and vitality:

> *'Twas the year of the famine in Plymouth of old,*
> *The ice and the snow from the thatched roofs had rolled;*
> *Through the warm purple skies steered the geese o'er the seas,*
> *And the woodpeckers tapped in the clocks of the trees;*
> *And the boughs on the slopes to the south winds lay bare,*

And dreaming of summer, the buds swelled in the air.
The pale Pilgrims welcomed each reddening morn;
There were left but for rations Five Kernels of Corn.
Five Kernels of Corn!
Five Kernels of Corn!
But to Bradford a feast were Five Kernels of Corn!

Five Kernels of Corn! Five Kernels of Corn!
Ye people, be glad for Five Kernels of Corn!
So Bradford cried out on bleak Burial Hill,
And the thin women stood in their doors, white and still.
Lo, the harbor of Plymouth rolls bright in the Spring,
The maples grow red, and the wood robins sing,
The west wind is blowing, and fading the snow
And the pleasant pines sing, and arbutuses blow.
Five Kernels of Corn!
Five Kernels of Corn!
To each one be given Five Kernels of Corn!

O Bradford of Austerfield haste on thy way.
The west winds are blowing o'er Provincetown Bay,
The white avens bloom, but the pine domes are chill,
And new graves have furrowed Precisioners' Hill!
Give thanks, all ye people, the warm skies have come,
The hilltops are sunny, and green grows the holm,
And the trumpets of winds, and the white March is gone,
And ye still have left your Five Kernels of Corn.
Five Kernels of Corn!
Five Kernels of Corn!
Ye have for Thanksgiving Five Kernels of Corn!

The raven's gift eat and be humble and pray,
A new light is breaking, and Truth leads your way;

One taper a thousand shall kindle: rejoice
That to you has been given the wilderness voice!
O Bradford of Austerfield, daring the wave,
And safe though the sounding blasts leading the brave,
Of deeds such as thine was the free nation born,
And the festal world sings the Five Kernels of Corn.
Five Kernels of Corn!
Five Kernels of Corn!
The nation gives thanks for Five Kernels of Corn!
To the Thanksgiving Feast bring Five Kernels of Corn!

Everyone cheered—in part, out of enthusiasm for the verses they had just recited and, in part, out of anticipation for what would follow.

"Let's bow our heads and give thanks," Priam reminded them. Abby was grateful to hear a real, heartfelt thanksgiving pour forth from him in place of the perfunctory grace he had always offered up in years past.

"OK. Enough of the preliminaries," Troy said. Bring on the food."

"Yeah. Bring it on Mom," Hector responded.

"Here, here," Priam agreed.

"Men!" exclaimed Cassie. "Is that all you can ever think about? Food?"

"Well, dear," Priam affectionately patted her shoulder, "at this particular moment, I can't really imagine anything else. Why? Got a problem with that?"

Again, Abby just smiled. She had always believed that the way to a man's heart is his stomach. There was, in fact, very little to her that was more revealing of matters of ultimate concern than what her family ate and how they ate it. Whereas most people tend to think of faith as a rather other-worldly concern, they think of food as a rather this-worldly concern.

It is difficult for many to see how the twain could ever meet. But for Abby, food and faith were inextricably linked.

She had even taught a topic Bible study on the subject at church this past year, believing that the younger women needed to fully comprehend the importance of the domestic arts that so many made light of. The word *faith*, she loved to point out, is used less than 300 times in the Bible. But the verb *to eat* is used more than 800 times. "You can hardly read a single page of the Scriptures without running into a discussion of bread and wine, milk and honey, leeks and onions, glistening oil and plump figs, sweet grapes and delectable pomegranates, roast lamb and savory stew," she often said. "Throughout, there are images of feasts and celebrations. The themes of justice and virtue are often defined in terms of food while the themes of hungering and thirsting are inevitably defined in terms of faith. Community and hospitality are evidences of a faithful covenant while righteousness and holiness are evidences of a healthy appetite. Biblical worship—in both the Old and the New Testaments—does not revolve around some esoteric discussion of philosophy or some ascetic ritual enactment, but around a family meal. As if to underscore this, all of the resurrection appearances of Christ occurred at meals—with the single exception of the garden tomb. On the road to Emmaus, in the Upper Room, and at the edge of the Sea of Galilee, Jesus supped with His disciples."

As she and Cassie brought the carefully prepared dishes to the table, they were greeted with wide eyes and ready applause—accompanied by the appropriate "oos and ahs."

The golden brown turkey was a plump thirteen pounder. It was stuffed with traditional southern cornbread dressing—but it was surrounded by a delicious ham and apricot stuffing as well. Dishes of homemade cranberry sauce, mounds of mashed potatoes smothered in giblet gravy, steaming bowls of green beans, carrots, and fresh corn, and a gooey sweet yam casserole filled the table to overflowing. There were also baskets of bread and biscuits, heirloom cut glass dishes of pickles, relishes, and condiments. It was a veritable feast of sights, sounds, smells, tastes, and textures fit for kings, queens, and princes.

Once everything had been passed around the table, silence fell over the room as everyone in the family concentrated on the vital task before them. They were all well on their way to finishing their first helping when Priam remembered that he had not yet offered a toast.

He tapped his small silver dessert fork on the side of his tall crystal goblet. "A salute," he declared. "To my wonderful wife, my dear children, and the amazing life we have built together."

They all raised and tipped their glasses together with glee.

"And to Dad, his new business, and all the amazing blessings we've enjoyed in the last few months," added Cassie.

"Amen to that," Abby concurred.

"Let's not forget to acknowledge the source of all the blessing—God showered us with this." Priam was more than usually expansive about his faith, Abby noticed with glee.

Then, they passed all the dishes around again. And again. And yet again. When they had all eaten as much as they could, Abby started clearing away the dirty dishes.

After a couple of minutes though she reemerged from the kitchen with a wry grin. "Do you want dessert now or later?"

"How about a little now and a little later," Troy kidded.

"Oh, I don't think I could eat another bite, Mom. I'm stuffed," Cassie moaned.

"I think I'm about to burst," Priam acquiesced.

"Well just wait until you see these desserts," Abby said. "I bet you'll be able to find some room for them."

She brought in a huge tray. On it were two deep dishes surrounded by flaky golden crusts—a plump pumpkin pie smothered in whipped cream and sticky pecan pie refracting a buttery sheen.

"Oh my," Troy exclaimed. "Awesome. I think I'm going to have to . . ."

"Wow," Hector butted in. "Can I have a piece of both?"

"Hang on guys. That's not all."

Cassie brought in a big cake plate. "This is the Mitford marmalade cake from the Jan Karon books we read last summer in the car while we were on vacation," she announced triumphantly. "I found the recipe in a bookstore newsletter I picked up the other day—they had a contest to see if anyone could produce something that tasted as good as it sounded in the books."

"Mom, it looks like something in a magazine," Cassie gushed.

"Can I have a piece of all three?" Hector blurted out.

"Easy for you to say," Priam complained, his eyes lolling and his waistline bulging. "I'm so full I feel like I am hardly able to walk as it is. I don't know how anyone expects me to choose in this condition."

"Well, you know, abundance always forces us to make hard choices," Cassie quipped.

"Hmm. You're right, Cassie. I guess I'm going to have to taste them all then."

Eleven

*"Greater love hath no man than this, that a man lay
down his life for his friends." John 15:13*

NOVEMBER 30, 1998

Franklin is a prosperous little town about thirty miles from Nashville—just to the south of Brentwood. Filled with antique shops, historic sites, and quaint restaurants, it is the quintessential southern town. Nestled in the rolling hills along the Harpeth River, the town's antebellum brick storefronts, broad town square anchored by the courthouse, and tall church spires are picture postcard perfect.

For several weeks, Noah had anxiously anticipated going there to attend the commemorative ceremonies that marked the anniversary of the Battle of Franklin—one of the bloodiest battles of the Civil War. Speeches would be made. Reenactments would be staged. Memorials would be adorned. Graves would be tended. Solemn parades would be observed. Valor would be remembered. Losses would be mourned. And glory would be regaled.

Growing up in California, he had never been particularly impressed by the tragedy of the war, its participants, or the turns of events that finally brought it to a shuddering resolution. Though it was likely that the blood flowing in his veins came from both slaves and slave holders, that epic struggle more than a century earlier seemed terribly remote and irrelevant. But here in the Deep South, it took on a vitality that surprised him.

In fact, the story of this particular battle and everything associated with it had become frightfully compelling to him. On November 30, 1864, the Confederate General of the Army of Tennessee, John Bell Hood, launched a frontal assault against the superior forces of Union General Hugh Schofield. The Yankees were dug in all along the southern approach to Franklin, at a once-prosperous cotton farm. The attack was a hasty, rash move and in a charge as dramatic as anything seen at Gettysburg, 18,000 Confederate soldiers were hurled against entrenched Union lines. It was a bloodbath and Hood lost 6,252 men in just five hours of fighting, including thirteen general officers and five generals. The battle marked the last possible hope of the Southern cause.

The farm where most of the fighting took place had been transformed into a historical museum years before. The home had been faithfully restored and several of the out buildings, though severely battle scarred, had been carefully preserved. The little visitors' center there told the remarkable stories of a number of extraordinary men who met their fate during those five tragic hours. Noah had spent hours pouring over its archives, examining its artifacts, and rehearsing its anecdotes.

The panorama of the whole drama gripped Noah's romantic sense of honor, chivalry, and nobility. And so, since he had moved into the area, he had become something of a Civil War buff. He studied the biographies of the men involved in the conflict. He poured over old battle plans, diary entries, letters, and eye witness accounts. He walked over the battlefield again and again, trying to imagine the white hot frenzy of battle. He was fascinated by courage under fire. He wanted to someday emulate their tenacity and steadfastness—and so he catalogued their social virtues and noted their moral vigors.

One of the most remarkable men he had read about—and one that the historians owed the most to—was perhaps the unlikeliest of all the heroes to emerge from the battle. He was the chaplain, E. M. Bounds. Still known today for his devotional writings on prayer, he was a pastor from Missouri before the war. But in the tense days prior to the outbreak of hostilities, Bounds was arrested by Union troops for opposing the confiscation of church buildings. His ministry in prison was so effective that following a prisoner exchange he was immediately sworn in as a chaplain and soon found himself under the Rebel General Hood's command. A more war-weary band of soldiers have rarely existed. These veterans had seen many a preacher appeal for converts in the quiet of the camp only to flee to the comforts of home when the firing began. Chaplain Bounds was a refreshing change. The soldiers learned that when the fighting broke out, they could find Bounds on the front lines, exposing himself to danger, and drawing fire as he shouted encouragement to his flock. The men loved him. He was barely over five feet tall and as thin as a rail, and when he made his rounds carrying a full backpack, the men laughingly called him "the walking bundle," for the man could scarcely be seen under the huge load. Bounds always smiled, waved, and turned to the next soul that required mending.

Many prisoners were taken after the terrible battle, and among them was Chaplain Bounds. For days afterwards, his heart-wrenching task was to dig mass graves for the very men whose souls he had tended. All the while, though, he sang hymns, quoted Scripture aloud, and offered encouragement to his fellow captives. Finally, after two weeks of this horror, most of the prisoners were released on condition that they not take up arms again. Bounds agreed and left for his home in Missouri. His business in Franklin, however, was unfinished.

Early the next year, he returned to Franklin. With all his heart he had loved the men in those horrible mass graves—he knew their hurts, the names of their wives and children, the shape of their fears—and he simply couldn't leave them there. He conceived a project to properly bury the dead and commemorate their lives. His vision moved local farmer, Ronald McGavok, to donate some land and during the hot summer of 1865 some 1,496 Confederate soldiers were exhumed and buried in the new cemetery on the hills of the Carnton Farm. He even raised seven hundred dollars to pay local men to tend the graves. But it was not enough. He made a list of all the men from Missouri he buried at Franklin and published it in the Missouri newspapers to inform the families and generate even more support. Tenderly, he placed the list in his own wallet where it remained until the day of his death forty-eight years later. Throughout his life, he visited the families of his men, wrote them letters, and even secured scholarships for the children of the men he had prayed with in those smoky Confederate camps. Following the War, Bounds became the pastor of Franklin's Methodist Church, and led a major revival in the town. Years later he would continue his dynamic writing and preaching ministry in Georgia and Alabama.

Noah often walked through the carefully tended cemetery at Carnton late at night. He was haunted, not so much by the cruel loss of life, but by the responsibilities undertaken by those who were left behind. Indeed, he thought of Bounds and his grim duty often. He thought of how he had set aside his own ambition, his own career, and his own life for the sake of others. He pondered the burden of such a Lost Cause.

Late that night as he wandered between the white markers glinting in the moonlight, he heard the mockingbirds call down at him from the nearly bare sugar maple that overspread the pathway. *I wonder if I will ever have a chance to do something so admirable, so sacrificial, and so noble as these men, as Bounds. I wonder if there will ever be a time when the stakes are so high and the needs are so great that such honor will be called for again. And if the day ever does come, I wonder if I will have the courage, the gumption, and the sense of honor necessary to do what I am supposed to do and be what I am supposed to be.*

The sweet smells of freshly mown hay—the last of the season—clung to the air and fragrant wood smoke from a nearby chimney wafted in the cool breeze. *I just wonder if leadership is even an attribute that is in supply any longer—it certainly doesn't appear to be so, if current events are any kind of a guide. Oh how I desire to stand above that. How I yearn for something more. I wonder. I just have to wonder.*

After the festivities were over, the crowds had returned to their homes, and the last huzzahs had been raised, Noah wandered through the cemetery for another hour or more. Finally, he went back to his truck and drove north toward Nashville, lost in thought.

HE COULD TELL SOMETHING was wrong the moment he pulled into the parking lot. HavaJava was abuzz with some kind of unpleasant furor. Clara Rachman was bustling around a table, obviously distressed. Several men were huddled around, gesturing in an obviously agitated fashion. Noah thought twice about going inside at all—he could have easily just put his pickup into reverse and slipped away into the night. But he decided he had better go ahead and go inside to see what the trouble was.

He was surprised to find that the object of everyone's concern was one of his old dumpster-diving acquaintances—the tall thin fellow he had last run into the night of his wild chase. He was alone, and looking even more haggard than before. His grimy coveralls were torn. His sparse hair was askew. And his taut features were lined with a sense of bitter horror. His hands shook as Clara refilled his coffee mug—while two of the other customers, one on either side, attempted to comfort or soothe or calm him.

Noah caught up with Clara as she headed back behind the counter. "What on earth is going on?"

"I'm not really sure," she replied, obviously shaken. "Jake came in about half an hour ago, saying that Hugo, his partner had been shot. Killed."

"Shot? How? Where?"

"I don't know, Noah. I don't really understand. He won't call the police. He's scared to death. He thinks whoever it was that killed Hugo is after him too. They chased him all the way to the freeway before he lost them—or they broke off."

"They? Who was it?"

"He doesn't know. They were just out digging in the dumpsters—looking for salvage. They saw some men coming out of a building. And they started chasing and shooting. They apparently got Hugo—but Jake made it to the car and escaped. That's all I know."

"Good Lord."

"What?"

"About six months ago, maybe more—that was the last time I saw Jake and Hugo—we were at a site together and almost the same thing happened."

"What do you mean?"

"I mean, we saw some men come out of a building. Jake and Hugo took off. But I stuck around to investigate. Big mistake.

I saw that the men had weapons—or at least a couple of them did. I tried to get away, but I stumbled, they heard me, and they came after me."

"Are you kidding?"

"No. And these guys were serious. I got to my truck and started hauling. But they were right behind me. They shot at me too. Once I got to the freeway, though, they just gave up the chase."

"And you didn't report this to the police." Clara had fire in her eyes. She was obviously scolding.

"Uh, no. I just figured that they were security or something. Or if they weren't security, I really didn't want to mess with them."

"You figured. You figured, huh?"

"Well yeah. I guess I figured wrong, huh?"

"I would say so, Noah, especially given the current situation. Sounds like they're the same guys Jake and Hugo ran into tonight."

"So how is he? Jake, I mean."

"He's pretty shaken up. The problem is, he'll have to answer questions from the police sooner or later. This is not the sort of thing that he can just ignore. He'll wind up being a suspect if he doesn't do something quickly to identify the real killers."

As they were talking, the customers with Jake convinced him to report the shooting to the police—if only for his own safety and security. He offered his thanks to Clara and then headed hesitantly toward the door. He was still pretty shaky when the other men grabbed his jacket, trundled him out to the parking lot, and drove away.

For a long time Noah and Clara leaned against the counter in silence. The shop was now empty and the hollow quiet left them with an eerie sense of discomfiture.

"All I wanted was a cup of coffee," he finally said. "I wasn't looking for adventure."

"That's the thing about life. You may have to go hunting for a good cup of coffee, but you never have to go hunting for adventure—it hunts you."

"That's just about the corniest thing I've ever heard in my life."

"Yeah. Corny, but true."

NOAH FINISHED THE LAST of his cappuccino and was ready to call it a day when he heard another late evening customer at the door of the shop. He swung around on his stool just as Cassie Priam walked in. Both of them registered their surprise.

"Noah, what are you doing here?"

"I was about to ask you the same thing, Cassie."

"Oh, well my dad is working late. I've been helping him some at the office—just around the corner. And well, we both thought that a cup of coffee might be pretty nice just about now."

"Well, you've come to the right place. Best coffee in town. I come here almost every night."

"Great." She placed an order for two tall lattes and then turned back toward Noah.

"You come all the way up here for a cup of coffee every night?"

"Almost every night. And besides great coffee, I can get great arguments as well—multicultural political correctness is Clara's other specialty. She serves it up stronger than a double cappuccino," he smiled over at her as she heated the milk for the lattes. "She's my favorite feminazi."

"Yeah. And he's my favorite fascist," Clara retorted over her shoulder.

"Gee. How affectionate," Cassie chuckled.

"So what's your dad doing working late downtown? I thought he had some sort of a computer consulting firm and worked out of your home."

"He does. He did. But business has really taken off. He had to hire a couple of people. He needed a place to meet with clients, to make presentations, and to put files and equipment. So a couple of months ago, he leased some office space here. It's already too small, so he's looking to expand next door."

"So, the Y2K business is booming, eh? That's good to hear. I guess companies are finally getting on the stick and repairing their legacy systems."

"Well, yes and no. See, my dad's company doesn't actually fix the Millennium Bug. That's a whole different thing. He decided to focus on analysis. He finds areas where companies are not compliant and then tells them what the most cost-effective and time-efficient ways are of repairing or replacing the systems might be."

"So there are actually several different courses of action that companies can take."

"Oh, sure. There are all kinds of Y2K solutions out there. My dad says they all have their strengths and weaknesses—but there definitely is more than one way to skin the cat."

"I thought you either had to search and replace every line of dated code on every computer system, or replace all the existing software with a compliant commercial package."

"Oh, no. One of the things my dad has recommended to his clients is a simple date-year expansion where every year field is allocated four digits instead of two in the data itself. Something similar is where the year field is expanded to four digits in the software. Those apparently are very time consuming processes, but they can be automated—essentially, with the right software, the computers can fix themselves."

"I heard that some companies—and even some government agencies—are just sidestepping the whole problem by back-dating—shifting all the years down by, say, 26, so that 2,000 appears as 1974."

"That's true. I think that's what NASA is doing. But of course, that doesn't fix anything—it just delays the problem for a few years. And it's not feasible at all for some applications. A lot of businesses—like banks, insurance companies, and broker-age houses—can't do that because interests, mortgages, annu-ities, premiums, dividends, and benefits are all date-sensitive."

"Gee, I hadn't thought about that."

"Yeah, so those companies have tried all kinds of things to get around the problem. One of my dad's customers had actually started to build duplicate databases—a two digit and a four digit version of everything for use with compliant and non-compliant applications. Another tried to code all years in binary—using, for example, the two bytes of a year field to code 65,536 years rather than two ASCII numbers."

"Wow. I'm impressed. I had no idea you knew so much about computers."

"Well, I don't really. Don't ask me what all this actually means. I'm really just repeating what I hear my dad talk about on the phone with his clients. It's all pretty complicated."

"Has your dad tried to do window pivoting?"

"Oh yeah. I think that's where you choose a pivot year—say, 1930—and then you interpret years ending in 30 to 99 as 1930 to 1999, and years ending in 00 to 29 as 2000 to 2029. Yeah, dad had a customer who wanted to try that. But it is just a tem-porary measure. In the end a more permanent solution has to be found."

"In some cases it seems like it might be easier just to shut everything down and return to manual methods: paper, pencil, and calculator."

"Wishful thinking, Noah. The problem is that virtually everything in our society is now run by computer—and there are even embedded computer chips in almost every appliance, every tool, every system, and in every aspect of our lives. So, even when it doesn't look like computers are around, they are. They're everywhere."

"Man, you know a lot about this stuff. I've done a good bit of research on Y2K, but most of it has to do with the problems that it will cause, not so much the solutions that there might be out there."

"Well, our whole family has been kind of living and breathing this mess ever since last spring. I guess like almost any new business, my dad's consulting company has required an awful lot of our time and attention. And, since I'm the oldest, I've had the chance to do some basic stuff around the office— you know, clerical-type work. It's meant that I've been able to pick up on a lot of information that I wouldn't ordinarily be exposed to."

"I guess not."

By this time the two lattes were starting to cool. "I'd better get going. My dad will be wondering where I've gotten off to. He wasn't too keen about letting me come down here in the first place."

"Cassie." The door of the coffee shop burst open and Bob Priam stormed in. "I was starting to get worried. What's taking you so long?"

"Ooops. Sorry. I was just talking with Noah—he's in several of my classes at school. I think we let the time get away from us."

Priam glared over at the two of them, obviously sizing up the situation, and obviously none too pleased. He always seemed gruff when he was worried about his kids' safety. "Let's go, young lady."

Noah looked back toward Clara and shrugged. He watched as Priam—with his daughter in tow—beat a hasty retreat into the night.

"You really like that girl, don't you?"

"What? Oh no, Clara. She's just a friend from school."

"Yeah. Right. You were dazzled. All that tech talk. She really had you going. I saw the look in your eyes."

"What look? Come on."

"Well, it doesn't matter much. Did you see the way her dad dismissed you with that glare?"

"Yeah. I think he was a little mad."

"He was more than a little mad."

"Yeah. I guess you're right. He was *very* mad."

"*Furious* is more like it. And I don't think he liked the looks of you talking to his lily white daughter."

"Story of my life. I think I'm quickly becoming the official chaplain of the Lost Cause."

Twelve

"A prudent man forseeth the evil and hideth himself;
but the simple pass on." Proverbs 22:3

DECEMBER 3, 1998

Hope for the best. Plan for the worst." That was the counsel Priam constantly gave. It was the byword of his entire consulting business. Again and again he reminded his clients to take every precaution, to explore every option, and to do careful contingency planning. Be prepared. That is what he told them. It was the product he sold day in and day out.

But then, one day, a simple question shattered his professional confidence and calm assurance.

"What are you doing to protect your family if worse comes to worst?"

He had just finished a major presentation to the board of a Fortune 500 primary care medical management company. It was his biggest client to date—and the amount of work Priam and his team had put into it stretched them all to the limit. Health Care International had never integrated its systemwide computing operations. To insure Y2K compliance would not only require a tedious inventory and repair of the legacy systems in fifty-seven widely flung hospitals and more than ninety clinics, it would require a comprehensive overhaul of the corporate network. The analysis alone had taken seven weeks of intensive work.

But the report was gratefully accepted by the board of directors. They had become convinced nearly a year before that their in-house Y2K efforts were moving far too slowly and that outside contractors would have to be brought in if they were to survive and thrive in the new millennium. They had studied the parameters of the problem and were painfully aware of the consequences should they fail to get their computers and embedded chip systems up to speed. As a result, they immediately recognized the competency and comprehensiveness of Priam's report. And they appreciated it. They had paid dearly for his services—but they recognized by the end of the presentation that he and his Apollo team had been worth every last dollar.

John Lockyear, the charismatic president of the company, openly and gratefully lauded Priam.

"I can't thank you enough, Bob. You've saved our bacon."

"Well, thanks, John. But it's not saved yet. Now comes the hard part: bringing all the systems into compliance. All we've done so far is point out what needs to be accomplished—when, where, how, and why. We've just given your information technology people a roadmap showing the location of all the potholes, dead ends, and speed bumps. The long arduous journey toward Y2K compliance has really only just begun."

"I have to tell you, that's a lot further along than we were seven weeks ago. I've been trying to get an accurate assessment of our real Y2K compliancy needs for two years now. That's how long our in-house people have been piddling with this thing." He shot off a glare toward his CIO who was fiercely concentrating on his Palm Pilot. Priam felt like slapping the poor guy's back on his way out and suggesting that he enter "Look for a new job" on tomorrow's to do list.

"You delivered in just seven weeks. Seven weeks. That's just amazing."

"Thanks."

Turning to the assembled board, Lockyear dismissed the meeting. "OK, gentlemen, the challenge before us now is to push ahead with this blueprint—and keep to a nonnegotiable schedule. And we have to be ready for testing our new systems at least six months ahead of time to work out the bugs. We've never brought in a software or hardware conversion, upgrade, or overhaul on time—not once in the history of this company. In fact, I don't know of any one else in our industry who has accomplished that feat either. But this time we have no choice. Our deadline is steadfast and unmovable. It is fixed in time like nothing else we've ever faced before. Spare no effort. Accept no excuses. Let's get at it."

Priam appreciated his businesslike attitude. Although the CIO was likely to lose his job, at least Lockyear resisted the tactic of humiliating him in front of everyone—in the way Menelaus would have. He appeared to be a real team builder. That was a refreshing change from what Priam had normally observed in the corporate boardrooms of America.

As they made their way down the hallway and out toward the lobby of the vast corporate headquarters, Lockyear traded pleasantries with Priam. Both men were tired but satisfied. Their leather heels resonated a syncopated clacking along the sparkling terrazzo and echoed into the soaring clerestory above. They stopped just shy of the impressive salmon granite and burnished curtain-glass entrance and looked out into the twilight that was beginning to settle over the Tennessee hills visible beyond the practically empty parking lot.

Just before they parted though, Lockyear squared his shoulders and looked Priam in the eye.

"I have to tell you Bob, this Y2K business has really got me spooked. The more I learn about it the more frightened I am that our economy is just not going to withstand the blows. In fact, your work here has actually caused me more alarm than comfort."

"How so?"

"Well, I'm not an alarmist. In fact, I'm an optimist by nature. I have to tell you that I'm pretty encouraged by the rapid strides that industry, the utility companies, and even certain agencies of the federal government have made toward compliance. Even though I realize that this thing is a weak-link problem—all it takes is for a couple of municipal utilities to lag behind and the nationwide system is compromised—I really don't think the power grid is going to go down. I'm guessing that we'll have a few brownouts here and there, maybe. But I don't think it's going down. And while we may have some disruptions across the rest of the service sector, I think we'll be able to limp through. I think technologically we'll be all right."

"I agree. So what is it that has you spooked?"

"The economy itself. And the mindset of the country. Right now the stock market is trading somewhere between 45 and 50 percent above earnings. We've had a runaway bull market like that for about two or three years now. It is ripe for a fall—a good corrective. It is well past time for the bears to come out of hibernation. The problem is that most companies are now spending millions of dollars off the bottom line for infrastructure repairs—from the best established Fortune 500 firm to the most recent IPO. The Y2K fix is slow and costly. And it adds nothing to earnings. Now that the IRS has ruled that companies cannot amortize those expenditures over several years, it means that they all have to take the hits this year and next."

"And that radically reduces their value in the market."

"Right. So, if traders ever reflect that fact on the floor of the stock exchange, we could see a panic selloff like we haven't seen since the Great Depression."

"And that might have a domino effect across the nation."

"Exactly. Worried families might try to get their savings out of their local banks—to get as much liquidity and cash as they can as fast as they can."

"And then we'd have a run on the banks. If that happened, we probably would have cash reserves on hand for a day, maybe two, at best. Then the feds would have to step in, close the banks—and that would really spook the general public."

"In other words, even before we actually know what any of the technological problems might be—even before January 1, 2000—we have the potential to have a virtual collapse of the economy. And if we have even a minor collapse there, Lord knows what will happen. Panic? Unrest? Rioting? Gangs taking over the cities? Martial law? Bob, it could be the undoing of our already fragile social fabric—or the collapse of order in our inner cities, at the very least."

"It could. I really don't think it will go that far though. Do you?"

"I have a hard time getting past the fact that we just don't have the kind of character capable of handling adversity. We're not the same country we were when the Great Depression hit. Just look at what happened just after Hurricane Andrew struck a few years ago, or the floods in the Midwest, or the fires in central Florida. Rioters and looters took to the streets almost immediately. And then there were the Los Angeles riots."

"Come on, John. Do you really think that it is going to get that bad?"

"I don't know. Nobody knows, I don't think. But I just keep thinking about your motto."

"My motto?"

"Yeah, you know. Your sales mantra. Your pitch. It's how you sold me on your company. It's why I was willing to place the future of Health Care International in your hands. *Hope for the best. Plan for the worst.* You said it. Not me."

"I did indeed. So, what's your point. I'm not sure I follow?"

"Well, I just wanted to know how you were planning for this thing? Personally. Surely, if the Y2K crisis poses the kinds of potential social and economic hazards that we've just described, we have to be as vigilant at home as at work—if not more so. Don't we? So then, tell me. What are you doing to protect your family, Bob—if worse comes to worst?"

PRIAM WAS STUNNED. He had spent so much time thinking through the implications of Y2K for specific business applications that he had hardly given a thought to the other, more practical concerns that the problem raised. It was almost as if he had missed the forest for the trees. Certainly, he was aware of the dire warnings about the fragility of the social structure—but somehow, he had convinced himself to think of that kind of liability almost exclusively in terms of the economic impact on business. Virtually every Y2K web site, every newsletter, every article that he had seen at least alluded to the personal and practical concerns of family—food supplies, family protection, electricity, potable water, and community stability. But he had all but ignored those dimensions of the crisis. He was no reactionary. In fact, he didn't have an alarmist bone in his body. From his business cut gray flannel suit to his cap toe oxfords, from his short razor coif to his crisp monogrammed sleeve cuffs, his every thought word and deed bespoke a sure and secure establishmentality.

He had very little patience with apocalyptic thinking. He was a nuts and bolts kind of guy. He believed that every problem had a solution. Hard work, creative thinking, and stick-to-it-iveness—that was the way to deal with a crisis. He had very little sympathy for anyone who harbored a run-for-the-hills mentality. Besides, he was absolutely intent on building a business.

He had been a veritable workaholic for as long as he could remember. His worldview had been shaped for so long by corporate concerns that it was difficult for him to even think in terms outside that environment. Even when he was at home with Abby and the kids, he always seemed to have a project to work on. And he had almost never yielded to pleas for family vacations. Instead, from time to time he would take them along on various business trips, conventions, or speaking engagements when he was scheduled to be in some locale he thought that they might enjoy—like the beach, the mountains, or overseas. As a result, his laptop was omnipresent and his concentration was ever-absent.

After he lost his job with OfficeCentral, he resolved to change his ways. And he did for a short time. He moved his office into the house. He spent an hour each morning with Abby in the garden—drinking in the coffee and the sunshine, watching the birds flutter around the tall flowers, talking over the day's projects, and listening to the astonishing sounds of silence. He played one-on-one basketball with Troy out in the driveway. He invited Hector to tag along for his daily runs—with Hector astride his bike and Priam pounding the pavement. He even read poetry aloud in the evenings with Cassie—even getting halfway through her favorite tome, the earliest edition of Arthur Quiller-Couch's *The Oxford Book of English Verse*.

But then the new business began to consume more and more of his time—and it began to command more and more of his attention. He started to slip into his old patterns of work. You can teach an old dog new tricks—but it is no easy feat. Lifelong habits are hard to break.

His best intentions slowly gave way to the tyranny of the urgent and the familiarity of the routine.

Those first few weeks of respite from the corporate rat race had reminded him of how homesick he had grown over the years. But it was a lesson that the anesthesia of ambition enabled him all too quickly to forget.

Now, he realized that his very worldview, his underlying perspective of life, his presuppositional framework, his foundational viewpoint had somehow become utterly twisted. The things that mattered most occupied him least. He was living a life consistent with what he thought in his head in contradistinction to what he felt in his heart and yearned for in his soul. He and Cassie's reading had turned up a haunting quote from the great English literary lion, Samuel Johnson, who once asserted, "Indifference in questions of importance is no amiable quality."

Whenever the subject of worldviews came up at home— usually at the behest of Cassie—he generally thought of it in terms of philosophy. Or as intellectual niggling. It made him think of the brief and blinding oblivion of ivory-tower speculation, of thickly obscure books, and of inscrutable logical complexities.

In fact, he now realized, a person's worldview is as practical as potatoes. It is certainly less metaphysical than understanding marginal market buying at the stock exchange or legislative initiatives in Congress. It is far less esoteric than typing a business plan into a laptop computer or sending a fax image across the continent. It is instead as down to earth as Abby tilling the soil for a bed of petunias she wouldn't even see for another six months.

The word itself, he remembered Cassie parroting her lessons from school, is a poor English attempt at translating the German *Weltanshauung*. It literally means a life perspective or a way of seeing. It is simply the way each individual looks at the world. Everyone has a worldview. It is the means by which they interpret the situations and circumstances around them. It is what enables them to integrate all the different aspects of faith, and life, and experience. Priam struggled to form an image he could use to help him understand his dilemmas.

All people carry in their heads some mental model of the world, some subjective representation of external reality. These mental models are kind of like giant filing cabinets. They contain slots for every item of information coming to them. They help people to organize their knowledge and give them grids from which to think. Minds are not *tabulae rasae*, blank and impartial slates. No one is completely open-minded or genuinely objective. When people think, they can do so only because their minds are already filled with all sorts of ideas with which to think. These more or less fixed notions make up their mental models of the world, their frames of reference, their presuppositions—in other words, their worldviews.

Worldviews are thus maps of reality. And like all maps, they may fit what is actually there, or they may be grossly misleading. The maps are not part of the real world, only images of it, more or less accurate in some places, distorted in others. For good or for ill, all good people carry around such maps in their mental makeup—and they act upon them. All thinking presupposes them. Most experiences fit into them.

Alas, Priam's worldview—and everything that it ultimately dictated in his life, thinking, and behavior—was out of whack. And he knew it only too well.

John Lockyear's question highlighted that fact in the starkest and most vivid manner imaginable. It caused him to awaken, as if from a dream.

WHAT ARE YOU DOING to protect your family if worse comes to worst?

The fact was, he had done nothing, planned nothing.

Now to be sure, he had provided for his family very well. And they were in excellent financial shape. They were debt free. They had paid off their house mortgage in record time. They had built a solid investment portfolio. They lacked for no material comfort or convenience. In other words, he had readied his family as if it were just another business venture. He had fallen into the trap of letting his job define him again—even evaluating his own family in terms of financial soundness and the outward appearances of success.

While he had designed careful contingencies for all of his clients, suggested failsafe measures for the companies he had consulted with, and developed long-term strategic plans for each of his corporate accounts, he had not really given a second thought to his family's welfare in light of the Y2K crisis. He had taken measures to insure the survival of businesses even in the face of widespread economic disruption. He had built into his advice buffer management systems so that they might weather any conceivable measure of social disarray. But he had not made the logical leap to similarly plan for his wife and children.

He thought of the old saws about cobblers whose children went about with no shoes, or carpenters whose homes remained in disrepair, or plumbers whose families were forced to dip water from the well.

As he drove away from the offices of Health Care International, night was beginning to settle into the glens, valleys, hollows, burns, and vales south of Nashville. Taking the long winding route along the Franklin Pike rather than the freeway gave him time to think about the predicament he had gotten himself into—again. A shock of Volunteer orange streaked the mackerel reefs of the dusky cobalt sky. And he recalled his life as little more than a famous regiment of victorious failures and successful catastrophes. He was dismayed by the stubborn recalcitrance that seemed to rule his heart with all manner of *das boot* totalitarian zeal.

What have you been thinking? What have you been doing? What are you doing to protect your family if worse comes to worst?

At last, he pulled into his subdivision. Carefully groomed homes lined both sides of the road. They were all lit up with the bustle of early evening activity—kids putting bikes away for the night, moms clearing away the day's clutter, and dads catching the evening news on television. Several families had already begun decorating for Christmas—trees adorned with glory faced front bay windows, twinkling lights and garlands draped eaves and columns, and wreaths emitted a fragrant balsamic welcome at door stoops. Several teens were kicking around a soccer ball under the dim glow of a street lamp. It all seemed so happy, safe, and secure on the surface. But he knew only too well from his own recent experience how fragile the veneer of prosperity actually was in most of those homes—stretched to the limit by debt, living beyond all reasonable means from paycheck to paycheck, and utterly dependent upon a continuing boon in the economy for even a semblance of their current standard of living.

Suddenly, the hubris of this upper-middle-class enclave appeared all too evident and terribly vulnerable. The houses looked less and less like paragons of success and more and more like pratfalls of pride. They seemed to him to be little houses of cards.

And that frightened him. His own house was indistinguishable from the rest of them.

He pulled up in front of his home. Through the lacy curtains on the dining room windows, he could see Abby setting the table for dinner. Hector was right there by her side—probably regaling her with adventure tales from his day at school. Cassie was sitting at the piano—he could barely make out the slight strains of the hymn she was noodling. Troy must have been around back—he could hear the thunk-thunk-thunk of the basketball on the driveway.

What are you doing to protect your family if worse comes to worst?

He sat there in his car for the longest time. He just stared and listened. He marveled at the odd paradox of being homesick right there at home. He pondered. He resolved. He wrestled. He wondered. He questioned. He prayed. He hoped for the best. But, he began to plan for the worst.

Thirteen

"Let us break their bands asunder, and cast away their cords." Psalm 2:3

DECEMBER 7, 1998

Contract repairs for Y2K projects proved to be an incredible economic windfall for Will Ajax and his Chernobyl team in more ways than one. First and foremost, of course, it offered them abundant work—and companies were paying a real premium for the various compliance, remediation, rectification, refurbishment, and installation services they offered.

Their style attracted Gen-Xers who worked in the corporate environment but were more comfortable with alternative dress, music, and lifestyles. Ajax delivered on his promises—and they loved watching him mock their bosses without them ever knowing. Even if they did catch on, though, they needed his expertise so badly that they were willing to ignore attitude for once.

By the time the autumn breezes had begun to chill the air across America, the media outlets had begun to chill the airwaves. Y2K became the latest in a long line of fashionable worries. And that was extremely good for business. Companies that assumed that they could procrastinate right up to the last minute suddenly realized in a panic that the last minute had actually arrived. And the suddenly incessant media carping would not let them forget it—try as they might. Dire predictions were offered by some of the most eminent and respected leaders in banking, business, and government.

The *Financial Times* reported, for instance, that sixty senior business executives from a wide array of multinational corporations had issued a warning that governments were not moving quickly enough to fix their Y2K problem. In a statement delivered simultaneously to the President of the U.S. and the Prime Ministers of Britain and Canada, the manifesto asserted, "We fear that governments lag in assessing and addressing the problem." They went on to caution that disruptions could extend to "delays in welfare payments, the triggering of financial chaos by a breakdown in revenue collection and debt management, and malfunctions in the air traffic control and defense systems." Among the sixty signing the statement were executives from Lloyds Banking Group, British Aerospace, BAT Industries, Thames Water, Bechtel Group, Unilever, Bom-bardier, Texas Instruments, and Ford Motor Company. Up to that time many skeptics claimed that Y2K consultants had been stirring up unwarranted fears in an effort to drum up business. Almost in an instant, the gravity of the situation struck home.

In Congressional testimony Edward Yardeni, the chief economist for Deutsche Morgan Grenfell, placed the odds of a serious global recession due to Y2K disruptions at 40 percent. But he was forced to quickly revise that estimate. After reading the federal government's third quarterly Y2K progress report he wrote that he would most likely raise the recession odds to 60 percent. Three months later, when the government's Office of

Management and Budget continued to suggest that vital computer systems operated by the government might not be ready for the century date change, he concluded that there was an increasing chance that important government services will be delayed, disrupted, pared, and curtailed by or in 2000. This precarious situation implied that foreign governments, as well as many business organizations around the world, may fail to meet the deadline too. Therefore, he raised the probability of a deep international recession to more than 70 percent. Indeed, he predicted that in the United States alone, real GDP could fall as much as 5 percent from peak to trough over a 12-24 month period starting late in 1999. That would mean dramatic domestic losses—somewhere between $300 billion and $700 billion—triggering huge production cuts, massive layoffs, and runaway deflation.

According to Yardeni, "The recession could begin before January 1, 2000, perhaps during the second half of 1999, if the public becomes alarmed and takes precautions. If stock prices fall sharply in 1999, in anticipation of a recession in 2000, the resulting loss in confidence could cause consumers to retrench in 1999 and trigger a recession sooner as well. It could start in 1999 if bankers cause a credit crunch by refusing to lend to companies that are most at risk of failing in 2000. If these companies are not bailed out by their key vendors or customers, they might start failing next year."

Such dire predictions were confirmed by IRS commissioner Charles Rosotti, who asserted, "It is a very risky situation. We have a very thin margin of tolerance to make this whole thing work. If we don't fix our computers, the whole financial system of the United States will come to a halt. It is very serious. It not only could happen, it will happen if we don't get this right."

And Frank Gaffney, director of the Center for Security Policy in Washington, concurred saying, "It is now too late to avoid altogether the myriad, damaging effects of the Millennium Bug on the United States, its people, and its interests. All that can realistically be hoped for is that a form of triage can be effected so as to reduce somewhat the possibly apocalyptic effects that will otherwise be experienced."

At last comprehending that the crisis was real, imminent, and disastrous, the minions of the press corps suddenly threw themselves into the maelstrom with a vengeance.

"But why? Oh, why?" reporters opined. "Why did we allow ourselves to get into this predicament? How could such a dire technological calamity occur at the advent of the twenty-first century? How could the experts of the information age have been so shortsighted? Wasn't there anything that might have been done to avert this kind of crisis?"

Their aching questions poured forth in a torrent. And almost as fervently, the ready responses poured forth in a torrent as well. Even if those responses were not exactly clear-cut answers, they were confident and emphatic guesses. Indeed, a myriad of experts and authorities weighed in on the network broadcasts, the 24-hour cable newscasts, the talk shows, the morning variety programs, the newspapers, the tabloids, and the news magazines. Already reeling under the tremendous pressure of meeting compliance deadlines, testing schedules, and shareholder expectations, the harried global technopoly was suddenly buried beneath an avalanche of analysis and apocalyptic hype.

Although most of the instant wits, wags, pundits, prognosticators, essayists, editorialists, commentators, and curmudgeons knew little or nothing about the Y2K problem, had never explored the technological issues involved, and had never thought through the immediate implications of the social questions it raised, they were quick to offer their opinions, explanations, conjectures, and theories concerning the coming calamity. Invariably they resorted to the sundry maxims and axioms of pseudoscience, pop-psychology, and fad-sociology. Most seemed more than happy to seize the opportunity to ride a political hobbyhorse or mount a social soapbox for one pet issue or another.

For several months the media's incessant handwringing commentary seemed to produce as many opinions as there were opinion makers. Experts seemed to come out of the woodwork, each ready to offer his or her authoritative voice to the cacophony of prognostication. A torrent of easy answers, quick retorts, and hasty analyses gushed forth. Alas, the modern media are set up for the rapid collection of emphatic guesses on the causes of disturbing news.

But whatever the woeful inadequacies of the media in reporting the Y2K crisis, Will Ajax was grateful to them for making it a matter of urgency and concern in corporate America—and thus affording him one astonishingly lucrative opportunity after another. He and his team had more work than they could handle.

Ajax had seized the chance to become one of the handful of contractors Bob Priam referred to his clients to do the actual Y2K repair work. Since Priam's consulting company only analyzed the problem, assessed the needs, and proposed a course of action, companies had to retain additional programmers to actually do the work of rewriting the code, installing the new hardware and software, and conducting the initial system tests.

The two men had met at an information technology expo several months earlier—and immediately they went about selling each other on their respective companies, their mutual interests, and their overlapping concerns. Priam recommended Ajax for a small job a couple of weeks later and was particularly impressed by the proficiency of the team's chief programmer, Athena Scully. The repair work was handled quickly, efficiently, and professionally. After that, Priam passed on as much work as he could.

B UT SUCH CONTRACT REPAIRS for Y2K projects offered more to Ajax than merely the prospect of good work, regular work, and lucrative work. They also offered him a constant stream of easy, albeit illicit, money.

One of the things that Y2K repair programming required was access to all the information, transmission, and processing systems within a given computing environment. The technicians had to have access to every line of code, every piece of software, every scrap of data, every password, every encryption device, and every shielding sequence. In other words, the programmers who walked in off the street to fix the Millennium Bug had to be able to put their hands on every detail of a company's vital information with full disclosure of all the firewalls and security measures.

In the Information Age, comprehensive access to so much sensitive data at any one time by any one person was unprecedented—and extremely dangerous. But then the Y2K crisis was itself unprecedented and dangerous—calling for drastic steps and extreme measures. And after all, such a situation would not actually pose a problem if the contract programmers actually doing the remedial work could be trusted.

Little did Bob Priam—or any of his unsuspecting clients—realize that Will Ajax could not be trusted. Regardless of whether he was bonded or not, he was like a kid in a candy shop who simply could not bear to keep his hands off the goods. For him, the Y2K crisis was a dream come true.

Ajax took full advantage of the extraordinary access he was given to the sensitive files of the clients. Recognizing the unique opportunity for what it was, he made the insertion of remote backdoor entries a part of the standard operating procedure for every system his team worked on. They wrote blind access codes for all of the accounting, billing, data transfer, fund supervision, portfolio management, client administration, product inventory, shipping and receiving, vendor conduct, customer tracking, and production control programs. They created a dense web of phantom accounts, clients, vendors, payables, and receivables. They manufactured reams of illusory data, profiles, balances, histories, backgrounds, and inventories. They fabricated a fog of disinformation designed to shield them from the scrutiny of auditors when they began siphoning off funds from the now-vulnerable and -accessible accounts.

While such data piracy might offer Ajax rich dividends from the padded purses of almost any large corporation, he realized that perhaps its greatest potential lay in the field of health care management. The lumbering bureaucracies that administered the multibillion dollar Medicaid and Medicare programs were already rife with corruption and mismanagement. The system was so big, so complex, and so disorganized, that it was an all-too-regular occurrence for vast sums of money to mysteriously disappear. Ajax saw the opportunity to get in on the getting while the getting was good.

And since Nashville was a critical hub in the national network of corporate hospital and primary care provision administration, Ajax began the getting—early and often. He had his programmers create a host of phantom claims that poured tens of thousands of dollars into his Chernobyl coffers every month. The convoluted path the electronic funds traveled before they made their way into the shielded accounts Ajax had set up for the cabal made them almost impossible to trace.

Of course, such a formula for success was not without its problems. If for instance, a careful portfolio manager or fund administrator were to regularly change the configuration of the security mechanism or install new firewalls sometime after the Chernobyl team's contract was completed, Ajax could lose his easy access. Even the blind back doors he had created might be blocked by an upgraded buffer program. In those instances, hacking into the system was still generally possible, but now, much more detectable. But sometimes, often in the most lucrative cases, access was blocked altogether. In such situations, on-site remediation was the only solution.

ONE OF THE THINGS that Bob Priam always recommended to his clients was that they alter all their information and transmission security measures shortly after Y2K repairs had been made. Perhaps the greatest risk he faced in his consulting business was legal liability—the prospect of being sued for a failed repair operation, lost data, corrupted code, service disruption, or embezzlement was not a terribly welcome one. But it was an all-too-real possibility that he was aware existed.

Legal experts worried that the Y2K crisis might provide the biggest litigation opportunity of all time. In an already litigious environment—Americans file about 15 million civil lawsuits and pay out nearly $125 billion in legal fees every year—that was more than a little frightening to Priam. *USA Today* reported, "Litigation resulting from Year 2000 meltdowns will be more costly than asbestos, breast implant, and Superfund cleanup lawsuits combined." He realized that costs could top $1 trillion in the U.S. alone—about a seventh of its entire economic output.

As a result, he was meticulously careful to protect himself against any and all liability. And the very best way to do that was to ensure that his clients' data was as safe as he could make it.

That meant that Ajax would have to content himself with a few initial hits from each of his contract repair jobs or he would have to find a way to extend his access through regular on-site remediation of his security end-run maneuvers. In other words, in order to maintain a steady stream of extorted income he would have to put together a crack team of data pirates to burgle passwords, reconfigure backdoor access, and to maintain phantom accounts. He would have to put together a kind of high-tech commando team.

Athena thought that the risks were too great. "Give it up Ajax," she told him several months earlier. "We don't need to be running around playing army. We're in the data business not the cat burglar business. We're all making more money than we ever dreamed of, anyway—legitimately."

"But the potential gains are enormous. We're not talking about taking anything—we're just going to put together a team that can manage and maintain our access."

"But why does that have to be done on-site?"

"The easiest way to find the passwords, the security arrangements, the firewall procedures is to simply look on the desks of the information managers in each department."

"How's that, pray tell?"

"Most administrators have so many numbers to remember that they write everything down—in an appointment book, a planner, a ledger, a notebook, an address book, or a journal. They even write passwords underneath desk blotters sometimes. It's laughable."

"Yeah, but think of all that we're jeopardizing. We've got a good thing going here."

"Look, Athena. You don't have to do this. You don't have to do a thing. Besides, it is a quick and relatively risk-free operation to bypass building security, shut down the alarms, slip into an office, scarf up the information we need, log onto the computer, reestablish our access codes, and then be on our merry way. We can be in and out in less than ten minutes—and never be detected."

"What if someone sees you, though?"

"No one will."

"But what if something goes wrong?"

"We'll take every precaution. We'll post surveillance ahead of time to determine the best times to go in. We're already familiar with the layout of the buildings we need to work—we're only maintaining access that we gained while doing the Y2K repairs. This is not a big deal. But it opens up incredible potential income streams. These Medicaid and Medicare billing operations can be cash cows for us over the long haul. But they have to be maintained."

"I still don't understand why it wouldn't be just as easy to hack into the systems from a remote location, Ajax. Is it really so necessary to remediate the systems on-site?"

"It's simple. When we hack into a system we greatly increase the risk of detection. We have to poke around to find the codes, our connection is extended far beyond the bounds of legitimate safety, and the possibility of a wrong move is greatly enhanced. If any of our transmissions can then be traced, our entire operation is exposed."

"There are precautions we can take to avoid that."

"But an on-site sting insures internal maintenance access— we are not outside the system, we're in it. It's faster. It's easier. And it's safer."

"Plus, you get to wear your macho commando outfits, carry your cool stealth gadgets, wave around a bunch of automatic weapons, and sneak around in the dark. It's male fantasy fulfillment, Ajax."

"Yeah, well. That too." He smiled broadly.

"You're just being a little boy."

"A rich little boy. And one who intends to get even richer with every passing day. If we stay ahead of the curve on this thing, the sky is the limit."

"I hope you're right, Ajax. But it sure doesn't have the appearance of wisdom. This is nothing but trouble. Mark my words. Nothing but trouble."

He recruited the team from an underground mercenary network. Such soldiers of fortune are generally not too particular about whom they work for so long as the pay is good, regular, and untraceable. Ajax made certain of that. Each man was weapons proficient, stealth trained, and technically apt.

At first, Ajax used them very sparingly. But gradually, they became a more vital aspect of his long-range plan for Chernobyl. And if the Y2K crisis ever became a full-blown social catastrophe, he would already have a security operation in place to push that plan forward even more.

At least that was how he rationalized it to himself, to the rest of his programmers, and to Athena.

Even after they began to run into a few glitches—with the dumpster-diver confrontations—Ajax was determined to use his muscle to expand his reach and his wealth. His appetite was insatiable. And his ego was enormous. He was thoroughly convinced that his supposed genius was sufficient to perpetuate his recent successes indefinitely.

Athena wasn't so sure. And she was beginning to grow restless. She was more and more uncomfortable with the unfettered voracity, the unheeding illusions of grandeur, and the untempered edacity that seemed to steer the wild coursings of Ajax through life. Indeed, such whirling dervishes of heart and soul and spirit were as repugnant to her as the latest pop-psychology fad. She was now checked by a grave internal caution.

Wisdom does not consist only of learning what one should do or even of what one could do, but also of knowing what one would do. And that is more often comprehended in one's consternations than in one's confirmations. Alas, Athena was only now learning that—the hard way.

Fourteen

"Thorns and snares are in the way of the froward."
Proverbs 22:5

DECEMBER 7, 1998

B ob, are you really convinced that we need to take such drastic measures?"

"I'm not, Abby. But I'd rather be safe than sorry."

"Well, I would too. But isn't there a way to play it safe without having to disrupt our entire lives?"

"I wish there were, Abby. If you can think of an alternative, I'm ready to listen. I'd love to be wrong on this."

"Maybe we should just slow down and think this whole thing through a bit before we jump to any drastic conclusions then."

Priam glanced up from his desk and looked long and hard into his wife's searching blue eyes. "I've been telling my clients for the past several months to hope for the best but to plan for the worst. I'm chagrined that I've not followed my own advice in the area that matters most: the safety and security of my own family."

"OK. I can buy that. But surely you don't think that the Y2K crisis is really going to create wholesale disruption and social catastrophe. There are too many people, too many businesses, with too much at stake. Surely, someone, somewhere is going to come up with reasonable, workable, and affordable solutions. Look at all the progress you've made with your clients."

"I have been pleased with what we've been able to accomplish—after starting so late in the game. I really do think that most computer systems at most big companies will be fixed in time. But Y2K is a weak-link problem. All it takes is for a few critical systems to fail—either because of lack of remediation, lack of testing, or lack of foresight. And Abby, I can say this with certainty: there are going to be some important systems that just won't be ready."

"I spoke with Rod Tardy at church just last week. He's an engineer at IBM. And he says that Y2K is just about all they are working on these days—and that everyone will be ready. Why must we be so alarmist if he's not?"

"Abby, think about what he said for a second. If Y2K is all IBM is working on these days, does that mean that all of the rest of the company's business has been put on the back burner? How does that help the bottom line? But besides that very basic business concern we have to face the reality that there are too many different software languages, programs, and computer systems than can be fixed with one simple, ingenious solution—even if IBM or Microsoft or some other company were to come up with one at the last second. Y2K solution companies can help their customers repair their noncompliant software. But the process is still time consuming, especially the testing phase. All

Y2K fixes require repetitive, time-consuming testing each time an application is modified to make sure it works with linked internal and customer-based and vendor-based applications that might have been repaired with a different technique. Some currently noncompliant systems are just so huge and complex that there simply isn't enough time left to fix and test them."

"So you really think this could be disastrous?"

"I don't know. I just don't know. Most folks don't believe Y2K is a serious problem. I hear it all the time: *You must be kidding. Somebody will surely figure something out. Right?* There is a great deal of confidence in American ingenuity: *This is a recognized problem and it will be fixed in time.* I want to be an optimist too. But the more I study it, the more convinced I am that there is no silver bullet. And there is no easy answer. I guess I have become a Y2K alarmist. I am definitely not a doomsayer though—even though doomsday scenarios are in the realm of the possible, especially if we fail to seriously assess the risks immediately. There's no point in us sugarcoating the problem, Abby. If we don't fix the century-date problem, we will have a situation scarier than the average disaster movie you might see on a Sunday night. I want our family to be as ready as we possibly can be. Just in case."

"But you would think that the federal government would step in if things were so dire, wouldn't you?"

"The problem is that the federal government is even more woefully unprepared than the rest of society. Medicare, the IRS, the Federal Aviation Administration, and other basic agencies are operating on utterly out-of-date technology. Most states begin their fiscal 2000 years on July 1, 1999. The federal government will begin on October 1, 1999. And a vast number of their mission-critical systems will not be ready by then. Here, look at these statistics. It's pretty horrifying."

Priam pulled a copy of a recent issue of *Forbes* magazine out of the pile of clippings, journals, and reports on his desk. As he flipped through it looking for the Y2K article, Abby scooted her chair in closer to look.

"Look at this. The government's Y2K compliance efforts recently received an F grade by the House Subcommittee on Government Management, Information and Technology, chaired by Representative Steve Horn of California. Only 63 percent of the 7,850 federal computer systems deemed mission critical—that is, vital to protecting U.S. national security, health, safety, education, transportation, and financial and emergency management—will actually be ready on January 1, 2000. So 37 percent of our vital systems are not going to make it—to say nothing of the thousands of less critical operations that are just being ignored right now. Only 24 percent of the Defense Department's mission-critical systems have been fixed so far. And, get this, only 36 percent are expected to by fixed by January 1, 2000. At this rate, our national defense mission-critical systems won't be completely fixed until 2009."

"Yikes." Abby finally seemed to be listening. She sat on the arm of his chair and looked with him at the report he was holding.

"Yeah. Yikes is right. The most recent General Accounting Office report said that the impact of Y2K failures could be widespread, costly, and potentially disruptive to military operations worldwide. And we're already seeing this. In an August 1997 operational exercise, the Global Command Control System failed testing when the date was rolled over to the year 2000. GCCS is deployed at 700 sites worldwide and is used to generate a common operating picture of the battlefield for planning, executing, and managing military operations. The kind of high-tech war we witnessed in the Gulf War may no longer be possible to fight if we don't correct these glitches—and quickly."

"I had no idea. Bob, this scares me. I've been telling all my friends not to be afraid because bright, good men like you were working hard all over the country. Unsung heroes."

"I know. This is bad news that is easy to brush aside and ignore. But it won't be for long. Of course, it is not just the government that is lagging behind. Serious problems face the private sector, too. According to surveys by the Information Technology Association of America some 94 percent of information technology managers see the Y2K computer issue as a crisis, 44 percent of American companies have already experienced Y2K computer problems, and 83 percent of all Y2K transition project managers expect the Dow Jones Industrial Average to fall by at least 20 percent as the crisis begins to unfold."

"But why? If this is a problem that can be solved, why aren't we solving it? What's the holdup? What am I still not understanding, Bob?"

"My experience at OfficeCentral provides the answer to that, Abby. At its core, this is not a technology crisis; it is a leadership crisis. We have the technology to fix or replace every computer and software program affected by the Millennium Bug—though it would be terribly expensive to do that. Estimated technical corrections range anywhere from $300 billion to $600 billion globally. Litigation, lost business, and bankruptcies might drive the costs even higher—some say as much as $1 trillion or more. But, it could be done—if we had the will. If we were willing to bite the bullet. But there are too many people wasting precious time trying to weasel out of blame, hoping that they can weather the storm, that the Y2K crisis will not hit on their watch. Politicians have been trying to limit public concern until after the elections—but the stakes are just too high for such partisan political games. What they ought to be doing instead is increasing defense funding to speed up compliance, creating Y2K compliance penalties and incentives for key federal agencies, require the Federal Emergency Management Agency to develop contingency plans for major disruptions in vital services, and informing small businesses of both the risks and the options. But, as we've seen in so many areas, our nation has a void of leadership—it's as if we're facing a leadership black hole."

"Arrrgh. This is so frustrating."

"I really think that as the sense of urgency becomes more widespread, most of the computer systems in this country will be fixed in time." Priam massaged Abby's neck and looked her in the eyes. "But even if only a small percentage fail, the resulting disruptions are bound to cause some trouble, and worse if the minority of noncompliant Y2K systems have an adverse domino effect on compliant ones. And in today's global economy, we've got a lot more to worry about than just U.S. companies and U.S. computers."

"What do you mean?"

"Well, the Millennium Bug has infected all the vital organs of our global body. It must be removed from all of them. A failure in any one system could corrupt other systems. The Year 2000 Problem will be a nonevent only if the global network is fixed 100 percent. Much will be fixed in time. But there is no doubt that some significant fraction will not be ready. In fact, most so-called embedded microchip systems will be stress-tested for the first time under real world conditions starting at midnight on New Year's Eve 1999. There are billions of these minicomputers embedded in appliances, elevators, security systems, processing and manufacturing plants, medical devices, and numerous other vital applications. Most are probably not date-sensitive. But many are and could seriously disrupt vital economic activities and create serious safety hazards."

"And we don't know which ones those are?"

"You guessed it.

"Again, the real problem is time—and the leadership to use the time we have wisely and avoid panic. All the money in the world will not stop January 1, 2000, from arriving at the rate of 3,600 seconds per hour. The President can't pass an Executive Order delaying the advent of the century. Congress can't legislate this problem away. There just is not enough time to fix and test all the systems, with billions of lines of software code around the world, that need to be fixed. Many businesses, governments, and organizations have become aware of the Year 2000 Problem only recently and may simply run out of time. Testing is much more time consuming than repairing noncompliant code. This might not be a problem for some standalone systems. However, the majority of software programs are part of a bigger corporate, industrial, national, and even global network. They are almost totally interconnected. They often depend on input information generated by other programs. They must all remain compatible as they are fixed. In other words, the sum total of all interdependent computer systems must all be compliant. A problem in one system could trigger a domino effect, which poses a great risk to all who fail to test whether their local compliant system is compatible with their global network. The networks that must function perfectly—at the risk of partial and even total failure—include: electrical power systems, telecommunications, transportation, manufacturing, retail and wholesale distribution, finance and banking, government services and administration, military defense, and international trade."

"So why can't we just go back to manual systems for a while—at least until the computers are brought up to speed? Thirty years ago, none of these computers even existed."

"I only wish it were that simple, Abby. The information revolution of the past four decades has contributed greatly to our global prosperity. I know that there are some people who question whether computers have really contributed to productivity.

But it is pretty clear, without computers, none of our most dynamic companies would exist today—Intel, Microsoft, Compaq, Dell, and Toshiba wouldn't be around, nor would the jobs they've created. FedEx, Wal-Mart, Sony, and American Express would exist today without computers, but they would all be much, much smaller. Our global and domestic markets for financial securities, commodities, products, and services depend completely on the smooth functioning of the vast technology infrastructure. Information is the lifeblood of our domestic and global markets. If the information flow is severely disrupted by Y2K, then markets will allocate and utilize resources inefficiently. Market participants will be forced to spend more time and money obtaining the information that was instantly available at almost no cost before the market was disrupted. Even the labor market—once dominated by heavy industry—is utterly dependent on information. Just-in-time manufacturing, inventory control, outsourcing, and globalization are all vital aspects of the modern division of labor. There are no low-tech alternatives if our high-tech information systems fail in 2000. We simply cannot manually collect, sort, store, process, and analyze all the data we must have to support, let alone grow, our global economy."

"Bob, can't you give me any good news? Is there no plan at all to get us through this crisis?"

"That's really the crux of the matter. There is no plan. Every company and government agency is responsible for fixing Y2K on its own. There are few industry alliances working to solve the problem collectively. Even worse, there is no global campaign to maximize awareness of Y2K, and very few national efforts to alert the public. Each Y2K-fixing entity independently establishes a triage process to identify mission-critical versus -noncritical systems. No authority, regulator, or industry association has defined the meaning of—or even established standards for—

what is meant by mission critical. The problem with that is simply that available resources are focused on fixing mission-critical systems, however defined. Y2K managers are free to reclassify mission-critical systems as noncritical."

"And they may do that just to avoid some of the heat?"

"Exactly. They might redefine vital functions under the increasing pressure of the looming deadline to show more progress than is in fact achievable. There is simply too little independent verification of progress. For example, the total number of federal government mission-critical systems mysteriously dropped from 8,589 to 7,850 over a three-month reporting period—simply because of reclassification."

"The old blame-shifting game—I can see it coming."

"Right. So, a company or agency could be telling the public that they've identified their mission-critical systems, that they are fixing the ones that are noncompliant; and that they expect to finish testing in time to implement them before January 1, 2000, but all the while they have committed their noncompliant noncritical systems to triage—even though some of those neglected systems really are vital."

"OK, OK. If all this is true then why isn't there more alarm? Why aren't people panicking over this?"

"I think we are all a bit wowed by the power of high technology—even though very few of us actually understand it. Plus, we don't generally realize how dependent we are on computers. Abby, don't forget, this is how I make a living, and I've only recently become concerned enough to reassess our family's plan of action. I thought it was all preventative and prudent. Now I'm taking my concerns up a notch or two."

"A notch or two, Bob? You're talking about changing our whole way of life."

"Even the most basic aspects of modern life are so connected to the full functioning of computer networks. My number one concern about Y2K is not whether the IRS is able to collect taxes or the Defense Department is able to deploy missiles or FedEx is able to deliver packages or America Online is able to keep the Internet running or even the local police department is able to dispatch a unit to the scene of a crime—as important as all those things may be. My number one concern about Y2K is whether the electric company will be able to keep the power on. Without electricity, we won't even know about—let alone be able to fix—all the other Y2K-impaired systems."

"Do you really think the power could go down?"

"I don't know. No one actually knows. But it is a distinct possibility. One that we need to prepare for."

"But surely the big utility companies are aware of the problem. Your very first client was Tennessee Electric Corporation. Aren't they compliant yet?"

"No. Not yet. But they are well on their way. And I'm fairly certain that they will make it in time."

"Whew. That's a relief. It's the first good news I've heard all day."

"Well, it may be good news. But . . ."

"But what? If our electric company is going to be compliant, what is there for us to worry about?"

"All of the other electric companies—including all of the little municipal utilities, all their vendors, all their suppliers, and all their ancillary networks."

"I don't get it. Why would we need to worry about electric companies in other parts of the country if our utilities are safe, secure, and compliant?"

"Because, even though TEC may be compliant, it is hardly safe and secure."

"Why is that?"

"Because the national power grid is so interconnected, one weak link can break the whole chain. All it takes is one or two noncompliant systems to jeopardize the integrity of the entire grid."

"Are you serious?"

"There are nearly six thousand electrical generating plants, five thousand miles of bulk transmission cable, some twelve thousand major substations, and innumerable lower-voltage distribution transformers. They are all a part of one giant, interconnected grid—and the whole system is controlled by computers. If one part of the vast network is compromised, all of the others are ultimately affected due to a domino effect."

"All of them?"

"Do you remember the massive power outage that plunged the entire Western region of the U.S. into darkness a couple of summers ago?"

"Yeah. I think I do recall that vaguely."

"It all happened because a tree had grown too close to a transmission line in Idaho. A power outage on that one line, combined with a record heat wave, caused a ripple effect that ultimately cut regional power supplies to fifteen Western states—including all of the major metropolitan areas of California—as well as parts of Canada and Mexico. All because of branches in the lines."

"Oh my. What a mess." Abby got up and began pacing around the room. Priam hated to scare her, but he knew that it was vital that they have all the facts on the table.

"It was a mess. It left commuters stranded in San Francisco's subway. It cut off the water in Los Angeles. Stores, banks, and restaurants were forced to close. Those that remained open had to do so without cash registers, lights, or refrigeration. It literally crippled the region."

"All because of branches in the lines."

"Having an interconnected power grid helps to make electricity more economical and efficient when everything is working right—which it does most of the time. But when something goes wrong, problems can cascade through the entire system, wreaking havoc."

"So, how will Y2K affect the grid?"

"Again, no one knows for certain. But we do know that many of the utility companies around the country have gotten off to a slow start on their compliancy repairs. And there is an awful lot for them to repair. In a nuclear power plant for instance, software that may be affected includes security control, radiation monitoring, technical specification surveillance testing, radioactive decay calculation, and accumulated burn-up programs. Even the conventional power plants are vulnerable. There are security computers. There are plant process systems. There are data scan, log, and alarm networks. There are dosimeters and readers, plant simulators, engineering programs, communication systems, inventory control mechanisms, and technical specification surveillance tracking systems."

"So where do we stand if the grid goes down."

"We don't stand in very good stead, that's for sure. If we have an extended power outage nationwide the economy stops in its tracks—banks can't operate, paychecks can't be cashed, and necessities cannot be purchased. If there is no electricity the water department can't pump clean, safe water to our homes. So much of what we take for granted would disappear in an instant."

"Enough, already. So what do we do? How do we prepare for something like this—something that might or might not happen? Get to the point, Bob," she snapped.

He tried to use a reassuring tone. "We carry insurance for our family—not because we think there is any imminent danger of us having to face a catastrophic health problem or sudden death. We have insurance because we know that it is prudent. We want to hope for the best but plan for the worst. We don't get to the end of a year and complain—or perhaps even cancel our coverage—just because we didn't use our fire insurance. Well, in the same way, I think we need to build a little insurance into our lifestyles. I know that we cannot make our family immune to every possible Y2K scenario. And we can't become radical survivalists. But we can take some basic steps to protect ourselves and our children just in case something does fall out from all this mess—and it is quite likely that at least *something* will indeed fall out."

"All right. So what's the strategy then?"

"I've thought about it a lot. And I have come to realize that if we merely did the things that grandma always said that we should do—exercising a little bit of simple prudence in some key areas—we would go a long way toward being prepared for just about anything unforseen in our lives short of absolute calamity."

"So the strategy is just to do what grandma said?"

"Right. Of course, for many Americans the grandma strategy may seem a little radical—get out of debt, keep a productive garden, have some food on hand in case of a storm, learn how to tend sicknesses at home, be able to defend yourself, have some basic tools around and the skills to use them, have a good contingency plan if times get tough, save up for a rainy day, and simplify your needs. It's what any grandma would recommend. We think we're so sophisticated that such advice is no longer of value. But it may be the very thing that enables us to pull through this one."

"So, it's basically just common sense?" Abby looked relieved.

"Sure. But of course, common sense has become rather

uncommon these days. Even *we've* neglected it for far too long—knowing all that we know."

"Well, let's get started then. Time's a-wastin'. Grandma strategy, here we come."

Fifteen

"What is a man profited, if he shall gain the whole world, and lose his own soul." Matthew 16:26

OCTOBER 5, 1999

Dazzling celebrations to mark the new millennium were being meticulously orchestrated in cities all around the globe. It was going to be the party to end all parties. At least, that was the idea.

In France, the Paris 2000 organizers announced plans to drop a massive cluster of television monitors through the center of the Eiffel Tower at the stroke of midnight against a backdrop of fireworks and lasers. As they had in the World Cup opening ceremonies there a year earlier, and the bicentennial celebrations a decade before that, the French would display to all the world their knack for the spectacular. And Paris would be the centerpiece.

Paris is a marvel of vintage sensory delights. The staccato sounds of the clicking of saucers in the Place de la Contrescarpe, the trumpeting of traffic around the Arch de Triumph, and the conspiratorial whispering on benches in the Jardin de Luxembourg seem to play a jangling Debussy score in the twilight hours. The nostalgic smells of luxuriant perfumes, wine, and brandy; the invigorating odors of croissants, espresso, and cut lavender; and the acrid fumes of tobacco, roasted chestnuts, and brasseries seem to texture a sweet and subtle Monet upon the canvas of *l'entente de la vie*. The dominating sights of the yellow towers of Notre Dame, the arched bridges cutting across the satin sheen of the river, and the stately elegance of the Bourbon palaces and pavilions scattered about the city like caches of mercy seem to sculpt a muscular Rodin bronze on the otherwise mundane landscape. The fountains fall with hallowed delicacy into a framing space in the Place de la Concorde. Blue hues creep out from behind the Colonades in the Rue de Rivoli and through the grillwork of the Tuileries. The low elegant outlines of the Louvre are a serious metallic gray against the setting sun. Well-tended branches hang brooding over animated cafés, embracing conversations with tender intimacy. Long windows open onto wrought iron balconies in marvelously archaic hotels, while gauzy lace curtains flutter across imagined hopes and wishes and dreams. Romance wafts freely in the sweet cool breezes off the Seine. Paris. What better place could there be to usher in the new year, the new century, the new millennium?

But as intoxicating as the French celebrations might be, the Italians intended to outdo them. And why not? Rome is after all, the Eternal City. Greenwich Mean Time may measure the minutes and hours, but the centuries take their cue from the Gregorian Calendar and the birth of Christ.

From the top of the Spanish steps you can follow the course of the winding Tiber as it makes its way between the Seven Hills. The dome of St. Peter's can be seen off in one direction, and that of the Pantheon can be seen in the other. The perpetual mewing of stray cats in the labyrinthine corridors along the floor of the Coliseum and the pigeons fluttering about the monuments to kings, emperors, and conquerors all along the Forum actually lend the city an exotic air of solemn permanency. The cradle of civilization, the wellspring of faith, the powder keg of ardor, and the terminus of time, there is virtually no other place on earth where so much has occurred for so long and affected so many. Visitors who happen to be in Vatican Square on December 31, 1999, will be standing upon the very apex of the millennial stage—just steps away from the Sistine Chapel, the Pieta, and the throne of the Holy See. And there may well be a vast throng of visitors there—officials estimate anywhere from 13 to 40 million tourists could make their way to the city and its environs in 2000.

Of course, if Rome proves too crowded, there is always Bethlehem. The town, now under Palestinian rule, already boasted the cavernous Constantinian-era Church of the Nativity, built over the grotto where Jesus was believed to have been born. New hotels, restaurants, shopping centers, and public spaces were being readied to greet the crowds of tourists expected to gather there—all of which were to be promoted by the renowned Saatchi and Saatchi public relations firm.

Not to be outdone, the Israelis were planning their own apocalyptic celebration at and around the mount of Megiddo. The idea was to use holograms, lasers, and actors dressed in the costumes of the Davidic Kingdom to create a virtual Armageddon. Christian tourists from around the world were sure to eat it up.

In California, an entrepreneur was hoping to use obsolete intercontinental missiles to launch thousands of artificial meteors, creating a pyrotechnic shower in the night sky fifteen miles wide. In Greenwich, officials planned to open the new Millennial Dome, promising the "greatest day out on earth."

Meanwhile, Rio de Janeiro was to offer the world's largest beach party, Kuala Lampur the biggest fireworks display, Reykjavik the tallest bonfire, and New York the most universal and beloved ceremony—the traditional Times Square ball drop.

But then even before the parties could get underway a pall fell over all the best laid plans of men and nations. Instead of celebrating the advent of the new millennium, people all around the world began to lament it. The high flying optimism was given a healthy dose of reality—and alas, it was anything but welcome medicine for an economic environment grown used to an unprecedented booming prosperity.

And it was just a taste of things to come.

IT WAS BLACK TUESDAY all over again. What appeared at first to be a minor bank run triggered a massive selloff that first panicked Wall Street and then the rest of the global trading network. Investors took a beating the likes of which had not been seen in a generation.

Of course, everyone had been expecting a downward adjustment in the market. In fact, most believed that it was long overdue. Stocks had been trading at outrageously inflated prices for several years running. Despite the Asian currency crisis, the revolution in China, the myriad of new secessionist movements in Russia, and the collapse of the unified European currency effort, the New York Stock Exchange continued to set record highs. Blue chips consistently traded at 45 to 55 percent above earnings. Speculative IPOs of selected high-tech and Internet stocks made millionaires of their principals—often before a single one of their products had been taken to market.

The appearance of economic vitality had long been balanced upon the crest of a very unstable house of cards. And on this fateful day, the cards all finally collapsed.

The news reports studiously avoided using the term "crash." The markets took a "nosedive." Share prices "dropped precipitously." Traders had "lost confidence" in continued economic growth. Investors were "disappointed" in their meager returns. But everyone was only too well aware that when the Dow "dipped" to a low of 7740, down from 9650, all the euphemisms in the would could not mask the seriousness of the collapse.

Precipitated by a slowly realized uncertainty that the telecommunications, utility, and computing industries would be able to absorb their Y2K losses—most publicly traded companies had been forced to spend upwards of 7 to 12 percent of their budgets on remediation and repairs over the previous two years—the stock price plunge demonstrated all too aptly the reality that economies are dependent as much on public trust as they are productive capacity.

The crisis had actually begun innocently enough the week before. Apparently a grassroots effort to prepare for Y2K disruptions had gradually begun to move people to action. As a result, bank withdrawals had reached their highest level in decades. In fact, withdrawals of private accounts had increased by 7 percent in just a few days—and while 7 percent might not have been particularly scrutinized under normal circumstances, it represented a fairly significant fluctuation of cash reserves for the banking system. In the highly charged environment of growing Y2K concerns, it seemed to agitate a whole host of gnawing fears. Some people began to speculate about the viability of their investments. Ultimately, their worries led many of them to literally take their money into their own hands. They simply decided that they would much rather have cash in hand than the mere assurance of ephemeral numbers in a computer network—especially when they were no longer confident that the network would function reliably in the days ahead.

When the banks opened after the anxious weekend, lines quickly appeared at branches all over the country. That Monday morning people began hearing scattered news reports about a possible bank run. Almost immediately they jumped to conclusions. A minor panic ensued. Small lines became big lines. Within hours, the number of withdrawals went from the thousands to the hundreds of thousands. By the next morning, more than one and a half million accounts had been closed out altogether.

By midday on Tuesday, the FDIC was flooded with calls from banks that had reached their marginal limits and needed assistance. But of course, the FDIC could not immediately meet the sudden demand. The supply of cash that exists at any one time anywhere in the U.S. economy is just over one and a half percent of all deposits and holdings. The fractional reserve system literally means that only about $16 of every $1000 is available at any one time—the other $984 is little more than code within a computer program. When the local banks—at the behest of the beleaguered FDIC managers—began to ration those scant resources to depositors, people became terribly nervous. The vicious cycle quickened. After waiting anxiously in long lines, customers were told that they would be unable to redeem their account values. Soon word spread that banks were out of money. And as a result, even more people panicked.

When word reached the trading floors on Wall Street that a bank run was underway, the selloff accelerated. Unable to get their money out of banks, small investors gave sell orders to their brokers. Because there were more small-stake individual investors than ever before in U.S. history, those orders dramatically accelerated the bust.

By the late afternoon, even large investment managers and brokerage houses were forced into the frenzy. Stock fund administrators were forced to sell holdings during the price plunge as redemptions continued pouring in. When the huge conglomerates began to sell into the imbroglio, the prices fell even faster.

Discount brokerage houses were flooded with calls. Internet traders were utterly swamped. Even the fax lines were busy. The entire complex trading system was frozen in uncertainty and panic. People watched helplessly as their retirement nest egg dropped 10 to 20 percent in a single day.

The day ended having well earned the moniker Black Tuesday.

The next day, the President appeared on the early evening news broadcasts to announce immediate federal intervention in the currency and stock crisis. He closed the banks and the trading floors for the remainder of the week. Always the consummate spin-doctor, he asserted that the federal action was merely an opportunity for America's financial community to take a well-deserved "holiday." During the short interval of "corrections to the investment infrastructure and market apparatus," he declared that there would be a complete commercial hiatus—no banking, no trading, no buying, no selling, nothing. He asserted that the bank run was actually nothing to worry about. It was little more than a self-fulfilling prophecy—one that was ultimately misguided and hasty. He assured the nation that things would quickly return to normal the following week when the Federal Reserve had the opportunity to insure that cash reserves could be appropriately apportioned to areas of peak demand and the FDIC had the chance to examine the institutions most vulnerable to disruption. He expressed utter and complete confidence in the economic health and stability of the country as well as in the dedicated information technology workers who would help to usher in a new century of prosperity for American businesses and American families. He encouraged seasoned investors to ignore the panicky, misguided reactions of the novices and to ride out this blip like they had so many times before. He didn't miss the opportunity to spread a little blame for the panic over a few choice political opponents.

But his soothing words did little to quell the fears of the citizenry.

AT TIMES OF CRISIS men naturally turn to the things of faith—for hope or solace or resolution or insight or courage. So, it seemed only natural that a fitful tumult of bells began to echo from church towers in urban centers all across the nation. Bells are more than the soul of a spire. They render the air about us sacred and turn the sky above us into a vaulted sanctuary. A single bell is like a small pleasure; a multitude of bells is like a large pleasure—either way, their pealing sound is a welcome emblem of grace in this poor fallen world. But even the ringing of bells failed to deter the American people from their sense of trepidation. If anything it seemed to exacerbate their sense of calamity, rather than restore their faith.

For one awful moment, men and women forgot that history consists not of the actions of crowds, nor the edicts of governments, nor the machinations of economies, nor the conquests of marauders. They forgot that instead it consists of ordinary people—each remarkable, each responsible, and each reciprocal—who make something of the circumstances that crowds, or governments, or economies, or conquests happen to give them in accordance with the outworkings of good providence.

They forgot.

Suddenly, they were blind to the evidences of surer truth all around them—the sights and sounds of the familiar. Their ancient legacies of savoir-faire, fortitude, and aplomb were shuffled in haste—thus losing their order. The dull certainties of experience were wrecked upon the shoals of trepidation—ignored against the backdrop of an ever-widening panic. And thus the whole land was riven with a kind of blind dread, deaf alarm, and dumb consternation. For the moment all they could think of was the fact that an unimaginable catastrophe had struck like a bolt out of the blue. In the midst of their own neighborhood, every man felt alone and unprotected.

Overnight there were riots in the poorest sections of Detroit, Chicago, Denver, Los Angeles, Oakland, Houston, New Orleans, Atlanta, Washington, Philadelphia, New York, and Boston. Looters shattered the quiet of the night in Miami, Jacksonville, Birmingham, Charlotte, Dallas, St. Louis, Cincinnati, Indianapolis, Baltimore, Newark, Phoenix, and Seattle. Police were called out to calm jittery protests in San Francisco, Portland, Las Vegas, Tulsa, Kansas City, Minneapolis, Gary, Milwaukee, Austin, Little Rock, Pittsburgh, and Hartford. The tenuously thin veneer of civilization was pierced by the wrath of the dispossessed and the discontent.

Before sunrise the next morning, the National Guard had been called out and placed on full alert. Citizens were asked to stay inside, to avoid all travel and commerce, and to remain calm while the officials worked to insure that life returned to normal as quickly as possible. But of course, in the inner cities, such a request was far easier to make than to enforce.

A culture coheres only so long as the people who comprise it continue to have confidence in their common callings, purposes, and destinies. It can maintain a semblance of amity and integrity only so long as a disposition of coherence remains.

Alas, America had all but lost its coherence.

THOUGH THE NATIONAL GUARD had begun irregular and sporadic patrols of the streets, Dr. Gylberd drove to the

Rivendell Academy as usual—though he was forced to do so without his normal cup of hazelnut coffee, cinnamon and raisin bagel, and cup of yogurt since virtually all the shops and stores remained closed. When he arrived in the parking lot, several students had already gathered—as had several parents. Somehow they looked to him like shivering, lost, and frightened immolations taking refuge from a storm.

He unlocked the building and everyone gathered expectantly in the main auditorium—as if Gylberd had called them together for instructions. It was an awkward moment for him—but he knew that it was simultaneously a defining moment.

Noah was the first to speak. "So what do you think, Doc?"

"I think things are a real mess. That much is obvious. How long the mess will last, I don't think anyone knows. But our social fabric is pretty fragile right now in many areas. I wouldn't count on things straightening out overnight. We may have quite a few challenges to overcome in the days ahead."

"But how can we possibly carry on if the banks remain closed—or if the rioting and looting continues? What happens if the President has to declare martial law?"

"Whatever comes, we'll just carry on. What else can we do?"

"But how?" one of the moms asked.

"The same way people always have in times of trouble—by depending on each other, caring for each other, and looking out for each other. Community is our greatest asset—something we can depend upon no matter how difficult things may get."

"Maybe we all should have packed up and moved way out in the country like the Priams did," Noah quipped.

"Well, perhaps that would have been nice. But that wasn't exactly an option for most of us. Besides, however wonderful their new little farm is, however secluded, and however well-provisioned, it will not afford them as much protection as community affords the poorest and most vulnerable among us. If we stick together, stand together, pray together, and work together we'll come out of this better than ever before. We really don't have to fear the future, because we have each other."

"Meanwhile, what do we do now?"

"Gee, that's easy. We have class. We do what we are supposed to do and we be what we are supposed to be. Look, we're hardly talking about the end of the world here. OK, so the stock market took a tumble."

"Yeah, and then the banks collapsed."

"Right. The stock market crashed and there was a run on the banks. But, we've known for a very long time that the stock market was foolishly inflated. And we've been only too aware that the fractional reserve banking system was unwise and insecure. Life goes on. We're not Marxists—so we don't believe that the value and purpose of life is determined by economics; we don't believe that the destiny of nations is controlled by labor and capital; and we don't believe history is driven by markets and governments. The ordinary man and his ordinary wife with their ordinary children fulfilling their ordinary callings are the most extraordinary forces in all the world—just like they always have been; just like they always will be. If we can simply remember that great lesson—which is taught in every age and in every culture—then we will have no reason to panic or despair."

"I think I'd still feel a little safer if I was tucked away at the Priam farm—with a good supply of food, water, generators, and weapons," Noah said with a wry grin.

"Well, Noah," Dr. Gylberd turned to look him square in the eye, "the fact is, the safest place in the whole universe right now is not in the center of the securest compound money can buy. It is in the center of God's will."

"I just wish I could be as sure as you."

"I have no doubt that you'll have your chance—as we all will. Tough times have the peculiar characteristic of confirming the truth for all those who have eyes to see and ears to hear. OK. Enough of this. It's time for class. Let's get on with it."

Sixteen

"Lay not up for yourselves treasures upon earth, where thieves break through and steal." Matthew 6:19

JANUARY 6, 2000

The lights stayed on—most of them anyway. Television viewers from around the world watching Dick Clark's New Year's Eve special did not see Times Square go dark at midnight. Phones continued to operate. Water and sewer services were not immediately disrupted. The collective sigh of relief at 12:00:01 was practically audible across the country, as every time zone proved the Y2K naysayers were right—most of the mission-critical systems necessary to maintain at least a semblance of normalcy were compliant in time for the century change.

Most. But not all. And thousands of small things Americans had come to take for granted had suddenly vanished from their lives. Though the power grid did not go down, over the next several days utility companies were forced to carefully ration their service to most sections of the country. Electricity became about as reliable in Chicago, Dallas, and Baltimore as it was in Chelyabinsk, Donetsk, and Bratislava. Water was available in most urban areas—but only three or four days a week. Phone service was soon limited to a few hours each day. Internet service providers were plagued by bugs, glitches, and brown-outs. At first, most stores were able to keep their shelves fairly adequately stocked with necessities, staples, and basics—but most convenience items were simply unavailable. As a result, waiting in long lines for everything from food and clothing to gas and other essentials had suddenly become a way of life.

And so, the Y2K doomsayers were also right—though mission-critical systems were indeed repaired in time, that was now of little solace. Life had taken a dramatic turn for the worse. And there was no indication that things would be able to return to normal any time soon.

For at least two years doomsayers and alarmists had been predicting major disruptions in basic services followed by a deep worldwide recession. The recession had come sooner than even they had expected—following the October stock market debacle and the bank failures. And though the disruption in services was not quite as medieval as they had predicted, it had essentially the same effect.

Troops had been called out—buttressing the National Guard presence that had been a necessary component of daily life since October. Travel was severely restricted. Most interstates were closed to all but essential military and transport services. Checkpoints were set up along all major thoroughfares. Strict curfews were established. Martial law was enforced with a vengeance and a number of constitutional liberties were tem-porarily suspended in an effort to maintain order. The American way of life came to a virtual standstill—even if it did not cease altogether.

As bad as things were in the U.S., they were worse through-out the rest of the world. Most of the African, South American, and Asian continents were plunged into total darkness—the thin veneer of technological development there practically disappeared altogether. Much of Eastern Europe was nearly as bad. And Western Europe was teetering on the verge of social chaos—only a patchwork of essential services remained there.

As *Newsweek* magazine had wryly predicted some three years before, New Years Day 2000 had indeed become "the day the world shut down."

A century before—on January 1, 1900—most Americans greeted the twentieth century with the proud and certain belief that the next hundred years would be the greatest, the most glorious, and the most glamorous in human history. They were infected with a sanguine spirit. Optimism was rampant. A brazen confidence colored their every activity.

Certainly there was nothing in their experience to make them think otherwise. Never had a century changed the lives of men and women more dramatically than the one just past. The twentieth century has moved fast and furiously, so that those of us who have lived in it feel sometimes giddy, watching it spin; but the nineteenth moved faster and more furiously still. Railroads, telephones, the telegraph, electricity, mass produc-tion, forged steel, automobiles, and countless other modern discoveries had all come about at a dizzying pace, expanding visions and expectations far beyond their grandfathers' wildest dreams.

It was more than unfounded imagination, then, that lay behind the *New York World's* New Year's prediction that the twentieth century would "meet and overcome all perils and prove to be the best that this steadily improving planet has ever seen."

Most Americans were cheerfully assured that control of man and nature would soon lie entirely within their grasp and would bestow upon them the unfathomable millennial power to alter the destinies of societies, nations, and epochs. They were a people of manifold purpose. They were a people of manifest destiny. And the experts of science, the gods of technology, and the minions of modernity would in short order make them the self-assured, self-reliant, and self-actualized masters of the universe.

As H.G. Wells, one of the leading lights of such sanguine futurism, asserted, "For some of us moderns, who have been touched with the spirit of science, prophesying is almost a habit of mind. Science is very largely analysis aimed at forecasting. The test of any scientific law is our verification of its anticipations. The scientific training develops the idea that whatever is going to happen is really here now—if only one could see it. And when one is taken by surprise, the tendency is not to say with the untrained man, 'Now, who'd ha' thought it?' but 'Now, what was it we overlooked?' Everything that has ever existed or that will ever exist is here—for anyone who has eyes to see. But some of it demands eyes of superhuman penetration."

For Wells, and all those who shared his Flash Gordon optimism, science was almost messianic in character. What they did not know was that dark and malignant seeds were already germinating just beneath the surface of the new century's soil. The rich ideological loam of scientism—the very source of their optimism—had sprouted a smothering kudzu of destruction and devastation. The emerging philosopher-kings of science, technology, and advancement would soon prove to be anything but the beneficent champions of the high ideals of progress.

Josef Stalin was a twenty-one-year-old seminary student in Tiflis, a pious and serene community at the crossroads of Georgia and the Ukraine. Benito Mussolini was a seventeen-year-old student teacher in the quiet suburbs of Milan. Adolf Hitler was an eleven-year-old aspiring art student in the quaint upper Austrian village of Brannan. And Margaret Sanger was a twenty-year-old out-of-sorts nursing school dropout in White Plains, New York. Who could have ever guessed on that ebulliently auspicious New Year's Day that those four youngsters would, over the span of the next century, oversee the spilling of more innocent blood than all the murderers, warlords, and tyrants of past history combined? Who could have ever guessed that those four youngsters would together insure that the hopes and dreams and aspirations of the twentieth century would be smothered under the weight of holocaust, genocide, and triage?

As the champion of the proletariat, Stalin saw to the slaughter of at least 15 million Russian and Ukrainian *kulaks*. As the popularly acclaimed *Il Duce*, Mussolini massacred as many as 4 million Ethiopians, 2 million Eritreans, and a million Serbs, Croats, and Albanians. As the wildly lionized *Fuhrer*, Hitler exterminated more than 6 million Jews, 2 million Slavs, and a million Poles. As the founder of Planned Parenthood and the impassioned heroine of various feminist *causes célèbres*, Sanger was responsible for the brutal elimination of more than 30 million children in the United States and as many as 2.5 billion worldwide.

The barbarism, treachery, and debauchery that will make their names live on in infamy forever shattered the fondest hopes and dreams for the twentieth century. The hopes and dreams for peace on earth were shattered on the battlefields of Europe, Southeast Asia, Central America, and the Middle East. The hopes and dreams for political utopia were shattered in the streets of Paris, Moscow, Gdansk, and Tehran. The hopes and dreams for medical and genetic perfectibility were shattered in the ovens of *Auschwitz*, the abortuaries of New York, and the streets of Zagreb. The hopes and dreams for winning the "war on poverty" were shattered in the ghettos, barrios, and purlieus of New York, Los Angeles, and Detroit.

The twentieth century began with optimistic shouts, assured whoops, and confident huzzahs. No grand illusions attended the millennial celebrations a century later. No amount of pomp and circumstance could rekindle a sanguine spirit quenched by the hard realities of experience. The twentieth century had been an unmitigated disaster—despite the great strides in wealth, technology, and medicine. And now that sad fact was once again evident for all to see.

PART OF THE REASON why the Y2K repairs did not allow a seamless return to normal life was the severe economic blow that the cost of those repairs had made. Desperate simply to survive, companies were forced to channel an inordinate share of their available resources into infrastructure projects that contributed nothing to their bottom lines. Share earnings plummeted, productivity fell, downsizing ensued, and a recession resulted. The chain reaction of deleterious effects put a fatal strain on the distribution and delivery systems so vital for the maintenance of economic vitality.

But the continuing brownouts and service disruptions were also largely due to the failure of embedded chip systems. Often called firmware, embedded chip systems are the tiny bits of computerized data that run virtually all our modern appliances and conveniences—answering machines, cellular telephones, photocopiers, fax machines, personal digital organizers, clock radios, microwave ovens, refrigerators, VCRs, air conditioning and heating systems, burglar alarms, elevators, security cameras, sprinkler systems, digital watches, stereos, and television sets. They are also integral parts of water and sewage systems, nuclear power plants, oil refineries, automobiles, flight avionics, marine craft, street lighting systems, train switching, traffic lights, radar, signaling systems, automatic teller machines, credit card authorization systems, heart monitors, pacemakers, intravenous drip machines, x-ray equipment, and sonogram machines.

The dirty little secret of the Y2K crisis was always the embedded chip system problem—not the much more easily accessed mainframe and desktop systems. There were at least 25 billion of these little devices deployed throughout the world on January 1, 2000. The good news was that only about 5 percent of them were date-sensitive. The bad news was that all of them had to be checked. Most of them could not be reprogrammed— the code is burned into the actual chip. They had to be replaced. Checking them was arduous. Programmers could not really even test them. In addition, the elusive little chips were more often than not running on proprietary systems—meaning that they were operated by thousands of different programming protocols. Programmers had to contact the manufacturers— assuming they were still in business—and see if the particular chip in question—assuming it was still supported by the company—was Y2K compliant. If it wasn't, it had to be replaced. If a replacement chip was unavailable, the entire device had to be replaced. The task of ferreting out the offending chips was thus so complex and so arduous that most Y2K compliancy programs ignored the embedded chip problem, focused on the mission-critical mainframe, network, and desktop solutions, and hoped for the best. As a result, no one actually knew which embedded chip systems were Y2K incompatible until they actually failed—meaning that disruptions were inevitable.

Bob Priam realized what a problem that might be early on in his brief Y2K consulting career. Though like almost everyone else in the industry, his agenda was driven by the tyranny of the urgent, he also spent a good deal of time trying to come up with solutions to the dilemmas embedded chip systems might pose for his clients.

Eventually he was able to develop a chip bypass device. He knew that it wouldn't be a universal fix. But he was confident that it just might come close. The device was simply a little minimicrochip that sat on top of the embedded chip—like a gnat sitting piggyback on a beetle. This electronic parasite intercepted the data stream flowing into and out of the chip. Its one job was to detect noncompliant dates in the data stream. When it did so, it automatically converted them to a Y2K compliant format. The little bypass could be installed by simply soldering directly into the input and output wires. It was extremely easy to manufacture and he was able to write the proprietary code that was burned onto the chip and made it work. Thus, it not only solved the Y2K problem, it provided a healthy income stream into Priam's fledgling business.

There were two problems with the solution. One was that the primary chip expects the date to be in a specific format. Ninety percent of the chips use the same date format, so the bypass could handle those—the year came first, then the month, followed by the day: 20000106. The last ten percent use a different order sequence for the date format—such as month, day, and year: 01062000; or even day, month, and year: 06012000. Alas, Priam's bypass chip wouldn't be able to tell the difference. All he could do was to use the bypass on all of the embedded systems and hope the 10 percent that didn't work weren't too critical. This made the whole thing a game of Russian roulette. But at the very least—and this is why people were so anxious to buy the bypass—it eliminated 90 percent of the problem. Once the year turned, programmers could isolate the remaining 10 percent and replace them with compliant chips. This was still way ahead of the only other option, which was to inspect every chip, call the manufacturer, wait for confirmation of the chip's Y2K vulnerability, and then replace the chip if necessary—an incredibly slow process. Not only would that mean missing the deadline of January 1, 2000, it would take somewhere in the neighborhood of eight years beyond that to manually replace all the chips—given the existing technology and manpower limitations. As a result, everyone who knew about it wanted Priam's bypass—however flawed it was. Companies had become desperate and the device seemed like the last, best hope.

The second problem with Priam's solution, though, was that he developed it so late in the game. Most companies never even got the chance to buy the bypass. There simply wasn't enough time to get the word out, to do the proper marketing, manufacturing, and distribution of the device before the advent of the new year. Scam artists were advertising instant cures and magic wand solutions through every available media outlet. Priam hadn't yet discovered a viable way to market his legitimate product. As a result, practically no one knew that the revolutionary solution existed.

But Will Ajax did. And now, he wanted it.

Ajax had discussed the bypass idea with Priam early on— when they were working together on a large regional telco project. At the time, it didn't seem to be a terribly vital aspect of the Y2K repair picture. But now that the economic outlook had changed so dramatically and the disruption of services had occurred, Ajax saw the genius of the plan.

After the first of the year, he was forced to reevaluate the function and purpose of his entire operation. He knew the majority of his income could no longer derive from embezzled Medicare accounts, filched portfolio trades, and stolen data transfers. But if he could get control of a silver bullet solution like Priam's bypass device, he could conceivably make more money than ever before.

He had dispatched his team of mercenaries to Priam's downtown office—just a few blocks from the Chernobyl warehouse a few days before. But the plush suite was obviously little more than a showpiece to meet with clients. There were several desktop systems linked to a network server—but the only sensitive data on any of the drives or the backup tapes were client records, invoice accounting, and job profile templates. The plans for the Y2K bypass were nowhere to be found.

Ajax feared that the schematics might be stored in Priam's laptop. And that there might actually be no backups anywhere, except perhaps at the manufacturing facility in Vermont, which was now—given the disrupted conditions of the nation's communications and transportation systems—impossibly remote. Since Priam had packed up and moved his family to some safe haven in the hinterlands, even getting to that laptop might prove to be a formidable challenge.

Fortunately, Ajax had had the foresight to plant a small transmitter onto the back sliding bay door for the port replicator on Priam's laptop some months before. He was a bit skittish about Priam's plan to bail out of the consulting business. He wanted to keep track of Priam's comings and goings—especially since he was sitting on so much cash from the final boom days of the consulting business. The little radio transmitter was about the size of an eraser head and attached to the plastic casing of the door with a self-adhesive strip. Ajax affixed it there one afternoon while surreptitiously admiring Priam's high-tech gadgets, toys, and hardware.

Athena thought that he had become downright obsessive about Priam. "Just let him go. There are lots of other issues we need to be worrying about right now."

"I'm telling you, the Trojan Horse transmitter I planted in his laptop is the key to our future prosperity," he replied. "We'll be able to get the plans for the bypass, solve all these embedded chip problems, make boodle, and come out looking like heroes in the process."

"Why do we need any of that? We've made enough money in the last couple of years to last a lifetime. What does it take? How much is enough for you?"

"Just a little bit more. Just a little bit more."

"I think this is crazy. Let it go, Ajax. You've been getting more and more reckless—and you're going to bring me down with you."

"We've done OK. It's hard to argue with success. Reckless is as reckless does. We're sitting pretty thanks to the risks I've taken on our behalf. And without a single mishap, I might add."

"You can't keep this up. It's simply not wise."

"I'll tell you what's not wise. It's sitting back while the silver bullet solution is within our grasp. I'm putting together the team. We're gonna raid the place tonight. I'm gonna get the plans to the chip, put Priam out of business once and for all, and we're gonna be big players in this wretched new world order."

"You're twisted, Ajax. This is going to be our undoing. This is going to be the end."

"You still don't have any faith in me? After all we've been through together? Trust me. This is going to be a bonanza for us. Just you wait and see."

AJAX ARRIVED WITH HIS team of eleven men on a ridge overlooking the Priam farmstead about an hour before sundown. They all wore winter woodland camouflage gear and were bundled up against the frigid elements. There they would wait for the full cover of darkness. In the interim, Ajax went over their plans one last time.

215

"Just remember what it is we're after. I couldn't care less what happens to the house, any of the things Priam may have in the house, or any of the people who may be there. All we want is the laptop, the docking station, and any storage tapes we may be able to find. This is to be a quick in and out. No dilly-dallying. No fraternizing. No aggrandizing. Just hit and run. We take out the barn as a diversion—and then, boom, we hit the house and be gone. Got it?"

"Yes, sir," the men uniformly responded.

"I don't want any screw ups. We'll be a long way from any help. The roads are impassible. Everything has to work like clockwork, or we're cooked."

"Anything else, sir?

"Oh, yeah. I almost forgot. Priam's some kind of survivalist nut now. He probably has some firepower on hand. Though, I am pretty sure he's a loner. So, it'll just be him. But, be on your guard nevertheless."

Ajax saw Priam walking in the little English cottage garden below. He was talking with someone. *A woman. No a girl. That's right. Priam has a teenage daughter.* The icy landscape around them was colored by the last rays of sunset and the first glints of the hazy moonlight.

The team settled into position and waited. A little wafting streak of smoke dissipated into the cold air above the house. Ajax took perverse comfort in knowing that in just moments the prosperous life Priam had secured for himself and his precious little family was about to be ravished. He had convinced himself that he despised that self-satisfied prig. He glanced down into the dell as Priam and his daughter made their way toward the house.

The harsh crackle of his radio headset interrupted his contumacious relish. "The team is in position, Sir."

Ajax looked off to his left. Through the trees he could see eleven men arrayed along the crest of the hill. "Right. Recheck the perimeter. Containment is essential. We don't go until they're all in the house."

Ajax allowed himself a hint of a smile. He took a deep breath and gave the signal to strike.

The men immediately scrambled to their feet and began to move across the frozen terrain down toward the house. Despite the weight of their gear, the steep embankment, and the necessity to maintain stealth, they kept themselves aligned in perfect formation all the way down to the house.

THE DOG STARTED BARKING. They were still a hundred yards away or more. But the dog sensed their presence and had begun an incessant, persistent yapping. Ajax signaled to the men to stop at the edge of the trees. They paused long enough to see how Priam might respond.

They got their answer quickly. A teenage boy stepped out of the house and yelled over at the dog, "Hush now, Trix. Be quiet."

The dog, unheeding, continued her barking.

"I said, hush. Dog, what is wrong with you? Be quiet, will you?" He turned back into the house and slammed the door behind him.

Ajax smiled. Everything was set.

The first team moved into the yard and toward the large storage barn. The second began setting charges along the fence line adjacent to the animal pens. The third split up, taking positions near the back and front entrances to the house.

Inside the barn, the first team found rows of storage barrels. "These are filled with grain. Looks like this guy was getting ready for the end of the world. I guess he thought he had it made."

"Not anymore. Not after tonight."

They too set a series of charges and then rejoined the men outside the house.

"All right. On my command," Ajax ordered. He looked around to make certain that each man was ready. He checked his analog watch. "Now."

Suddenly, the silence of the happy little valley was sundered by a series of convulsive explosions. The barn was engulfed in flames almost instantly. The fence line was decimated, and the goats and chickens came charging out of their pens in a panic.

Priam burst out of the house ahead of the rest of the family. "My God. What's happening here?" He stood on the stoop and watched as all of his careful plans and provisions were devastated in a single moment. Shock registered on his face. Before he could take a step toward the scene of disaster he was grabbed by two of the men.

"Hey. What the . . ." His protest was quickly muffled as he was ignominiously dragged off the porch and roughly bound.

"Bob. Bob, where are you?" Priam's wife came out behind him. "Oh, Lord. What is going on here?"

Again, she was restrained before she even knew what was happening. Ajax had the men pull the two of them off to the side as the assault team entered the house from both the front and the back. Inside, they subdued both boys. Troy put up a pretty fierce struggle, but he was after all, no match for the mercenaries. Hector merely whimpered as his hands were bound behind him.

Priam's office was just off the kitchen at the foot of a narrow staircase. The laptop, the docking station, and a cache of backup tapes were easy to find—they were sitting atop a long low shaker-style desk beneath a bowed window overlooking the garden. On a table next to the desk were Priam's shortwave and CB radios. One of the men, a technician, smashed them with the butt of his rifle. Then he grabbed the computer equipment— along with all the cables, an external keyboard, and a trackball— and headed back outside. Before he could reach the door a deafening blast erupted from the top of the stairs. The technician stumbled through the doorway and fell at the feet of Ajax— the laptop and all the rest of the gear scattering across the frozen lawn. Blood trickled out of the corner of his mouth.

"Someone inside is shooting," one of the men shouted.

"No kidding."

"It's the girl. Get the girl."

A furious report ripped through the house a second time. And then a third. The men who had come through the front door scrambled out of the line of fire. But not before Cassie struck one of them squarely in the chest. He lay face down in the kitchen, his own blood pooling beneath him.

"Get her. I don't care how you do it. Just get her." Ajax was screaming at the men. "And then let's get out of here. We've got the goods."

One of the men laid down a withering stream of fire from his automatic weapon as two others positioned themselves along the side of the staircase. Cassie ducked out of the way and down the hall. The men ascended the stairs and rounded the corner. Though the hallway was dark and shadowy, an eerie light from the blaze outside filtered into the bedrooms off to each side. Cautiously, the men checked each room, all the closets, the two bathrooms. They were joined by two others. And they double-checked every nook and cranny.

"She's gone."

"But how? There's no other way out. There's only one staircase. All the casement windows are shut up tight as a drum and the storm windows are closed."

"Look. A laundry chute."

"A what?"

"A laundry chute. You throw dirty clothes in here and they go down into the basement where the laundry is done. She must have climbed in and slid all the way down."

"You're kidding, right? A person can't fit down this."

"Well, it might be a pretty tight squeeze. But remember we're talking about a teenage girl here."

The men ran down the stairs. Three more members of the team joined them in their search. At the back of the stairwell, at the end of the kitchen, they found the doorway that led to the basement. The moment they opened the door another gun blast echoed in their ears.

"She's down there, all right. Is there another exit?"

"None. Let's take her." They dropped a canister of tear gas into the basement and stepped back. In less than two minutes, Cassie came up the stairs, choking, coughing, and crying. The men manhandled her to the ground and bound her hands and feet.

"Well, well, well. A feisty one." Ajax stood over her, laughing at her diminutive size. He frowned menacingly. "You've cost me two men tonight, little girl. For that, you're gonna have to pay. And pay dearly." He reached down and stroked her cheek with the back of his hand. "Yes, indeed. You're gonna have to pay."

He turned to the rest of the team and gave the signal to move out. "We've done enough damage here for tonight. I've had about as much fun as I can stand. We're taking the girl with us. A hostage. The spoils of war. Leave the others."

The men made their way back over the crest of the hill. Ajax looked back over his shoulder at his handiwork. Priam's security—ablaze; his plans—absconded; his daughter—abducted. *There is nothing quite so satisfying as a productive day's work.* Again, he smiled.

Seventeen

"To me belongeth vengeance." Deuteronomy 32:35

JANUARY 7, 2000

Somehow during the wee morning hours, Hector managed to wriggle one of his hands free. He had been working at it for hours when at last he was able to slip his wrist out of the restraints and pull free. He then dragged himself toward the kitchen, pulled himself up to the cabinets, and retrieved the long butcher's knife from the countertop—the one his mother never allowed him to handle. Troy watched anxiously from across the room as he sawed feverishly at the ropes around his ankles, waist, and chest. Once freed, he ran over to cut Troy's fetters.

"Quick. Let's find Mom and Dad," Troy commanded once he had been ungagged and unbound.

"Right."

They ran through the house, checking each room but found that they were alone. Hector was headed toward the stairs when he remembered. "Outside. Maybe they're still outside."

They burst through the door, hardly even noticing the effects of the mayhem a few hours before. Priam and Abby were still tied to the tree, shivering, where they had been left by Ajax and his men. The bodies of the two men who had been shot in the scuffle with Cassie were gone. And so, apparently was Cassie. The barn had burned nearly to the ground. The embers were still bright and the smell of destruction was everywhere around them.

The boys freed their parents and helped them move into the house where they could warm up. They had practically turned blue. Abby was hysterical. Hector worried about hypothermia— he had just learned about it in school. So he ran into the master bath and began filling the tub with hot water.

Still shivering and shaking Abby asked about Cassie, "Where is she? Is she all right? What happened? Were there gunshots? Where is Cassie?"

"It all happened so fast, Mom," Troy tried to explain. "I don't know, exactly. But I think she shot a couple of them. Then they tossed a tear gas grenade or something and choked her out. Then they took her with them."

"Took her? Oh my God. Oh Lord Jesus. My baby. They took my baby."

Finally able to think, Priam tried to stand, but he was still stiff and shaky. "Has anyone called the police yet?"

"No, not yet, Dad. We just got free a second ago."

"Call now. No, bring me the phone. I'll call."

"Who were those men?" Abby was crying now. "What did they want? Why did they take Cassie? Oh Lord. What is happening?"

Hector tried to comfort his mother as best he could, but she was sobbing uncontrollably now.

"Hector, help your Mother get into the bathroom so she can soak in the tub. Troy, hurry up with the phone." Priam was now beginning to thaw, and was just about ready to spring into action.

"Bad news, Dad. The phones are dead. And the radios are smashed."

"What? Oh great. That's just great. Now what are we gonna do? Help me find my keys, guys. Abby, get warm. You need to be able to think clearly."

Still weeping, Abby went into the bathroom to try to get warm. The sun was not yet up but already she had an uneasy suspicion that it was going to be a long day.

"Look, wherever they were headed, they had to pass through one of the National Guard checkpoints. There are really only two possible directions they could have gone— toward one or the other of the interstates. There is only one road out of here and only one road that connects the two inter- states—and there are checkpoints going in both directions. I'll head out and see what the men posted there can tell me. At the very least, they will be able to notify the police. It's gonna be OK. We're gonna find Cassie." Priam headed out the door and toward his Jeep. "Troy, take care of your mother and brother."

The night shift was still on duty when Priam arrived at the first checkpoint. The men there averred that they had not had very much traffic all night. Certainly there had been no large parties that fit the description of the raiders. And there had been no sign of Cassie. However, they were able to place a call to the local sheriff's office.

The men at the second checkpoint said essentially the same thing. There had been very little traffic, none of it matching Priam's description of the attackers. And no Cassie.

As he drove back toward the house, Priam's mind was racing. He was angry, confused, and afraid. There literally was no other way to or from the farm. The men had to pass through the checkpoints—no matter where they had come from or where they were going. That's all there was to it. The Guardsmen on duty seemed competent enough and honest enough. It just didn't add up.

By the time he arrived at home the sun was up and Abby and the boys were outside surveying the damage. The barn was a total loss. Troy had rounded up several of the chickens and put them into a small holding pen on the opposite side of the garden. The goats had all returned of their own accord—looking for food.

"Any word on Cassie?" Abby asked anxiously.

"Nothing yet. There has been no sight of her at either of the National Guard checkpoints. But they were able to contact the police—actually the sheriff. At this point there isn't much else we can do."

"Are they on their way out now?"

"I don't know. I would imagine so."

"What is taking them so long?"

"I don't know, Abby. I just don't know."

Priam tried to comfort her, but he felt as helpless as she did. He looked around at the horrid wreck of his hopes and dreams and ambitions. "The plan was supposed to be foolproof."

"What? What plan?"

"Our plan. It was supposed to be foolproof. I had weighed every eventuality. I calculated every probability. I checked on every possibility. I had checklists, timetables, systems, and contingencies. I had everything worked out. I was so sure, so confident. I was the Y2K expert."

"Bob, you can't blame yourself for this."

"Well, who else am I going to blame? I was gonna make absolutely certain that my family was well taken care of. Now practically everything is gone. Up in smoke. Gone in a single instant. Our food, our pure water supply, our auxiliary fuel."

"And our daughter."

"Right. And to top it all off, our daughter. All the effort. All the planning. All the money. All for nothing. Nothing at all. Well, so much for the grandma strategy."

THE GRANDMA STRATEGY started out simply enough. Priam thought that if he followed some basic common sense guidelines—the sorts of things his grandparents would have done as a matter of course—he could create a hedge against the worst effects of the Y2K crisis. Essentially, the strategy consisted of a dozen simple preparations.

First, he secured hard copies of all the family's important papers. He did not want to have to count on computer records to prove his age, citizenship, marital status, property owned, debts owed and paid, and bank balance. He got copies of birth certificates for each member of the family, a copy of his and Abby's marriage license, the baptismal certificates for each of the children, social security cards, the deed to their home, the titles to their cars, loan statements showing exactly what he owed, credit card statements, and three years of tax returns. He even got a copy of the Personal Earnings and Benefit Estimate Statement from the Social Security Administration—though it entailed a good deal of red tape. Once he had each of the documents in hand, he placed them in a fireproof box which he kept in a secure location at home—he didn't want them in a safety deposit box just in case the banks ultimately closed.

Second, he began to build an emergency preparedness library. Priam believed that his best weapon against uncertainty was knowledge. If the computers went down because of the Y2K problem, and if they went down as long as he thought they might, he wanted to be certain that he could function in a low-tech world. There were so many things his grandparents knew and took for granted that he didn't. For example, he really didn't know how to dress a wound or set a broken bone or cure an infection or treat someone for food poisoning. He didn't know how to secure a source of water should the tap suddenly dry up. He didn't know how to distinguish edible plants from those that were deadly. He didn't know how to deliver a baby, pull a tooth, or lance a boil. He had no earthly idea how to dress a deer, butcher a pig or goat, pluck a chicken, or even to clean a fish. He certainly didn't know how to dispose of garbage properly—much less sewage. As a result, he knew that he would have to educate himself. He needed handbooks, how-to manuals, and encyclopedias. And so, he began collecting the clearest, most informative, and best illustrated resources he could find.

Third, he tried to objectively evaluate the desirability of their home's location. He knew that even in the best of times, large cities are not always the best places to live. When the infrastructure breaks down they can be absolutely horrible—and dangerous. It did not take a great deal for him to realize that they might not want to live in the inner ring suburbs once the Y2K crisis hit. He tried to imagine what it might be like to live in their neighborhood without electricity, water, or the benefit of police protection. It was not a pleasant thought. He and Abby had always talked about moving further out, perhaps to a small farm in the country. He decided that it was now or never. He wanted to relocate someplace nearby where the crime rate was low, where there was a volunteer fire department, where the population was sparse, and where land values were good. He put their house on the market, found an idyllic farm, and made the move. He had a new barn and storage facility built, gave Abby free reign and a mission in the gardens, put in security fences, gates, and locks, installed an auxiliary power generator, and remodeled and refurbished the house. And after all that, he still made money on the deal.

Fourth, he made preparations for self-defense. He had never owned a gun before in his life. In fact, he was very nervous about the whole issue of gun ownership. But the very thought of a compromise in rapid response law enforcement due to Y2K breakdowns made him reconsider all his options. At first, he simply bought a couple of small caliber handguns and some ammunition. He and Abby took a few classes at the local shooting range and began to familiarize themselves with weapons, safety issues, and legal questions. Gradually, over the course of the year, Priam built up a small arsenal of weapons including several hunting rifles, rapid fire pistols, and one high powered automatic. He hoped that they would never have to be used for anything but a deterrent—but he wanted to be prepared, regardless.

Fifth, he knew that he needed to find a reliable source of water. People can live for weeks without food but only a couple of days without water. Even though there were several running streams on his new farm, they were seasonal and thus dependent upon regular rains—which were not always dependable in the heat of the summer in Tennessee. The average American uses an astonishing fifty-four gallons of water a day. He knew that if the municipal water department was unable to provide safe, clean water on demand after the Y2K crisis struck, he had only a handful of options. He could try to buy water once the crisis hit—a very unreliable, untenable solution; he could depend on local authorities to distribute emergency supplies of water—again rather unreasonable; he could try to use the water already stored in the house—which would be fine if the crisis lasted for just a day or two; he could store emergency water supplies—a far more complex task than it might seem at first blush; he could purify whatever water he could find or gather—again, a job easier said than done; or he could secure an alternative source of pure water. In the end, he decided to spend the money to dig a well on his property. He also made certain that he had a ready supply of halizone tablets, clean storage bottles, and air tight stoppers, just in case.

Sixth, he began to stockpile basic food staples, household goods, and essential supplies. He reasoned that gathering such things ahead of time when they could be found in abundance was not hoarding—it was merely wise preparation. At first, he and Abby simply bought a few extra items each time they went grocery shopping. They stocked up on canned goods, dry goods, condiments, toilet paper, personal hygiene items, soap, shampoo, pet food, matches, and candles. Later they bought some bulk grains, dehydrated vegetables and fruits, cereals, and freeze-dried meats. They stored their supplies in airtight metal canisters in the barn. Priam knew that they probably could not store everything they might need, but they could insure a basic diet of staples.

Seventh, he thought through the clothing purchases they might need to make over the course of the next year or so, and began to buy in advance. He knew that the Y2K crisis, if it struck at all, would start in the middle of winter. He wanted to make certain that every member of the family had an adequate supply of jackets, sweaters, socks, boots, sweatshirts, jeans, thermal underwear, gloves, and hats. Cassie and Abby enjoyed this part of the preparation process—they poured over the Land's End and L.L. Bean catalogs for hours, compiling lists, and creating wardrobes. *Even if disaster struck, they would be well dressed,* he chuckled.

Eighth, he prepared an inventory of emergency medical supplies. In the beginning, he thought that a really complete first-aid kit might be sufficient. But then he realized that he would need far more than mere first-aid items if the Y2K crisis cut them off from basic primary medical care for any length of time. He would need extra rubbing alcohol, hydrogen peroxide, cortisone, pain relievers, antacids, allergy medications, cough syrup, and cold remedies. He also wanted to make sure he had on hand several prescription medicines as well as extra prescription eyeglasses. He even signed up for a class at the local community college to learn CPR and the bare basics of EMT.

Ninth, he determined how he might dispose of waste. Few things can spread disease faster, attracting flies, cockroaches, rats, and other vermin, than the improper disposal of garbage, trash, and human waste. Even with his well, there was a very real possibility that water would have to be rationed in a crisis. Septic tanks are useless without an abundant and ready supply of water. Bucket and chemical toilets are only a very temporary solution. Priam had several large compost bins built adjacent to the garden for organic matter, he put an old fashioned out-house at the edge of the woods, stored bags of lime and kitty litter, and he installed a small incinerator in the barn for anything else.

Tenth, he collected some barter alternatives to currency in case the fiat money system failed in the wake of Y2K disruptions. Although he was fairly certain that the dollar would survive the crisis—and thus kept a cache of several thousand in cash on hand—he wanted to make certain that he had something besides Federal Reserve notes and credit cards if he needed to purchase something in an emergency. Hard money, particularly junk gold and silver coins, was always attractive, even during the worst economic disasters. But barter items were perhaps even more desirable. He kept a large crate filled with such things as extra ammunition, lighters, coffee and tea, whiskey, batteries, sugar, and salt.

Eleventh, he insured a steady flow of information and communication. If the electricity went out, how could he get news? What if the phones were down too? A battery-operated radio is a good place to start. But what if the radio stations are forced off the air once their back up generators fail? He decided he might invest in a short wave radio and a citizen's band radio. Both would provide a link to the outside world in an emergency situation—and thus, offer him a level of security that nothing else might be able to afford.

Finally, he began to acquire a basic selection of hand tools. Prior to this, Priam had been anything but a handyman, barely taking the time to change the light bulbs. Every time the family needed a plumber, a carpenter, an electrician, a mason, a mechanic, or a repairman, Abby would chide him about his inattentiveness to the basic upkeep of their home. But every time he tried to tackle a job, he found that it took so much time and effort, it was actually more efficient to hire the task out. If the Y2K crisis actually hit, though, that would no longer be an option. So he slowly began to accumulate a selection of saws, hammers, drills, chisels, rasps, planes, hammers, and screwdrivers. He collected a heavy toolbox full of wrenches, pliers, wire snips, files, nails, screws, and staples. Out in the barn he stored a couple of hatchets, a large axe, several shovels, and an assortment of rakes, hoes, shears, pitchforks, and clippers. He even bought an old fashioned rotary push mower for the lawn. High grass meant snakes, and Y2K was a minimal threat compared to snakes as far as Abby was concerned.

He had thought of everything. At least, that is what he had convinced himself of. His grandma strategy was practically foolproof. He was ready to withstand just about anything and everything that the Y2K crisis could conceivably throw at him.

The problem was that he had failed to prepare for the one inconceivable thing that the Y2K crisis *did* throw at him. And now all those careful preparations, as wise and as important as they might have been, seemed rather futile to him. Like so many of the best made plans of mice and men, his brilliant grandma strategy was only as good as the context within which it was placed.

AROUND NOON, PRIAM DECIDED to go back out to one of the National Guard checkpoints. The sheriff had still not arrived. The phones were not working. And he had been unable to raise anyone on the CB radio the Guardsmen had lent him. He simply had to do something to find Cassie.

Again, though, the guards on duty could offer little help. They placed another call over their police band radio to the sheriff's office, but could do little more for him. At his insistence, they let him fill out a crime summary and a missing persons report. Reluctantly, he returned to the farm, forlorn.

When he pulled off the road and onto the long winding drive through the trees and over the ridge, he was surprised to see several pickups and cars parked near the house. There were seven or eight vehicles off to the side of the driveway and another four or five in the side yard in front of the still smoldering remains of the barn. As he pulled up closer he could see that there were a number of people walking back and forth all over the property. He thought he recognized one or two of them, but the rest seemed to be total strangers.

When he clambered out of the Jeep he saw Abby and the boys surrounded by several women and children engaged in animated conversations. There was a flurry of activity along the fence line where several of the men seemed to be hard at work on something or another.

"What's all this?" he asked as he walked toward Abby. "Who are all these people? What are they doing here?"

Abby turned toward him with tears in her eyes. "Any news? Any sign of Cassie?"

"None. They put in another call to the sheriff's office. What's going on here?"

"This is the most important part of the grandma strategy, Bob. The part we somehow forgot about."

"What do you mean?"

"Neighbors. Friends. People who care. Community."

"Community? But we don't even know these people. Who are they? Where did they come from?"

"See the tall man over there by the barn? That's Dr. Gylberd. He's one of Cassie's teachers. He got a message on his CB from one of the school's graduates—a National Guard officer—who heard about what happened here. Dr. Gylberd got hold of some of the families from the school, several from church, and several more from the neighborhood. And well, here they are. They said that they just wanted to help."

Priam was thunderstruck as he looked around. Several of the women were laying out food on a table covered with a clean red and white checked tablecloth. He heard tracking dogs baying throughout the surrounding hills obviously in search of any trail left by the raiders. And a number of teens were attempting to gather the rest of the stray chickens into the temporary coop a few of the men had just fashioned from two-by-fours and chicken wire, each group being careful to avoid—as Dr. Gylberd had so explicitly instructed them—the areas of the house and surrounding yard which might contain vital crime-scene evidence.

"I can't believe it."

"I know. Isn't it amazing?"

"See that young man over there by the chicken coop? That's Noah. He's one of Cassie's friends. He showed up with half a dozen teenage boys—and they went to work. Just like that. The man over there working on the coop, he's the manager of the feed store where I buy food for the animals, seeds for the garden, and tack for the barn. The men scouring the property for signs of an escape route are neighbors with hunting dogs. And the ladies over here at the picnic table are all from my Sunday school class."

"I don't know what to say."

"I'm not sure there is anything that we can say. Except maybe *thank you*."

"All right, ya'll," one of the ladies at the picnic table yelled. "Time to eat. Gotta take time to eat. Cassie needs us to keep our strength up and our wits about us."

As everyone gathered around, one of the men announced, "First, we're gonna pray for Cassie's safety. She's a very smart girl, but she needs the Almighty's protection." And so, together they prayed.

Their spare common sense and encouragement forced Priam and Abby to overcome their sick panic and eat gratefully. They would need their strength, after all, for Cassie.

Eighteen

"Whosoever will save his life shall lose it." Mark 8:35

JANUARY 6, 2000

There was something devilish in his eyes—malignant, unearthly, and most hellishly clever. Cassie was gripped with a cold fear. Ajax ordered the men to bind and gag her. Her shoulders and wrists ached. Her head was pounding. Her sense of direction was completely awry. But most of all, she was afraid. The next hour or so seemed like an eternity. She had no earthly idea where they were taking her, but wherever it was, she felt as if they might never arrive.

When they finally got to the Chernobyl headquarters, Ajax instructed the men to carry her inside. "Take her up into the building. Lock her up in the storeroom until I decide what to do with her," she heard Ajax say. "Untie her carefully—I don't want her bruised."

As the crow flies, the warehouse was less than thirty miles away from the Priam farm. But even to the practiced eye it seemed much, much further than that. Indeed, it appeared to be a universe apart. If this wasn't the end of the world, it was a pretty fair approximation of it.

Along the riverbank, beside the Chernobyl site, were several rows of old warehouses and decaying industrial buildings—apparently, long since abandoned. The men rounded the corner and approached the metal sheathed wreck of a structure. A series of makeshift docks jutted out into the water, and a few tarp-covered skiffs were moored to the shadowy pylons. Along the backside of the building was a gaudy tower sporting a jumbled array of antennas, microwave disks, solar panels, and loupe feeders.

Negotiating a rusting tangle of chain link, barbed wire, and scrap metal half buried in the muck and mire, they rapped on the vast bay door atop what appeared to be an old loading dock. A sliver of iridescence suddenly pierced the darkness at the edge of the portal. After identifying themselves, the door scraped all the way open.

"Welcome back," chimed the beautiful young woman before them. "Hmmm. Looks like Ajax got a bit more than he bargained for. Why am I not surprised?"

The men jumbled inside. Widening her eyes in astonishment was about the only response Cassie could muster to the sight before her. The vast cavernous warehouse was a ramshackle clutter of complex hardware: tangles of cables and wires, banks of monitors, mounds of processors, and tables laden high with every imaginable device—all tossed about willy-nilly. It appeared to be the set for a mad confluence of the X-Files and the X-Games—a gadget playground fit for the X-Gen. It was an electronic arena of delights—built to the staggering proportions of Babylon. It had the delectable taste and smell of chaos, danger, anarchy, and taboo—like General Powell's high-tech military command center, or a digital pleasure dome fit for a modern day Kubla Khan, or perhaps a hip-hop version of

Nebuchadnezzar's Hanging Gardens, or maybe even all of them rolled into one.

A bevy of programmers, hackers, and otakus were scurrying about, ankle deep in the debris of heedless activity. The place was a hive of frenetic energy populated by angels of light. Cassie noticed that Ajax was now striding toward the center of it all. He seemed to be conducting the random confusion like a symphony.

They unbound her before tossing her into her little cell—a dusty, unused storeroom at the back of the building—though perhaps not as gently as she might have expected. She certainly was not unbruised by the process. At least she would be able to move around a bit. Perhaps she would even be able to get some rest, which she suddenly realized she desperately needed just about now.

The storeroom was a damp chamber in what had been an old factory or assembly plant of some kind. There was nothing covering the uneven floor but the crumbled remains of some old boxes, newspapers, and packing materials. Perhaps it was part of an old shipping and receiving department. It was black as pitch, though there were several heavily shuttered windows all along one side. Her captors turned the key in the door, and she could hear them shifting their feet as they stood guard outside. Cold, sore, and exhausted, she soon fell into a fitful, uneasy sleep.

EARLY THE NEXT MORNING Cassie awoke with a start. For a brief, tortured moment she was altogether disoriented. Only gradually did the horrors of the night before coalesce in her mind. Still immured in darkness, she began to explore the room, discovering as she groped about that the walls were lined with boxes and barrels and canisters filled with heavy metal engine parts, iron slag, and machine tools. The whole place smelt of mold and disuse.

She wracked her mind to try to figure out just what had happened and why. She worried and fretted for her family. She knew they were sick with worry over her, and that even now her dad would have the police searching for her.

She wondered how in heaven's name she had ever screwed up the courage to pick up her father's revolver, much less to fire it. Somehow she got the odd feeling that the entire scenario that was played out the previous night and the wretched scene she now faced were familiar—that she had actually encountered them beforehand. Surely she was imagining things—but she couldn't shake the notion.

Waiting in the dark, she played all sorts of mind games— anything to pass the time. She tried to recall the plots of her favorite adventure stories. She coursed through her vivid memories of Robert Louis Stevenson's *Treasure Island*, Walter Scott's *Waverly* and *Ivanhoe*, Daniel Defoe's *Robinson Crusoe*, John Bunyan's *Pilgrim's Progress*, Thomas Mallory's *Le Morte d'Arthur*, and Herman Melville's *Moby Dick*. She thought she saw glimmers of a semblance in Homer's *Iliad* and *Odyssey*, but she wasn't quite sure. Then she remembered a remarkable tale by the Scottish historian, diplomat, adventurer, and novelist, John Buchan. *The Thirty-Nine Steps* had been her favorite assignment in her Sophomore literature class. The intrepid hero had been captured by the enemy and locked up in a storeroom. The fate of Western Civilization, it seemed, depended on his escape. Utilizing his considerable ingenuity, spunk, and gallantry, he made good his narrow escape and ultimately was able to save the day. And everyone lived happily ever after.

Agitated by her situation, and newly inspired by her recollection of all her literary heroes, she determined that she too had to find a way to escape her captivity. She tried the shuttered windows, but of course they were locked and barred. She groped among the boxes, but was unable to find anything that might be of use to her. Behind them, though, were several tall shelves and cupboards. She tried to open one of the doors but it was either jammed or locked—she couldn't tell which. Nevertheless it seemed flimsy enough. She tried to force it. She found a small crowbar-like tool and pried at the edge until it burst open with a crash. Afraid that the noise might arouse the suspicions of her captors, she waited for a bit. But when they failed to investigate, she reached into the cabinet to see what she could find.

In the corner there were several flashlights. She tried each in turn, but none of them worked any longer. As she groped around, her hand touched something familiar—a smallish, rectangular cardboard box. She shook it gently and heard a distinct rattling sound. Wooden matches. But would they work, having lain around who knew how long in this dank place? She drew one out and struck it on the side of the box. No luck. The striking surface was too damp. Could they possibly be . . .

She took another one out. Only four left now, her fingers told her. She briskly struck it against the concrete floor. The match head sputtered and died out. Now there were only three, but she uttered a small prayer of thanksgiving nonetheless. At least they were the right kind—Ohio Blue Tip strike-anywhere matches.

She held the third one in her hand, her fingers shaking. She would have to drag it across the floor with just the right amount of pressure. Crack! Too much—or a weak spot in the wood.

Only two left now. Slowly she lifted the next to last one from the box. With a firm resolution, she swiped it against the floor. Poof! A small flame burst forth. Holding it in front of her, she noticed several bottles of odd-smelling chemicals—no doubt for some kind of experiments. There were several coils of copper wire, a few rolls of tape, and a couple of bolts of cotton fused cording. There were also quite a few boxes of old blasting caps and detonators. Then way at the back of the shelf she found a stout cardboard box, and inside it was a small wooden case. Just before the flame extinguished, she managed to wrench it open, and within lay a handful of little gray briquettes, each a couple of inches square.

Her sense of *déjà vu* was overpowering. It was as if a Buchan plot was coming to life before her very eyes. She gingerly picked one of the little briquettes, and found that it crumbled easily in her hand. She smelt it—she even touched it with her tongue to taste it. After that she sat down to think.

The resemblances were uncanny. But unmistakable. She knew that she had stumbled upon a small supply of lentonite. She had never seen it before—the old explosive had hardly been used since before the Second World War. Maybe that's why Ajax never cleared the old supplies out of the storeroom—they just looked like dusty remnants of a distant and antiquated industrial past. But she had read about such things. Lentonite was terribly outdated technology, but perhaps, if she could somehow get it to work, it just might do in a pinch. Indeed, it had been the salvation of the Buchan hero. Maybe, just maybe, she could blast her way out of trouble the way he had.

The problem was that the substance was very unstable. The characters in the books she read were mining engineers or war heroes or spies. She, on the other hand, was just a romantic teenager with a taste for poetry and chivalry. She trembled with fear. She could easily kill herself fiddling about with such things. She didn't know how to use lentonite. She was only vaguely familiar with its potency. She had no idea what an appropriate charge might be and was clueless about timing.

But it was a chance—perhaps the only chance she had. It was a mighty risk, but against it was a black certainty that the man with the evil eyes would be up to no good with her and with her family. If she used the explosive, the odds were, as she reckoned it, about a hundred to one in favor of her blowing herself to smithereens. If she didn't, she would likely meet a worse fate at the hands of Ajax. The prospect was pretty dark either way. At least with the lentonite, her fate was in her own hands.

Recalling the horrible events of the night before settled her. She was resolute. Even so, she was trembling from head to toe when she picked up a second briquette, a length of the cotton fuse, and a detonator. She laid the lentonite against the door into the warehouse, fixing the detonator in it. She strung a length of the fuse around a stack of the heavy boxes.

She ensconced herself just below the sill of one of the windows wedged behind the boxes. She drew a deep breath and said a prayer. It was admittedly a prayer of desperation—but then, it was a desperate moment. She took the final match, struck it firmly, and lit the fuse. She waited for a moment or two. There was dead silence—even the fizzling of the fuse had stopped. There was nothing but the shuffle of heavy boots outside the door. She sighed, partly in relief, partly in despair.

Suddenly a great wave of heat seemed to surge upwards from the floor and hang for a blistering instant in the air. Then the wall opposite her flashed into a golden yellow and dissolved with a rending thunder. The wall of boxes tumbled on top of her and around her. Light burst in everywhere.

She felt herself being choked by thick yellow fumes so she struggled out of the debris and to her feet. Just behind her she felt a cold draft and she turned to see that the jambs of one of the windows had collapsed and through the jagged rend the smoke was pouring out into the winter noon. She stepped over the broken lintel, and found herself outdoors just feet away from the riverside dock she had been carried across the night before. All around her was a dense and acrid fog.

She staggered up the bank toward the street. There were confused cries from within the warehouse. She knew she had only a moment or two to make good her escape. Though reeling from smoke inhalation and giddy from the effects of the lentonite, she still had enough sense of mind to steer clear of the front of the warehouse. She aimed herself toward the street where a crowd was already gathering. There were a row of industrial buildings across the street—most of them had recently been converted into artist studios and galleries. She thought that if she could just cross over the street and duck into one of the storefronts, she might actually have a chance. But she never quite made it that far.

Overwhelmed, she slumped over, nearly unconscious, into the arms of one of the dark figures that suddenly rushed toward her. She realized she no longer had the will to care if she were recaptured. So, she wasn't quite the Buchan hero—at least she had tried. She looked up with bleary eyes—but she couldn't tell if she had fallen into the grip of friend or foe. Not that it really mattered at this point.

THE ABDUCTION OF PRIAM'S daughter was the last straw for Athena. She had watched with mounting dismay the depraved obsessions of Ajax jeopardize their operation. Lord knows, she never claimed to be a saint. She willing participated in his scams, his rip-offs, and his stings. She enjoyed the challenge of beating the system. She got a kick out of sticking it to the big corporations. And she loved it that they were gypping the government out of tens thousands of dollars every year. Those were just desserts, she figured.

She had to admit that she had been sweet on Ajax at one time. He was after all incredibly appealing, a real sweet talker, and passionate about nearly every aspect of his life. For almost a year, she held on to illusions that she would be able to channel his creative zeal and zest for achievement toward some positive end. Alas, her hopes were dashed time and again. She was forced to face the fact that he was entirely self-consumed. He was the sort of man incapable of loving or of being loved. Eventually, the only feeling she could muster for him was pity.

She would have left Chernobyl long before but the collapsing economy, the restrictions on travel, and the tenuous social situation made her decide to bide her time. She would look for an appropriate opportunity somewhere down the line and until then simply occupy her space and enjoy her accumulated wealth.

The Priam raid changed all that. The loss of two members of the team was bad enough. But then Ajax came traipsing in with this teenager in tow. What he intended to do with her, she could only guess. Whatever it was, Athena had no intentions of being around to witness the debacle. She had already moved several of her things—her laptop, her decoding system, her solar powered battery chargers, some clothing, and her cappuccino maker into a friend's loft across the downtown historic district. She had just come back for a few more things when the explosion ripped through the side of warehouse.

The smoke was so smotheringly thick that at first no one inside seemed capable of responding to the surprising turn of events. Athena ran out of the front of the building. A dense yellow fog billowed out along the dock and up toward the street. That was when she saw her. She had staggered out of the rubble and was trying to make her way toward the crowd that was quickly converging on the scene. But she was clearly in bad shape, stumbling and disoriented. Athena reached her just as she collapsed.

Now she was breathing in the acrid fumes as well. She knew she had to beat a hasty retreat—for both of their sakes. She dragged the limp body over the curb, onto the street, and across to the other side. Already the smoke she had breathed was making her lightheaded. She began to feel faint. She managed to round the corner just as several of the men from Ajax's operations team emerged onto the street, scouring the crowd in attempt to recover their escapee. She moved down the alleyway to a fire escape landing. Struggling to keep her grip on the girl, she pulled her way upward. Though the teenager was slight, the dead weight was almost too much for Athena who was now coughing fitfully. She reached the third landing, but she just couldn't go on. She had hoped to make it up to the roof where they might be able to keep out of sight for a few hours. But she foundered there on the rusty metal landing—and she too fell into a stupor.

When she awoke it was already dark. She looked at her watch and was astonished to see how late it was. Cassie was just beginning to stir beside her. She knew that they couldn't stay here—they were too close to Chernobyl and too far from any possible help. It was a wonder that they had not already been seen.

Athena tried to explain to the teen what their situation was and that what they needed to do to get across town. She was surprised by how alert the girl was. Indeed, she marveled at her spunk and tenacity. She was even more impressed once Cassie recounted the events that lead to her capture, imprisonment, and eventual escape.

After tending a few cuts and bruises, they were ready to take leave of their temporary shelter on the fire escape. Gingerly, they made their way back down the creaking, rusting hulk.

Together they walked along the edge of the dark cluttered alleyway. Stepping gingerly past a couple of homeless drunks, addicts, and vagabonds and steering past the heaps of rubbish, they noticed a newly installed surveillance loupe on the corner of the adjacent building—it was probably a part of a perimeter defensive system for Chernobyl. Athena casually reached into her satchel, pulled out a pistol, and fired off several rounds, shattering the camera and sending a dazzling spray of sparks and shocks upward into the night sky. Now they were going to have to hurry. They had probably been noticed. She hadn't counted on that.

They rounded the corner and onto the street where all the commotion had been earlier in the day. Snow had begun to fall again in flurries. Dusting the doorways and flocking the storefronts, its shocking whiteness seemed to somehow bestow a pristine purity on the dreary neighborhood. It was a wry deception. Covering over the ugly, obscuring the dull, and taming the pretentious, the damp blanket began to transform the concrete wasteland before their very eyes. Were it not for the task before them, they might have actually taken pause to marvel; they might have actually reveled in the wonder of it all; they might have actually enjoyed it. The moist flakes twinkling past the decrepit neon hustle and bustle cast a spell of transfixing beauty over the entire cityscape. But they had no eyes for beauty just now. The desperate, like the dispossessed, seldom do.

Around the next corner, the first sight that greeted them was a street fight. A small crowd had gathered in front of a National Guard command post to watch two emaciated youths lunge and slash at each other with cheap gravity-blade knives. The onlookers seemed to divide their attentions between the petty struggle before them and the prospect of a hustle around them. They made for a motley crew.

Several teens wove in and out of the spectators peddling everything from pot to heroin. "Got coke, man. Good coke. Ludes. Reefer. Dust. Crank. You name it man, I got your high. Ups. Downs. Got what ya need. Got it, man. Best price."

Oblivious to this grating litany, two overworn middle-aged men circulated through the disinterested and restless throng, distributing handbills for a bar on Broadway. Most of them fell to litter the sidewalk after only a moment or two.

It seemed as if everybody was working some angle or another.

Athena and Cassie crossed over to Second Avenue and made their way away from the riverfront as quickly as they could. It was almost midnight now, and the streets seemed to just be starting to come to life. A garish kaleidoscope of flashing lights mixed with the wheedling jive of hawkers and the choked cacophony of the dense revelers. Along Eighth Avenue from Broadway to Wedgewood, Cassie had seen several porno shops, live sex theaters, peep show parlors, and X-Rated movie houses. There were countless bars, all full, and shops specializing in street gear: knives, chains, chukka sticks, belo balls, handcuffs, machetes, ninja stars, slam jacs, and cudgels.

The hourly National Guard sentry slowly rumbled past in one of the now-omnipresent Hummers, armed to the teeth against the threat of rioting, looting, and pillaging. The soldiers aboard looked past the commonplace corruption, perversity, and decay that now gripped the cityscape—as long as the sin there was orderly, it was both tolerable and tolerated.

But they moved on, barely glancing up at the eye-popping debauchery around them—though they were admittedly not altogether incognizant of it. Indeed, they were struck by the cruel irony of it all—the fact that the city's thin veneer of prosperity had been so quickly and easily stripped away here along the fringes of downtown, like a fresh snowfall swept from a dingy stoop. The effects of the Y2K crisis had hardly begun and already an air of hopeless decrepitude, frustrated inevitability, and totalitarian resignation had set in.

The two women who made their way through the depressing landscape were actually exhilarated by their new prospects. Each had somehow, against all odds, shaken free from a cloying captivity. It was not a liberty that either would willingly surrender—regardless of the battles that might yet lie before them.

Nineteen

"Bear ye one another's burdens." Galatians 6:2

JANUARY 7, 2000

D r. Gylberd sat at the table and confessed. "I have a partic-
ular weakness for barbecue. I've eaten at Arthur Bryant's
in Kansas City, at Sonny's in Atlanta, at Red Bryan's in
Dallas, at Corky's in Memphis, at Luther's in Houston, at
Herbert's in Franklin, at Dreamland's in Birmingham, and at
Bar-B-Q Baron's in Midland."

Noah looked at his teacher appreciatively. He knew he was
attempting to distract the family distraught over their still
missing daughter.

Gylberd looked up at the others, a respectable smear of
sauce at the corner of his mouth. "I've had shredded pork in
Knoxville, pit-roast in Richmond, honey-back in Charlotte,
pollo loco in Miami, yankee links in New York, braised hot
wings in Buffalo, and charred cabritto in Santa Fe. I've even
sampled Chen's Mongolian barbecue in London and Ferrot's

Canadian ribs in Ottawa. But my favorite—by far—is Texas-style brisket."

With that, he took another bite of his sliced brisket sandwich, and let out a great sigh of satisfaction. Though the others at the table, the teens spread out on the ground around them, and the adults scattered about in lawn chairs were not nearly so adamant about their lunch as he was, each expressed gratitude for the meal.

Besides the barbecue, there were bowls of German potato salad and creamy cole slaw. There were large pots of baked beans. There were deviled eggs, saucy fruit compote salads, creamy vegetable dips, and homemade whole-wheat rolls. There were desserts too. A moist carrot cake, a silky banana pudding, and a tangy key lime pie complemented the luscious strawberry shortcake, the fresh chocolate chip cookies, and the rich pound cake.

It was the sort of feast that was generally only available at those rare celebrations of life, faith, and community—dinner on the grounds. No royal fête had ever been better, no stately banquet had ever been finer, and no gourmet repast had ever been more satisfying.

Priam was still speechless. As he looked around at the plain, country faces, he recognized the great benefits he had never allowed himself. He noticed the people he had never had time for before. He saw the country bumpkins, the low-level functionaries, the trivial teenagers, and the soccer moms he had never given the benefit of a doubt before. Their kindness to him—in his greatest hour of need—was a stern and accusing rebuke. At the same time it was what he most desperately needed—a warm and forgiving embrace.

As they finished their meal—but before anyone was quite ready to return to their work, Dr. Gylberd asked Priam if he had any news on Cassandra.

"Nothing at all. We've notified the sheriff's department. I've filled out the paperwork. But they've not even sent out a squad car to investigate. I am getting awfully frustrated. And every minute that passes is another minute my daughter is in who knows what kind of trouble."

"Well, the police and sheriff's departments are just completely swamped. There is just not a whole lot that they can do right now. Things are so confused. Communication is so haphazard. We'll keep hunting for her ourselves—and then call in the law once we have something."

"Are you kidding?"

"At this point, do you have a better suggestion?"

"You're talking about forming a Wild West posse?"

"I hadn't actually thought of it in those terms, but yes. That's actually a pretty good description of what we might need to do."

"Bob, we have to do something," Abby interjected. "We can't just sit here and do nothing at all."

"Right. OK. What do we need to do then? Where do we start?"

"Bob, you told the police that you thought you might know who the men were and where they were headed. Is that right?"

"Maybe. Well, yes. One of the men looked vaguely familiar. I couldn't see his face—they were all wearing ski masks—but his voice and the way he carried himself triggered a memory. I think it was someone who used to work with me. A programmer that our company referred for work on Y2K repair jobs. He had a small company. They kept a warehouse near downtown on the river. That's about all I know. It's not much to go on."

"It's a start. Noah, bring me that map we were looking at in the car earlier, will you? Let's look at it and see if we can't determine a plausible route they took when they left here last night."

"Or perhaps, how they even got here in the first place—without passing the National Guard checkpoints."

"Right." The men waited for Noah to return with the map. Several of the others returned to their work.

"Here you go, Doc."

"Thanks, Noah."

They spread the map out on the table. They followed every possible route that the men might have taken. Eventually, all of them passed by one or another of the Guard checkpoints.

"See, I told you. There is no way they could have done this without passing the checkpoints. The men on duty last night either missed them or forgot or were bribed into looking the other way or something."

"Hmmm. It does look rather impossible. Maybe the men came from right around here—and maybe they never went out toward either of the freeways at all."

"It doesn't seem likely."

"Or maybe," now it was Noah who was scrutinizing the maps. "Maybe they didn't use roads at all."

"I don't think so, Noah," Gylberd responded. "It would be awfully slow going and terribly tedious to try to go overland in middle Tennessee. From the sound of it, this was a pretty professional, efficient, and fast-moving team. I don't think they would attempt to go cross-country like that."

"Just because they didn't use roads doesn't necessarily mean that they would then have to go overland or cross-country, Doc."

"What do you mean?"

"Well, didn't you say, Mr. Priam, that you thought one of these guys had a warehouse right on the river downtown."

"Yes, but . . ."

"What if they traveled by water the whole way here?"

"By water?"

"Yeah. Look at the map. They would have had to go way to the north and west of downtown along the Cumberland before they hit the mouth of the Harpeth, but then they could have come all the way to this point," he pointed to a spot on the map just adjacent to the farm property. "How far away is this from here?"

"A mile. Maybe less. Just over the ridge and through a couple of pastures and a bit of woodland. The dogs kept pulling us that way, but no one could figure out why."

"There you have it. I bet they came in and slipped out by boat."

"Noah, you're a genius. That's it. I think you're right."

Suddenly a plan began to emerge. Two of the men working on the barn had bass boats sitting in the driveway. They would try to find the spot where the men had put in. They would then send four men in each of the boats along the same route. Meanwhile, four more men would attempt to reach downtown by car, and alert the appropriate authorities. Then, they would all meet at the warehouse, where hopefully, Cassie would be waiting for them.

GYLBERD, NOAH, AND THE others had no trouble whatsoever finding the place where the boats had put in the night before. The dogs led them straight to a wide sandy embankment, well shielded from view. They found all the telltale signs of a carefully planned operation—lots of equipment, a large team, and a well-conceived strategy.

"What do you suppose they were after?" Gylberd asked.

"I don't know, Doc. Mr. Priam seemed pretty clueless. He said the only thing taken was his laptop and some computer peripherals. Maybe the guy thought there was something on the hard drive that was very valuable."

"Obviously, there were all kinds of things at the house of value. They definitely knew what they were after. Blowing the barn was probably just a diversion to get the family out of the house quickly and easily. Looks like Cassie gave them more than their money's worth, though."

Noah chuckled. "Anybody who knows her could have told them not to mess with that girl. Well, they know now."

"That they do."

The bass boats began to skim across the surface of the little river. The men watched carefully along the banks as they passed, looking for any signs of ingress or egress. It was difficult to believe that they were passing through the heart of a major metropolitan area. Trees overhung the water, wildlife abounded, and the sights and sounds of the city were obscured from view almost continuously. In fact, they would have had a hard time believing they were anywhere near civilization at all except for the few times when they passed under bridges or alongside roadways.

The journey to the place where the Harpeth emptied into the Cumberland took a meandering route and lasted nearly an hour. From there, the ride continued for nearly half an hour more before downtown Nashville came into sight.

They had a pretty fair description of the warehouse site from Priam. But it was difficult differentiating one building from another along the riverfront. They all looked rather decrepit. When Noah spotted the radio tower, though, he was fairly certain that they had found the right place.

"Look over there, Doc," he pointed toward the back of the building. "See all those antennas, microwave disks, solar panels, and loupe feeders? There shouldn't be high-tech gear like that on an old industrial warehouse loading dock. Looks like our friendly data pirates have set up quite a clever hedge against Y2K."

"Clever indeed. Let's just hope that Priam and the others made it through the Guard checkpoints and rousted out the cavalry. I'd hate to be caught snooping around this place without backup."

They docked their little boats at a slip within sight of the warehouse, but several spaces distant. They clambered out onto the docks and tried to get a good view of the street up ahead. There was no sign of Priam or the police or the National Guardsmen. But there was a good deal of activity alongside the warehouse.

"Looks like they're doing some kind of structural repairs there. See the new strips of sheet metal on that lean-to shed?"

"Yeah. It looks like there may have been a fire there—see the charred window jambs? And look at all that twisted sheathing. Do you suppose there was an explosion?"

"I can't really tell from here, Noah. I think I may need to take a little closer look. You stay here with the boats. Jim and I will take a little stroll to see whatever we can without arousing too much suspicion."

As the two men made their way up to the street and along the sidewalk across the way, Noah kept his eyes trained on the warehouse. He had an eerie feeling that he had seen the men working there somewhere before. Just then a tall, striking figure emerged from the warehouse. He began giving the other men orders. Though Noah could barely make out the tenor of his voice, he knew immediately where he had seen the men before. They were the burglars who had shot at him—and then chased him—when he was dumpster-diving nearly a year and a half before. And they must have been the same men who shot at Jake and killed Hugo a few months later. *So these are the guys who snatched Cassie. Now what do I do,* he thought.

A memory played at the edges of his mind. He was standing in the graveyard on the hills of the Carnton Farm, recalling once again all the suffering those men had endured. And their courage. He thought of Bounds, striding around at the front lines of the battlefield, bolstering the men. And then a strange thing happened. He began to see in his mind's eye all the great men from the past he'd read about: Patrick Henry, Robert E. Lee, Teddy Roosevelt, Winston Churchill. Suddenly, he knew he had to do something to help Cassie.

He snatched an automatic pistol from a black nylon knapsack lying on the bottom of one of the boats. "What are you doing, Noah?" one of the men asked. "Dr. Gylberd said to stay put till he got back."

"I'm just going to try to get a little better look," Noah fudged.

He wasn't really sure how he could actually help matters by tangling with the men at the warehouse. He knew that prudence demanded that he wait for Priam and the police to arrive. But he was suddenly filled with an unexpected resolve.

He skirted the edge of the water toward the tarp-covered skiffs. Through the open bay door he caught a glimpse of the interior of the warehouse. He saw the tangles of cables and wires, banks of monitors, and mounds of processors. *Whew. This guy's got quite an operation here.*

He was so overtaken by the sight of the equipment inside the warehouse that he stood gawking in plain view of the docks. One of the men saw him standing there and called out to him. "Hey. What do you think you're doing over there? This is private property. You'll have to move on."

Ajax turned and looked over at him. Noah was seized by a fierce loathing. He slowly raised his pistol and took careful aim.

What happened next went down so quickly that it was little more than a frenetic blur. Shots were fired. He wasn't sure whether they came from Ajax and his men, from his friends in the boats behind him, or from Gylberd across the street. All he knew was that he was suddenly in the middle of a furious life-and-death exchange.

He dove into the tall weeds beside him in an attempt to take cover. Bullets whirred over his head and scored the hard ground around him. He hadn't gotten off a single shot. He was abruptly paralyzed with fear. He heard a tumult of voices and the awful cries of the wounded. At one point he tried to see what was happening by parting the weeds slightly and was rewarded for his curiosity with a stinging wound to the shoulder. He was bleeding profusely. He was terrified. It seemed that the gunplay would never end.

After what felt like an eternity, he heard the piercing sound of sirens. The shooting seemed to intensify for a moment and then slowly died away. There were loud shouts. Scrambling along the street. And then silence.

Slowly, he lifted his head and saw a swarm of police, troopers, and National Guardsmen on the dock and in the warehouse. The programmers, otakus, and engineers from Chernobyl were being loaded into a couple of paddy wagons. There were several ambulances in the front of the building and a number of paramedics were running purposefully to and fro caring for the wounded.

He tried to stand, but he was weak and collapsed back into the weeds. Thankfully, his friends behind him were already calling over to the paramedics—and in short order he was being tended to. "Just a flesh wound," he heard one of them say. Well, it hurt an awful lot for "just a flesh wound."

Priam was there. He had arrived with the police just after the shooting had begun. Apparently, Gylberd saw Noah raise his pistol and had opened fire from the street to distract Ajax and his men. He was hit almost immediately, the first casualty in what turned out to be a brutal gun battle. Thankfully, the police were able to bring it to a quick conclusion.

Not surprisingly, all the noise, tumult and, commotion had drawn a huge crowd there on the edge of downtown. Clara Rachman had a pretty good view of the action from the sidewalk in front of HavaJava five blocks down Broadway. When she realized what was happening, she ran around the corner and up to her loft apartment where she found her new roommate, Athena Scully, and their young guest, Cassandra Priam.

Together the three of them warily made their way through the crowd. The entire intersection of First Avenue and Broadway was blocked off by emergency vehicles. But they elbowed their way to the front of the throng of gawkers. When they rounded the corner they caught sight of the chaotic scene.

It almost seemed like the set of a movie or video, common sights in Nashville. But this was all too real. The surreal shroud of smoke in the air was punctuated by the crackling sounds of radio dispatchers and the hurried efficiency of police and paramedics. Onlookers strained to get a better view.

The girls arrived in front of the Chernobyl warehouse just in time to see Ajax cuffed and shoved into one of the paddy wagons, and Gylberd, laid out on a gurney, hurried into an ambulance. Cassie thought she saw Noah being tended to by paramedics. She slipped past her new friends, ducked under the hastily strung crime-scene tape barricade, and ran toward him. She was sobbing uncontrollably.

When Priam saw her there a moment or two later his heart leapt with joy, with relief, with thanksgiving.

"Cassie. You're all right. Oh, thank God. Cassie." They wept aloud as they embraced.

IT WAS AN ODD GATHERING of people assembled around Gylberd's hospital bed in the ICU. Noah was there, of course, as was Cassie. Athena and Clara stood on the other side, backlit by the window. Priam, camped out at the foot of the bed, sat with his head bowed, seemingly in prayer. The others too kept a kind of silent vigil, waiting for some sign from the professor. Together, they were more than a mere assemblage; they were a kind of . . . community. Bound together by exigency, necessity, need, they formed a bond beyond that which brought them together. A bond of love.

As they watched, and waited, and prayed, Tristan Gylberd slowly opened his eyes.

Twenty

"Thou shalt be called the repairer of the breach."
Isaiah 58:12

JANUARY 9, 2000

Ever since men first learned to measure the passing of time, the *fin de siecle*—or the end of the century—has been filled with expectation and portent. Every culture across the globe has invariably attached special significance to the fact that another hundred years have passed. Some because they thought the earth was coming to an end. Some because they thought the earth was coming to a beginning. But all because they thought the earth was coming to something—perhaps even, something significantly new and different.

As the twentieth century came to an end—and with it, the second millennium since Christ—all those primordial fears, foibles, fancies, and fascinations seemed to redouble their hold on the attentions of the wise and the foolish alike.

As at the end of the fourth century, men were frightened by the minatory movements of barbarians pouring over once safe

263

borders with an alarming prolificacy and profligacy. As at the end of the thirteenth century, men were unsettled by the specter of unchecked plagues rampaging through the population. As at the end of the fifteenth century, men were uncertain about those things men are usually most certain of: doctrines and dogmas—their careless admixture of faith and faithlessness had wrought remonstrance, schism, confusion, and inquisition. As at the end of the eighteenth century, men were shaken by the terrible swiftness of geopolitical change—by the revolutionary emergence of startling new alliances, the stirring of age-old animosities, and the plotting of fierce contemporary conspiracies.

The more things change, the more they stay the same.

Then, as now, the speculations of men ran to the frantic and the frenetic. Ecstatic eschatalogical significance was read into every change of any consequence—be it of the weather or of the government. Apocalyptic reticence was chided as faithlessness, while practical intransigence was enshrined as faithfulness. Fantastic common wisdom replaced ordinary common sense, and plain selfish serenity replaced plain selfless civility.

Interestingly, the *fin de siecle* that heralded the advent of Y1K witnessed a frenzied, catastrophic effect on the culture. Apparently, New Year's Eve 999, found Christians everywhere in decrepit churches and chapels, awaiting with utmost anxiety whatever the pregnant darkness would bring forth on the stroke of midnight. The suspense of that hour united Christendom in a single community of faith and fear. From Gibraltar to the Baltic, from the English Channel to the Bosporus, from Rome to Constantinople to Jerusalem, the fearful and the faithful gathered their loved ones about them and looked up expectantly toward the celestial vault of the medieval heavens.

All of the experts were fully convinced that the end was nigh unto them. They had examined all the data—from the

Scriptures to the state of affairs around the known world—and were sufficiently persuaded that judgment was near. They worked the populace into a panic.

Of course, their prognostications were wrong.

When nothing particularly remarkable happened, when the world entered intact upon the year 1000, Sylvester II at his special midnight Mass in Rome turned to the astonished congregation, who lifted their voices to the Lord in the *Te Deum* and hallelujah choruses while clocktowers chimed in the second Christian millennium and bells rang out from all the steeples.

But, the people were not merely relieved. They took their new lease on life as a mandate to make a difference in their tired old medieval world. Grand sighs of relief became even grander breaths of fresh air as people turned to the rebuilding of the dilapidated chapels, the foundation of monasteries, and the creation of Romanesque cathedrals, until the landscape was cloaked in a white mantle of churches. Hungary, Poland, and Russia converted to the True Faith in one miraculous gasp. European society, redeemed and transformed, expanded outward under full sails, soon unfurling crusader flags to reclaim Jerusalem from the heathens. Viking raiders vanished into thin northern air, the international climate softened, and sweet winds blew across the wilderness where serfs energetically cleared away first growth for a surging population bound now for that series of renaissances which would propel them into modernity. If ostensibly anticlimatic, the calendrical millennium turned out to have been extraordinarily convenient, a supernally notable year in which the West, after the doldrums of the Dark Ages, at last shook off the shackles of the barbarians who had not so much succeeded the classical world as ridden roughshod over it.

To be sure they had great obstacles to overcome. Economic disruption, tumult, and disarray resulted from all of the anxious build up to Y1K. Panic wreaks havoc and unleashes tribulation—at least for a time. But in the end, the changes portended for good.

So, as it turned out, that *fin de siecle* was not an *annus terribilis*—a year of horrors—as almost everyone had expected. Rather it was an *annus mirabilis*—a year of marvels.

What was it that made the difference? Was it merely the turning of the page of the calendar? What translated the gloom and doom of that generation's best and brightest into the dawning of a new hope? Was it the razzle-dazzle hat trick of exchanging zeros for nines on the ledger board?

No.

In the end, that *fin de siecle* came and went like all the others had—a mere backdrop to the real drama of green grocers, village cobblers, next-door neighbors, and grandfathers. Despite all the hype, hoopla, and hysteria, the ordinary people who tend their gardens and raise their children and perfect their trades and mind their businesses simply went on with life. Thus, the paradoxical convulsion of that time was not manifest in what happened between two dates, but what happened between two peoples—between the eponymous and the anonymous, between the profound and the simple, between the wise made foolish and the foolish made wise.

In fact, that is the great lesson of each *fin de siecle*—throughout all of history, not just those of the tenth and twentieth centuries. It is simply that ordinary people gathered together in community are ultimately the ones who determine the outcome of human events—not kings and princes, not masters and tyrants, not even clocks and calendars. It is that laborers and workmen, cousins and acquaintances can upend the expectations of the brilliant and the glamorous, the expert and the meticulous. It is that plain folks, simple people, can literally change the course of history—because they are the stuff of which history is made. They are the ones who make the world go round.

That irony, that paradox, that remarkable reversal is woven into the very fabric of God's good providence in the world. Because some people cannot comprehend that, they condemn it.

The more things change, the more they stay the same.

SUNDAY DAWNED BRISK and bright. As Priam walked in his garden, there was an evident bounce in his step. All was hardly right with the world. The deep global recession wrought by the Y2K crisis was still in full force—and probably would be for some time yet. Electrical power was still an iffy proposition in most places around the country. Phone service was still unreliable. Martial law was still a smothering imposition on the constitutional liberties of most Americans. And the Priam barn— with all its carefully selected contents—was still a heap of charcoal and rubble behind his house. Lives had been lost. Heartache had been shared—and would be again.

Nevertheless, he was as content as he had ever been. And as confident.

He looked over toward the chicken coop where Hector was scattering feed for the appreciative hens. He glanced back at the house where Abby was bustling about, trying to get ready for church. He listened to the thunk-thunk-thunk of Troy's basketball on the porch. And he turned and faced the edge of the driveway where Noah Kirk's truck had just pulled in to give Cassie a ride to Sunday school.

He gave thanks for the trials and tribulations of the *fin de siecle*—for the Y2K crisis—and all that it had wrought, both good and bad.

The Beginning